R⊕YAL
HEIR

a novel

OTHER BOOKS AND AUDIOBOOKS
BY TRACI HUNTER ABRAMSON

ROYAL HEIR

a novel

TRACI HUNTER ABRAMSON

Covenant

Covenant Communications, Inc.

TO PAIGE EDWARDS
AND
ELLIE WHITNEY

Thank you for always encouraging me to
make the next book better than the last

Acknowledgments

WITH EACH BOOK, I AM truly honored to be blessed with so many readers who have supported me on the journey from one story to another. Thank you for reading and for asking the question, What happens next?

Thank you to the wonderful people at Covenant who continue to allow me to do what I love, especially my amazing editor, Samantha Millburn, as well as Amy Parker and the many people working behind the scenes to make each project a success.

Thanks to my critique partners, Paige Edwards, Ellie Whitney, and Kyla Beecroft, for helping me polish those early drafts. Also, thank you to Sarah Eden, Annette Lyon, and Janette Rallison for giving me the excuse to research Europe in person. You always make the adventure memorable.

Also, I want to thank the many staff members at the Rouse Center who tolerate my crazy antics when writing while walking on their treadmills.

Thank you to my husband, Jon, and to my children, Diana, Christina, Lara, Gabriel, and Luke, for tolerating my time on the computer and my crazy schedule. You make life the best adventure of all.

CHAPTER 1

Princess Cassandra of Sereno crossed the Aubusson rug that ran the length of the wide hallway in the palace residence. She didn't look at the guard stationed a short distance away; she knew he was there, but she was already focused on her intended destination. She smoothed a hand down her pale-pink ball gown and knocked on her father's door.

His deep voice called out an instant later. "Come."

Cassie pushed open the door and entered her father's apartment. It smelled of leather and aftershave, the lingering perfume her mother had always worn now a distant memory.

She passed through the living quarters and stopped at the bedroom door. Her lips curved when she saw her father standing in front of the oval mirror on the wall, his fingers tugging on his crooked bow tie.

"After all these years, I would have thought you'd figure out how to tie one of those."

Dark eyes met hers in the mirror. "I can tie one."

"Since you taught me it's bad manners to contradict a king, I'll ignore that comment." She put her hand on his shoulder, nudging him so he would turn to face her. "Let me." Cassie undid the tie and started over.

Her father's voice softened. "Your mother always did this for me."

"I know. I miss her too." Cassie tugged on the bow tie, ensuring it was even and straight. "There you go. Perfect."

He checked the mirror before nodding his approval. "Thank you."

"Are you ready?"

"I should be asking you that. I'm sorry so many duties have fallen to you."

She heard the unspoken words at the end of his sentence, "since your mother's death." Even though it had been over a year, the thought that her mother was no longer in this life could still cut her off at the knees. Her mother's illness had been so quick, so unexpected. The doctor had barely uttered the word *cancer* before they were standing at her graveside.

"Have you spoken to Victoria and Anabelle today?" her father asked.

"Yes. I think they were both relieved you let them stay at school for summer term."

"It's hard for them to walk the halls and not have their mother here."

The sorrow washed over her. Not wanting to dwell on the hurt, she said, "Anabelle did mention something about extra guards following her around. What's with that?"

"A few rumblings. Nothing to worry about."

"Papa, you keep too much from me."

"You will bear the burden of leadership soon enough. Let me shield you a bit longer," he said. "You're only twenty-six. You should be traveling and learning more about the world instead of acting as hostess for state dinners."

"Some things can't be helped." She tucked her hand into the crook of his arm. "But as hostess, it's my duty to make sure the king is on time."

"Bossy little thing, aren't you?"

"You taught me well."

"Let's go." He led the way out of his private quarters and into the main hallway, where one of his assistants was waiting. "Is everything in place, Theo?"

"Yes, King Alejandro."

A guard took position in front of them, leading the way from the family's private residence into the heart of the palace.

Framed masterpieces hung on the walls, the influence of the French, Italian, and Spanish all represented, as well as a few of Sereno's own stars.

They reached the section of their home open to public tours, and the artwork here transitioned to being enclosed in protective cases. They were halfway through the wide entryway when the heavy wooden doors opened, the hinges creaking.

Why were the guards allowing anyone to enter when the king was walking through? When two men in white chef's uniforms stepped inside, Cassie's confusion deepened. Food preparations should be nearly completed by now. Why would two chefs be arriving minutes before hors d'oeuvres would be served?

Cassie anticipated the guards demanding answers to those exact questions, but instead, one shouted, "Get down!"

The guard's words only added to her confusion, leaving her frozen in place. Then she saw it, the guns in the newcomers' hands, as well as the dark, almost blank expressions they wore.

Her heart caught in her throat, and she reached for her father's hand only to find he was no longer beside her.

Weapons raised on both sides. A guard jumped in front of her, and another grabbed her arm. Gunfire sparked. Bodies fell. Alarms sounded.

Fear swamped through her, even as she was yanked to the side of the foyer. The heel of her left shoe caught on the wood floor, breaking cleanly when a guard shoved her behind a suit of armor. An instant later, the guard dropped to the ground.

Gunshots sparked against metal.

More gunfire. More shouts. More sparks as bullets hit the armor protecting her. The helmet took a direct hit and clanged to the floor.

Cassie fought for breath, unable to see anything beyond the hallway behind her and the guard lying at her feet. She focused on the guard, his chest rising and falling in an irregular pattern, blood visible on his uniform a few inches below his right collarbone.

Cassie knelt, hooked both hands beneath his shoulders, and pulled him toward her. She squeaked in alarm when a bullet impacted only inches from her head, but she didn't release him until his body was out of the line of fire.

"It'll be okay," she murmured, not sure if she was trying to convince the injured guard or herself. She saw the handkerchief in the man's pocket. Quickly, she drew it out and pressed it against his wound.

She glanced up in time to see a fresh wave of guards arrive from the hall opposite her. This time, the gunfire lasted mere seconds, and none of the royal guards fell. In an instant, Darius, the captain of the guard, appeared at her side.

"Call an ambulance," Darius yelled to the man behind him. As his companion did so, Darius leaned down. "Your Highness, are you okay?"

"I think so." Her gaze swept the room, taking in the two assailants lying on the ground, along with three more guards. A tremor worked through her. "My father?"

The king answered for himself, his voice booming through the foyer. "Cassandra!"

Relief washed through her at the familiar sound.

"She's unharmed." Darius signaled to one of his men, who took Cassie's place at the injured guard's side.

Cassie stood, and immediately, her father gripped her arms, checking for himself to make sure she was indeed okay. Then he swept her into his embrace.

Keeping her close, her father motioned to the foyer. "What happened here? How did those men get past our guards?"

"We don't know yet, Your Majesty."

"Find out."

The guard bowed. "Yes, sire."

* * *

King Alejandro paced his office, his phone to his ear as his palace manager gave him the update on their dinner guests. Despite the shooting, the meal had been served, but instead of dining with royalty, those present had been joined by several local police detectives.

Alejandro finished his call, but his restless pacing didn't cease. What he wouldn't give to have his wife's calm presence beside him, to have the fresh perspective a woman's eye could give.

The thought of discussing tonight's events with Cassie surfaced only to be pushed firmly away. His daughter had suffered enough trauma. Even now, she was locked in her room with two guards posted outside her door. He wasn't taking any chances with her safety or the safety of his other two daughters.

Deep down, though, he knew extra guards wouldn't be enough. They wouldn't be safe until he understood what the assassins wanted. If he gained understanding, he could mount a defense. Until then, his entire family was vulnerable.

Questions rolled through his mind on repeat. Was this attack on him because of some decision he had made, or had it been an attempt to force a change of power? Was the hostile force from within his sphere of influence, or had it come from another nation? And who would have benefited had the assassination attempt been successful?

The last question lingered in his mind.

He circled his office again, his gaze drawn to a seascape that had graced his wall for the past three months. The painting had been a gift from the Meridian royal family, given to him when Prince Garrett had visited with his new bride.

The two countries had been allies for centuries, but those relations had strained when King Eduard had allowed the Americans to build a naval base on his coast, ultimately increasing the military traffic in the area. Despite the recent challenges, Alejandro had hung the painting in his private workspace as a reminder of the constant battle between land and sea, a battle that man often recreated.

The thought that the Americans could be behind tonight's attack rooted in his mind. Although several countries had expressed interest in partnering with

Sereno to harvest the rich fields of natural gas in their territorial waters, the Americans had also tried to home in on his small island country, eager to explore and exploit.

More questions rose within him, but he fought them back. He didn't need speculation. He needed details, both on how the assassins had made it past his security and on the condition of his injured guards.

A knock sounded on his door.

"Come."

The door opened, and his captain of the guard stepped inside.

"How are your men?" Alejandro asked.

"Three dead, two wounded." Darius clasped his hands together. "Antonio is still in surgery."

"And the other survivor?"

"No news yet."

The grave tone of Darius's voice spoke volumes.

"What do you know so far?" King Alejandro asked. "Who were those men? And why did they want me dead?"

"It wasn't you they were shooting at," Darius said.

"Are you certain?"

"When they entered, they had a clean shot at you. They didn't take it."

"If I wasn't the target, who was?"

"Princess Cassandra."

A sharp pain pierced his heart, and he dropped into the chair behind his desk. Alejandro looked up at Darius, fighting to keep his voice calm. "Are you sure?"

"Antonio was shot pushing her out of the way. When I reviewed the security footage, their intention was quite clear. More than a dozen shots were fired at your daughter. None were fired at you."

"Why would someone want to kill her?" Even as the question escaped him, he knew. Not waiting for an answer, he said, "Double the guard on Victoria and Anabelle."

"I already did, and I arranged to have them moved to the villa in Switzerland."

"Good," Alejandro said, approving of the move. The family getaway in the Swiss Alps was heavily guarded and not known to the outside world, not even the family who would ascend to the throne if his family was no longer able to rule. "Tell me how those men made it past the gates."

"The guards at the side gate were drugged, and another was killed by the east entrance."

"And the patrols? How did they not see what was happening?"

"Someone told them you had requested an audience with the chefs."

"Who?"

"I don't know." Guilt and frustration laced his words. "The call came from the phone at the guard house where my men were drugged."

"So it could have been the attackers."

"We believe that is the case," Darius confirmed. "Sire, if I may. Perhaps it would be wise to have Princess Cassandra moved to a safe location until we can identify the security breach. If one of my men . . ."

"You think this is an inside job?"

"I would like time to rule out the possibility."

Alejandro contemplated the wisdom of his captain's suggestion, his heart torn between ensuring his eldest daughter's safety and keeping her close to him. Logic made the decision for him. "Where do you suggest I send her?"

"Somewhere unexpected," Darius said without hesitation. "If someone on the inside did help these men gain access to the palace, we have to assume the traitor knows the family's patterns well."

"Thank you, Darius. I appreciate your insight." Alejandro's gaze landed on the painting on the wall. "I'll take care of the arrangements myself."

"Yes, sire."

CHAPTER 2

LEVI STROLLED THROUGH THE MANICURED gardens that spanned the wide area between the royal chateau and the Mediterranean Sea, his gaze constantly sweeping past the shrubbery, the arched trellises, and the climbing roses. As though he didn't have a care in the world, he took a circuitous route around the garden's edge before approaching the sea wall that separated the royal chateau grounds from the private beach.

He put a hand on the stone wall and soaked in the view. To his left, the wide stretch of sand gave way to rocks and cliffs. In the other direction, the pristine sandy beach dominated. The fingers of early-morning light played off the waves, and a half dozen fishing boats dotted the horizon. How had he grown to expect to see them there, to see the sun rise each morning over the Mediterranean?

He would miss this. He could hardly believe his time in Meridia was nearly over. For the past two years, the royal chateau had been his home. He had endured three major threats against the royal family and watched the king's two sons marry and begin their happily ever afters. What had started as a short-term assignment had extended twice already, and each time, he had been relieved to find he didn't have to go back to the United States and the memories that always haunted him when he was in the country of his birth.

He sensed rather than heard someone approach. Even as he turned, his hand moved to the pistol holstered in the front of his waistband. But he recognized the long red hair before his eyes landed on Janessa's face.

"It's just me," Janessa said, taking position beside him as though she had nothing better to do than to get up and watch the sun rise. Levi knew better. He had worked with the woman for three years before she had married and given up her position with the CIA.

He nodded to her. "Your Highness."

"I don't think I'm ever going to get used to being called that."

"Sure, you will," Levi countered. "You've been married for almost a year. I'd think it would be old hat by now."

"Not quite."

"What's going on?" Levi asked. "It's not like you to be down here this early."

"Did you hear about the incident with the Rossi family in Sereno?"

"Yeah. Assassination attempt on King Alejandro."

"That's what the news is saying anyway." Janessa glanced behind her before continuing. "We think the target was actually Princess Cassandra."

"Princess Cassandra?" The image of the dark-haired beauty immediately popped into his mind. He had seen her briefly when accompanying Janessa and her husband, Prince Garrett, to a formal dinner in Rome several months ago. Janessa had offered to introduce Levi to the princess, but he had refused. A few minutes in her presence had been enough to understand the princess wasn't likely to acknowledge anyone in the working class, much less take the time to learn their names.

Levi pulled himself from the memory and noted the intensity in Janessa's expression. His eyes narrowed. "You want something."

"Yes." Janessa wandered forward, laying a hand on the wall. She stared out at the Mediterranean for a moment, not speaking until Levi adopted a casual stance beside her. "Princess Cassandra is arriving by boat sometime late tonight or early tomorrow morning. I want you to take over her security until the investigation is over."

"Excuse me?"

"You heard me."

"Why me? I'm supposed to be on a plane in two days."

"I know," Janessa said. "I also know you don't want to leave."

Levi didn't contradict her statement.

"You know I tried to convince Director Palmer to extend your assignment here," Janessa said, referring to the CIA director.

"I know." Levi nodded, an unspoken sign of his appreciation. "With the US naval base fully staffed, I'm not needed here anymore."

"But you are needed," Janessa countered. "You know tensions have been high between Sereno and Meridia since the agreement finalized on the naval base. You can help bridge that gap."

"You're going to have an American protect a princess who doesn't like Americans? I'm not following your logic."

"First of all, she doesn't know you're American," Janessa said. "You speak Italian like a native. If you don't tell her any differently, she'll assume you're Meridian."

"And second?" Levi asked.

"Belinda is back at headquarters."

The flash of memory erupted in the form of flames exploding through shattered windows. "How did you . . . ?"

"She's still a friend." Janessa let out a small sigh. "She also hasn't changed. She can't see the whole picture of what happened that night. She doesn't want to see it."

"I know." Levi shook away the memories of the one time he had tried to give her the truth.

"There's one more thing."

"What's that?"

"The two hit men who were killed last night—" Janessa paused and lowered her voice even though they were alone. "They were American."

"You can't be serious."

"Both former military."

"You think someone hired them to feed the hostilities between Sereno and the US?"

"That's my guess," Janessa said. "So what do you think? Are you willing to spend a bit more time rubbing shoulders with royals?"

Recognizing Janessa's attempt to lighten the mood, he shrugged. "I don't know. Princesses can be such royal pains."

"Yeah. We try." Janessa motioned to the chateau. "Come on. Let's get some breakfast, and we can talk about Princess Cassandra's living arrangements."

"Shouldn't we talk to Director Palmer before we move forward?"

"I already did."

Levi simply shook his head. "Of course you did."

"Did I mention that Patrice made your favorite blueberry scones this morning?"

"What did that cost you?"

"Not a thing." She smiled sweetly. "Sometimes being royal has its advantages."

"So it seems."

* * *

Cassie stared out the window of the private yacht, the spray of water rising into view as the vessel cut through the waves. The rhythm of the sea and the faint rumble of the yacht's engines should have soothed her, but the memories of last night wouldn't stop playing over and over in her head. Someone had tried to kill her. Someone had nearly succeeded.

The guards who had protected her had survived the night, though one of them was still in critical condition. Two men suffered because of her, three guards had died, and she didn't even know their names.

She closed her eyes against the tears that threatened. This was no time for a show of weakness.

She blinked several times and looked out the window again. The faint outline of the coast in the distance indicated she was already inside Meridia's territorial waters. What she didn't understand was why her father was sending her here or how he expected to get her ashore without the world knowing exactly where she was. She hated not having control of her life.

How she wished she could have joined her sisters at the hideaway in the Swiss Alps. Unfortunately, fear that someone might try to follow her there was enough of a deterrent to cause her father to make other arrangements for her. Now, here she was with a destination in mind but no idea what she was supposed to do when she got there.

Her father's declaration that he was sending her away had come only an hour after the gunshots had ceased. Amidst the confusion of the guests leaving the palace, Cassie had been escorted out a side entrance and taken to her father's yacht, where she'd spent a restless night in her stateroom while waiting for the proper crew to be assembled for today's journey.

Cassie wasn't sure how many people on board knew of her presence, but so far, she had seen only her private steward. As much as she often craved privacy, this wasn't what she'd had in mind.

For thirty hours, she had remained in her stateroom with nothing to do but relive the memories. She had managed a few hours' sleep yesterday afternoon and into the evening, but when the sun had gone down, she had showered and changed into a simple pair of navy slacks and a tan button-up shirt. With her long hair hanging loose, she supposed she looked as common as anyone else. But she wasn't common, and she never would be, no matter where her father sent her to hide.

She lifted her chin and straightened her shoulders, reminding herself of her duty. She was the oldest, the royal heir. It wasn't only her father's job to keep her family safe. It was hers too. If that meant spending a few weeks in a foreign land, then that was what she would do.

The engines stopped, the yacht's forward progress slowing. A sailboat crossed into view and approached from the port side.

Her heartbeat quickened, and she stood. They were still at least a half mile from shore. Why were they stopping? Was something wrong with the boat, or was she being set up again?

She hurried to the door and opened it to find her guard raising a hand to knock, a porter beside him. "Your Highness, your escort has arrived."

Cassie eyed the porter, a balding man in his forties. "My escort?"

"Another vessel will take you on the next leg of your journey," he explained. "Your father was explicit in his instructions that no one from Sereno know your end destination."

"I see."

"Come with me, please."

Though her trust was in short supply, she mustered her courage and stepped into the hall. The guard led the way while the porter retrieved two of her suitcases.

Questions and doubts plagued her. What if this was all part of an elaborate scheme to kidnap her or worse? How could she know for sure her escort was really someone who could be trusted?

She headed for the stairs leading to the lower deck, but the guard continued forward and led her outside.

Apparently sensing her confusion, he said, "The sailboat rides too high in the water to board from below."

Trapped between obligation and fear, she followed him onto the deck, stopping three feet from the starboard railing. Though the sailboat's deck was several meters below where she stood, she was able see the three people on board. To her surprise, she recognized two of them. Prince Garrett and Princess Janessa.

Her guard motioned to the metal ladder bolted to the side of the yacht. "I'm sorry, Princess, but I'm afraid the only way to get you onto their boat is for you to climb."

A new panic clawed through her, her fear of heights rising steadily. She watched a seaman attach a rope to the first of her suitcases and lower it down to the sailboat while the porter went below deck to retrieve the rest of her luggage. One by one, all four of her bags were transferred.

"It's your turn, Your Highness." Her guard held out a bright-yellow harness. "You'll need to put this on so we can attach the safety line while you climb down."

She could do this, she assured herself. She had to do this. She took the offered vest and slipped it on, clipping the front and ensuring the straps were pulled tight.

"Ready?"

Cassie drew a deep breath and blew it out, then took small steps to approach the railing before gripping it tightly.

In her mind, she chastised herself for her childish fear of heights, but she still couldn't keep her heart from racing or her palms from sweating. The sailboat was only three meters below her, but it might as well have been a hundred.

She tried to look down at her intended destination, but immediately, her eyes darted up and over the water. Several seconds passed as she gathered her courage. Muffled voices carried from below, followed by a shout from an unfamiliar voice. "Wait a minute."

Relief poured through her, no less dramatic than if she had been in front of a firing squad and had been given a stay of execution.

A dark-haired man appeared in front of her, both hands on the railing beside hers, his feet on the ladder.

"Look at me," he said with a quiet authority. "I'll be right here with you. We'll go one step at a time."

Mortified that she hadn't been able to hide her fear, she lifted her chin. "Fine."

Apparently unaware that gravity could plummet him down onto the boat below, he reached out his right hand and gripped her left arm. "You can do it."

When she looked at the ladder, she realized he had moved to the side to make room for her, only one foot and one hand keeping him in place.

Wanting nothing more than to have this experience behind her, she placed her left foot on the top rung. She felt a hand on her back, but she wasn't sure if the newcomer was trying to hold her in place or give her a signal of encouragement.

"Now the other foot."

She followed his instructions, her gaze now on her guard and the porter who stood on deck. The dark-haired man guided her down the first three steps, but when she reached the point where she had to let go of the railing, she stalled.

"You can do it," he repeated.

Her knuckles white, her stomach churning, she whispered, "I can't."

"You can. Trust me."

Before she realized what he was doing, his arms reached around her on either side, and her body was trapped between him and the ladder. The scent of man mixed with the ocean breeze, and the wall of solid muscle pressed against her back. His hand touched one of hers. "Let go with this hand. I'll guide it to the rung."

With his body holding her in place, she drew a deep breath and did as he asked. Her fingers found the top rung below the railing.

"Again."

He guided her other hand, taking her a step lower.

One movement at a time, they climbed down, pausing twice for Cassie to regain her bearings and her courage.

"Almost there," the calm voice said. "One more step."

She lowered her foot, and suddenly, another set of hands reached out to steady her.

"Here you go," Prince Garrett said, holding her arm until she gained her balance.

The man who had helped her leapt onto the deck, unclipped her safety harness, and signaled the yacht.

Cassie's gaze darted from the larger vessel to Garrett, her anxiety rising again. Her guards as well as her sense of security were gone, and now she was in the care of people she barely knew.

"Your Highness," the man said gently. "We need to get you below deck and out of sight."

It took a moment for her to realize he was speaking to her. "Yes, of course."

She didn't protest when he took her arm and led her to the hatch. He waited for her to go first before following her into the berthing compartment.

He retrieved a bottle of water from the minifridge, twisted the cap open, and handed it to her. "I'll be by the hatch if you need anything."

"Thank you." Cassie watched him ascend the stairs and close her inside. She lowered herself onto one of the couches that ran along either side of the room and stared at the stairs. Once again, someone had come to her rescue, and once again, she didn't know his name.

CHAPTER 3

LEVI HADN'T HEARD A PEEP from the princess for the past hour. He had expected her to be higher maintenance.

Garrett had dropped the sails a few minutes ago and was now powering the vessel using the on-board motor. Levi stood beside him as a wooden dock came into view.

Thick foliage flanked the narrow dirt road that connected the dock with the main street. The only sign of recent human presence was the silver sedan parked beside a cluster of trees. He hoped he would have enough room for all of Cassandra's luggage.

Why a woman would need four suitcases was beyond him.

He retrieved his phone and checked in with his security team.

As soon as he hung up, Garrett asked, "Is everyone ready?"

"Yeah. We're all set." Levi glanced at the closed hatch. "I don't suppose either of you wants to go check on the princess, do you?"

Janessa shook her head. "I'll help Garrett tie off the boat."

"But I should stay up here in case there are any problems," Levi said.

"Nice try." Janessa smiled in triumph. "You already said your men are in place."

"I think she's pulling rank on you," Garrett said.

"She was a lot easier to deal with before you married her."

"Insulting me isn't going to get me to go down there." Janessa lowered her voice. "Some people in the royal circles aren't happy Garrett married a commoner."

"Are you telling me she's one of them?" Levi asked.

"She wasn't very warm when we visited Sereno."

"You'd better go make sure she's ready," Garrett interrupted.

Recognizing the royal command for what it was, Levi knocked on the hatch. When Cassandra didn't respond, he waited a moment and knocked a second time. Again, he was met with silence.

Levi opened the hatch and started down the stairs. "Your Highness?"

He ducked down to see into the compartment, his eyes instantly drawn to Cassandra. The princess lay on one of the couches, a blanket tucked around her, both shoes on the floor. Her thick sable-brown hair fanned out behind her. Dark eyelashes contrasted against porcelain skin. He didn't know how someone from an island nation could remain so fair.

He reached the bottom of the stairs and cleared his throat. "Your Highness?"

Her eyes opened slowly, her disorientation evident. The royal air she always carried with her was absent now, replaced by a flash of vulnerability.

"I'm sorry to disturb you, but it's time to go."

She sat up and raked her fingers through her hair. "Where are we?"

"About an hour up the coast from Calene." Levi lifted two of her suitcases. "It'll take a minute to get your luggage transferred."

Leaving the princess to orient herself, Levi hauled the first of her suitcases topside. He handed the bags off to Garrett and returned downstairs to retrieve the remaining luggage.

During the minute he had been gone, Cassandra had transformed from a sleeping beauty into the princess he had come to expect. She now sat on the couch, her shoes on her feet, her hair smoothed into place, a royal air surrounding her.

"Give me a minute to get these loaded," Levi said. "I'll come get you when we're ready."

The princess stood. "Before you go, can I ask you a question?"

"Of course."

"What's your name?"

"Levi Marin."

She extended her hand. "It's nice to meet you, Mr. Marin."

Not sure what had prompted the formal introduction, he took her hand in his, noting the softness of her skin. "Nice to officially meet you too."

* * *

Fear and doubt once again churned through her as Cassie mustered all her energy to adopt the calm facade she had been trained to wear in public. She followed

Levi to where Garrett and Janessa stood by a simple sedan, her luggage nowhere in sight.

Garrett waited for her to reach him before he spoke. "Levi will take you the rest of the way."

"The rest of the way where?" Cassie asked.

"To our home in Bellamo," Garrett said. "Janessa and I will spend the next few days at the palace to draw any paparazzi away from the chateau where we live."

"Then what?"

"You will be our guest as long as you want," Garrett said.

"Or as long as my father wants," Cassie corrected, already feeling more like a prisoner than a guest.

"A suite has been prepared for you," Garrett continued. "Levi can show you around and answer any questions you might have."

Cassie swallowed her frustration and reminded herself that these people were doing her a favor. She let a little piece of her public mask chip away. "Thank you for your hospitality."

"Of course." Garrett took his wife's hand. "We'll see you in a few days."

Cassie watched the couple walk toward the dock.

"Ready?" Levi asked.

"Yes." She approached the car and waited by the rear passenger door. Levi passed her and opened the front door.

"Sorry. The back is full of luggage."

Though not accustomed to sitting in the front, she stepped forward and slid into the passenger seat. When Levi took the seat beside her, she said, "I thought you would have had more security here."

"I had my men do a sweep before we arrived. They're stationed on the main road." He started the car and turned around before heading for the opening in the trees.

"Your men know I'm here, then?"

"No. They think they were securing the area for Prince Garrett and Princess Janessa," Levi said.

"I see." Cassie wasn't sure what to think about the idea that her safety had been entrusted to only one man. Forcing that thought away, she asked, "What am I supposed to do while I'm in Meridia?"

"Whatever you want. Enjoy the pool or the stables. Go for a walk in the gardens, or go to the beach."

Her body stiffened. "Is that how you think royals spend their time? Lounging around in the sun all day?"

"Not at all. In my experience, royals work far longer and harder than most people realize," Levi said. "That doesn't change the fact that it's in your best interest to stay off everyone's radar for as long as possible."

Her posture relaxed. "Regardless, I don't have time for a vacation. I chair the energy commission in Sereno. We are in the middle of a major project right now, one that is extremely time sensitive."

"Your suite has a workspace in one of the bedrooms, but if you prefer, I can arrange for you to have a separate office. Or you can work in the chateau library."

"Thank you." They drove in silence for a minute before Cassie asked, "How many people know I'm here?"

"Besides the royal family, only me and Martino, the chateau manager."

"Can he be trusted?"

"Yes. He has been a loyal employee of the royal family for nearly three decades," Levi said. "I did a background check on him myself when we had some difficulties last year."

"I'm sorry if I seem paranoid."

"You've been through a traumatic experience. It takes time to sort things out and learn to trust again."

"You sound like you're speaking from experience." When Levi didn't respond, Cassie asked, "What is your position with the royal family?"

"I'm the head of security at the chateau where you'll be staying." Levi glanced at her. "Although, at the moment, my primary job is to keep you safe."

"So you're my bodyguard."

"Something like that."

She fell silent for a moment. "You realize that as soon as I arrive at the chateau, your entire staff will know I'm there."

"Not necessarily," Levi said. "Everyone thinks you're coming to visit me."

"What do you mean?"

"I mentioned I was picking someone up from the airport." Levi glanced at her. "The staff knows we have a new security officer due to start soon. They all assume that's you."

"Me? Security?" She shook her head. "No one would ever believe that. Not to mention, I have responsibilities. I wouldn't possibly have enough time to pretend to do one job while trying to keep up with another."

"It's either that or pretend to be my girlfriend," Levi said. "We need a plausible reason for your presence, or rumors will start. That's the last thing we want when we're trying to keep people from knowing where you are."

She took in his strong profile, all angles and planes. His wasn't a face she would ever see gracing the cover of a magazine, but with his firm lips and chiseled features, he certainly wasn't hard on the eyes. She supposed he would best be described as "ruggedly handsome."

Pulling her thoughts away from the man beside her, she focused again on the issue at hand. "It doesn't matter what role you try to put me in. Someone is bound to recognize me. The paparazzi have splashed my face on the internet often enough for me to be noticed."

"I'm sure that's true in your country, but Meridia has its own royals to watch. You show up in a regular car with a regular guy, people will believe what we tell them."

"Are you sure about that?"

Levi's lack of response was enough to indicate he too had doubts.

Following impulse, she said, "It'll be more believable if we say I'm your girlfriend."

The words were barely out of her mouth when Levi slammed on the brakes, and the car came to a screeching halt. Cassie's body jerked forward, held in place by her seat belt, her hands gripping the center console and the door. Out of the corner of her eye, she saw a deer bound from the road into the trees.

Levi put his hand on hers. "Are you okay?"

Her heart pounded, but the simple touch comforted her. "I think so."

His gaze remained intense on hers for a moment before he withdrew his hand and took his foot off the brake. They started down the road once more in silence. After a moment, he said, "Are you sure you want to fake a relationship? It's not as easy as it sounds."

"Surely it can't be that hard," Cassie countered. She wasn't going to mention that her entire dating history had been carefully orchestrated by her father's social secretary.

"Okay. What's our story going to be?" Levi asked.

Cassie pondered the question. "Maybe we could say we met in college."

"It would be more believable if we pass this off as a newer relationship," Levi suggested. "That way everyone doesn't expect us to know everything about each other."

"True."

"You said you head the energy commission for Sereno. Do you have a background in engineering?"

"Natural resources, actually."

"Perfect. I was at the energy summit six months ago with King Eduard. We can say I met you there."

"But I wasn't there."

"Even better."

"Excuse me? You want me to say I met you someplace where I wasn't?"

"You aren't you right now, remember?" Levi said. "If I'm going to be your boyfriend, is there anything I need to know before we try to pull this off in front of the staff?"

"Yes. My friends call me Cassie."

"Then Cassie it is."

CHAPTER 4

FOR THE PAST HOUR, LEVI had tried to adjust the scenario of what his life would entail over the next few weeks. His comment about posing as Cassandra's boyfriend had been a flippant attempt to gain her cooperation. He still wasn't sure how she had turned the tables on him. Cassie, he corrected. He needed to start thinking of her that way now.

He glanced at her sleeping in the passenger seat. Even at rest, a worry line marred her otherwise smooth brow. Early-morning sunlight streamed through the car window and highlighted the blonde streaks in her brown hair. Dark eyelashes fluttered against flawless skin.

Her eyes opened, and she straightened in her seat. Levi could see the brief moment of confusion, followed by her awareness of her current surroundings.

"I'm sorry. I didn't mean to fall asleep."

"You needed the rest." Levi studied her for a brief moment. Even though she wore only a light dusting of makeup, her inherent confidence and regal posture made him wonder if she was correct about being recognized by the chateau staff.

"How much farther?"

"We're almost there."

"Do you have one of those things to pull your hair back? It might help to hide who you are."

"No, but I don't need one." She combed her fingers through her long hair and proceeded to tie it in a knot to create a ponytail. She then retrieved a pair of sunglasses from her purse and slid them into place. "How's that?"

"Good." He turned into the long drive leading to the chateau and stopped at the security booth long enough to offer the proper paperwork to bring Cassie inside.

After he passed that obstacle, he instinctively reduced his speed so he could enjoy the scene before him. The French-inspired architecture of the chateau included towers and turrets, manicured gardens, and a wide lawn.

He entered the circular drive and stopped at the bottom of the steps leading to the main entrance. One of the wooden double doors opened, and Martino, the chateau manager, emerged.

Tall and distinguished, the older man reached the car as Levi climbed out. Levi handed him his car keys. "Can you please have the staff bring in her luggage?"

"Of course." Martino lifted a hand and waved at the butler who had followed him outside.

Levi circled to the passenger side and opened Cassandra's door. He offered his hand, her long, narrow fingers grasping his as she placed her feet on the ground. Despite her casual clothes, the moment she stood, her regal posture left no doubt as to who and what she was.

Levi released her hand. "This way." He escorted her into the spacious entryway, past the enormous great room, and up the sweeping staircase. He stopped at an open doorway on the left. "This is yours. If it doesn't suit you, I can ask Martino to make other arrangements."

Cassandra walked through, her steps slowing as she passed by the cluster of chairs that created a seating area, a couch opposite them.

She didn't look through the doorway to her right but crossed to the window seat. "I can see why Garrett and Janessa choose to live here. The views are stunning."

"Yes, they are." Levi continued farther into the room. "Although, I imagine you have similar views from your bedroom window."

"Of the ocean, yes, but not of the gardens." She pushed one of the gauzy white curtains farther to the side. "Could we go for a walk down there?"

"I thought you would want to settle in first."

"It'll be a few minutes before my luggage is delivered," Cassandra said. "Besides, wouldn't that be a normal thing to do? Take your girlfriend on a tour of your home?"

"I guess it would." Levi motioned to the door. "I'm ready when you are."

"No time like the present."

* * *

King Alejandro pushed the pain that radiated through his leg and into his torso to the back of his mind. He needed to know his daughters were safe, and he despised being forced to rely on others for that information.

He paced his living quarters from one end of the expansive living room, through the archway into the dining room, and back again. If the possibility of an internal breach didn't exist, he could have called his younger girls at the hideaway to check on them before following up with King Eduard to verify Cassandra had arrived at her final destination. The chance of being overheard or, worse, his calls being traced, tied his hands.

A knock sounded at his door. Alejandro paused beside his favored chair and called out, "Come."

Darius entered.

"Any news?" Alejandro asked.

"Everyone has safely arrived at their destinations," Darius said.

Relief poured through him. "They're all okay?"

"Yes, Your Majesty. They are all fine."

"Any other updates?"

"I'm afraid so."

"That doesn't sound promising." Alejandro sat and motioned for Darius to do the same. "What do you know?"

"I mentioned a guard was killed by the east entrance."

"Yes. What about it?"

"It appears the shooting in the main hall may have, at least in part, been a diversion."

"A diversion for what?"

"A robbery. Sire, I'm sorry, but the vault was broken into."

"What is missing?"

"We are only beginning the inventory; however, the founding jewels are gone," Darius said. "I'm so sorry, Your Majesty. The guards in that section of the palace abandoned their posts to respond to the shooting."

Alejandro digested the implications. The jewels were one of the protections in place to ensure his family's safety. Apparently, the precautions he had taken only last month had been more warranted than he had realized. "They were doing their duty. Their first priority was to protect me and my family."

"Yes, but one of them should have remained."

"Perhaps one did," Alejandro said. "You mentioned one was killed not far from there."

"Yes, but he wasn't assigned to vault duty," Darius said. "With your permission, I would like to reach out to Interpol. Recovering such a treasure is something they can help us with."

"You may enlist their help, but there is one thing you should know."

"What's that?" Darius asked.

"The thieves didn't get all of that particular treasure."

"How can you be so sure?"

"Trust me on this."

Another knock sounded.

Alejandro nodded his permission for Darius to answer the door. A moment later, he returned with Dr. Marois and another man Alejandro had never seen before.

"If you will excuse me, Your Majesty, I should return to my duties," Darius said.

"Of course. Please inform me as soon as you have any further developments."

"Yes, sire."

Alejandro turned his attention to the other two men. After being up all night with worry, the last thing he wanted was to deal with more people, especially his medical staff. "Dr. Marois. I don't recall having an appointment scheduled with you this morning."

"Your assistant indicated you would have a few minutes to meet with us, and I didn't want to miss this opportunity." Dr. Marois lifted a hand toward his companion. "Dr. Lewis was in Paris at a convention and agreed to consult with me on your case."

Dr. Lewis nodded his head. "It's an honor to meet you, Your Majesty."

Though the words were spoken in Italian, Alejandro couldn't miss the English accent. "Where are you from, Dr. Lewis?"

"Montreal."

"Dr. Lewis has made some wonderful strides in the treatment of cases like yours," Dr. Marois said.

Alejandro fought back his impatience and the never-ending sense of dread. "I appreciate your making time to see me." Alejandro shook the man's hand. "Please, sit down. I am interested to hear about these wonderful strides of yours."

"Thank you, Your Majesty. I hope my research will be of some help to you."

"As do I."

* * *

Cassie stopped beside a climbing rosebush and ran her finger along one of the silky blooms. The riot of flowers scented the morning, competing with the salty air.

"It's so peaceful here."

Levi leaned down and plucked a purple anemone from the flower bed to his right. He twirled it between his fingertips before he offered it to her. "Garrett and Janessa often enjoy spending time here at the end of a long day."

"I'm sure they have a lot of those." Cassie considered the new Meridian princess. "How is Janessa settling into her royal duties?"

"Very well." Levi's gaze returned to the path in front of him. "It doesn't hurt that the royal family has all been so welcoming to her."

"I have to admit, I was surprised by that," Cassie said. "The announcement of Garrett's engagement was entirely unexpected."

"I understand some weren't happy that he married a commoner."

"This certainly isn't the first time such a thing has happened." Cassie wasn't about to admit she'd had her own misgivings about the match, although not for the reasons Levi implied. Rather, she was more concerned that Janessa's upbringing in the United States would influence Meridia's foreign policy. Already they had to deal with the impact of having a US naval base in close proximity, thanks to the alliance.

She and Levi strolled past the swimming pool. "Does the family often have time to swim?"

"Not as much as they would like, but when Prince Stefano and Princess Alora bring their children, it is a common occurrence."

Cassie thought of Stefano and his new bride and two stepchildren. "The Meridian royal family has certainly been through a lot of changes over the past year."

"Yes, they have," Levi agreed. "It has been good to see them enjoy some peace after the struggles of the recent past."

"You're talking about the bombing attempts."

"Yes."

Cassie shuddered at the reality that she had nearly died a few hundred feet from here when she had attended Garrett and Janessa's wedding, which had included multiple explosive devices.

"I was at Garrett's wedding."

Levi glanced at her. "Yes, I know."

"You said you are the head of security here."

"That's right."

"Is it you I owe for saving my life and the lives of the others in attendance that day?" Cassie asked.

"Some might blame me and my staff for not preventing the presence of the bombs in the first place."

"After Friday night, I know better." Cassie looked out at the Mediterranean and reminded herself that she was safe now. "I didn't think anyone could penetrate the security of Sereno's royal palace."

"Unfortunately, no security is infallible." Levi motioned toward a path on the other side of the pool. He waited until they walked by a cluster of palm trees before he continued. "I promise you, the security here has been enhanced repeatedly to prevent any reoccurrences."

"Yet we are still relying on hiding my identity to keep me safe," Cassie said.

"You are safe here." Levi stopped by the sea wall and waited for her attention to focus on him. "Hiding your presence buys us time to investigate who might want you dead."

The bluntness of his words struck her. "You don't sugarcoat things, do you?"

"You are next in line for the throne of Sereno. Truth is necessary to rule effectively."

"I said almost the exact thing to my father only two days ago. He didn't agree."

"I'm sure he's trying to protect you." Levi glanced behind him before his gaze returned to her. "King or not, heir to the throne or not, you will always be his little girl."

"You sound like you are speaking from experience. Do you have children?"

"No, but I do have a younger sister."

"Then you can understand my position," Cassie said. "My father wants to protect all of his daughters, but eventually, it will be my responsibility to ensure the safety of Victoria and Annabelle. I can't learn how to do that unless he lets me."

"Then perhaps our dates should include expanding your understanding of how royal security works."

"Our dates?"

"I'm your boyfriend, remember?"

An unexpected ripple of anticipation fluttered inside her. "How could I forget?"

CHAPTER 5

Julien sat in his streamlined office and seethed. News of the shooting in Sereno had broken thirty-six hours ago, but no one had confirmed the identity of the casualties. Why hadn't he heard anything yet?

He stood and wandered to his window. Three stories below, pedestrians and cyclists made their way along the banks of the canal that cut through Copenhagen. The location had served his purposes well since graduating from university, but after six years, he was ready to take his place at the head of the country that should be his.

A knock sounded at his door.

"Come in."

Pratt entered, took off his hat, and cast his eyes to the floor. The man was average height, his light-brown hair and common features serving him well when he didn't want to be noticed.

"Is she dead?"

"I'm afraid not." He turned his hat in his hand. "The princess escaped without harm."

"How could you miss her?" Julien slammed both hands on his wooden desk, the movement causing several papers to take flight. "I gave you a fool-proof road map of precisely where she would be."

"The princess was later than expected, and my men encountered more resistance than anticipated."

"I paid you to plan for every contingency." He looked at the clock on his wall to see it was almost nine in the morning. "Why am I only hearing about this now?"

"You didn't want any electronic connection between us. I got here as soon as I could."

His temper boiled inside him. It was too late to stop the second stage of his plans. His people were already mobilizing. "I was counting on you."

"I know, sir." Pratt retrieved a cloth pouch from his pocket and offered it to Julien. "We were successful in retrieving these."

"The founding jewels." Julien took the cloth bag and opened the drawstring. He retrieved a glass breakfast tray from the buffet and set it on his desk. He then gently emptied the bag into the tray. A half dozen jewels sparkled in the light. Diamond, emerald, sapphire, garnet, topaz, and amber, each with impressive size and uniquely shaped.

Julien did a quick count. "Where are the rest of them?"

"This is all we found."

Suspicion surfaced. "This is all you found," Julien repeated.

"I promise you, sir, this is all there was," he insisted. "We searched the vault for another container, but nothing else was there."

"There should be four times this many."

"Perhaps King Alejandro split them up in case of a theft."

"If he did, he's more clever than I gave him credit for," Julien said. "What about the other item I sent you after?"

"It wasn't there either."

A new wave of frustration rose within him, and he fought to keep it in check. "Tell me what happened last night."

Pratt set a flash drive on Julien's desk. "The video from my men's body cameras is on here. I have some of my staff searching now for Princess Cassandra's whereabouts."

"She isn't at the palace?"

"We aren't certain, but she hasn't been seen since being rescued from the shooting."

"Find her," Julien demanded, slamming a fist on his desk. "And finish the job."

"Yes, sir."

* * *

Levi waited in the hall outside Cassie's rooms. Dinner would be her first test in close proximity to the staff.

After their walk in the gardens, Levi had escorted her back to her room, where they had eaten a late breakfast together and made dinner plans. Levi hadn't heard from her since.

Her door opened, and Levi struggled to keep his mouth from dropping open. Gone were her sunglasses. Her eyes were no longer blue but were a vibrant green. Her hair, now heavily streaked with blonde, hung in a loose braid.

Her regal posture remained, but with the simple cotton dress she wore, Levi hoped the staff wouldn't look beyond the clothing to see her true identity. He noted the way the ties at her waist accented her slender figure and reminded himself that their relationship was based on fiction.

"What do you think?" Cassie touched her braid. "Girlfriend material?"

"Absolutely." Levi offered his arm, and she tucked her hand through the crook of his elbow. "How did you . . . ?"

"I had some hair color and colored contacts in my luggage. You never know when it'll be necessary to make a clandestine exit from somewhere."

"I'm impressed."

"You should be. It's been a long time since I've had to braid my own hair."

The reminder of her social status doused the flicker of attraction he felt like a bucket of cold water. "You normally have a servant do that for you?"

"My sister, actually," Cassie corrected. "Annabelle loves that kind of stuff."

"Did you manage to get any rest?" Levi asked.

"I did, thanks." She fell into step beside him as they moved down the hall toward the main stairwell. "It was the first time in days I have fallen into a deep sleep. It was a bit disheartening when I awoke and didn't realize where I was."

"I can imagine." Levi guided her down the stairs and into the hallway that led to the kitchen.

"Something smells amazing."

"Patrice mentioned something about lasagna."

"That isn't often on the menu at state dinners."

"I know. I thought it might be a nice change for you," Levi said. "No one at the dinner table tonight will judge you on whether you know the right way to eat pasta."

"So, who are we eating with?"

"The Saldera family. Patrice is the cook here; her husband, Enrico, is the head chauffeur; and Paolo, Enrico's father, manages the stables." Levi opened the door to the kitchen and waited for Cassie to walk inside. As expected, Patrice was standing by the stove, a spatula in hand. "Patrice, this is Cassie."

Patrice wiped her hands on her apron and bustled across the room to greet Cassie. Patrice took both of Cassie's hands in hers. "It is so good to meet you. I hope you are hungry."

"Famished."

"Good, good. I always make too much."

"I have never heard anyone complain about that," Levi said.

Patrice's wide face split into a grin. "This one likes to steal my leftovers."

Cassie squeezed Levi's arm. "I've always known he was a very smart man."

"Go, sit." Patrice waved at the doorway on the far side of the room. "The rest of the family will be in shortly."

When everyone else arrived, Levi made the introductions, then managed to take only one bite before the questions started.

"Cassie, what brings you to the chateau? I thought you were the new security person."

"No, although Levi tried to convince me to take that job."

"She's here to visit me for a few weeks," Levi offered.

"Then you're dating?" Patrice asked.

"Yes." Cassie spooned some vegetables onto her plate.

Levi lifted his fork for another bite. "Patrice, this lasagna may be your best ever."

"Don't try to change the subject on me," Patrice said in her mom voice. "Why didn't you tell me you had a girlfriend?"

"Cassie and I haven't known each other that long." Levi reached for the bread basket and broke off a piece of baguette. "Only since the energy summit last fall."

"That was six months ago," Patrice pointed out.

"Poor Brenna is not going to be happy when she finds out," Paolo said.

"Brenna?" Levi asked. "She's too young for me."

Enrico took a sip of water. "She didn't think so."

"How old is Brenna?" Cassie asked, a touch of amusement lacing her voice.

"Twenty," Patrice said. "She is one of the house servants."

Paolo shook his head. "Poor girl."

Levi noticed the look on Cassie's face. "Do you find this amusing?"

"You're so cute when you're embarrassed." Cassie put her hand on his and spoke to Patrice. "Isn't he cute?"

"And this is why I haven't brought you to meet my friends before," Levi grumbled.

"I like her," Paolo announced.

"I do too." Levi glanced at Cassie before adding, "Most of the time."

Their dining companions chuckled.

"Well, I for one am glad you are here, Cassie." Patrice picked up the spatula and served herself a second piece of lasagna. "Maybe you can teach Levi how to take a day off every now and again."

"I will certainly do my best."

* * *

"I like them," Cassie announced as Levi led her past the various seating areas in the great room and out the french doors leading to the terrace.

"I'm glad. They liked you too."

Cassie tilted her head to the side. "Really? How can you tell?"

"Patrice asked about your favorite foods, Enrico offered to take you into town when I'm working, and Paolo invited you to the stables tomorrow. All telltale signs that they enjoyed your company."

"It's an odd sensation to think someone feels that way and know that it doesn't have to do with who my father is."

"I never thought about it that way." Levi put his hand on the small of her back and led her toward a lighted path in the garden. "Surely you have friends."

"I have my sisters."

"And . . . ?"

"We have family associates and people who I have been close to over the years, but always in the back of my mind, I can't help but wonder if they want to spend time with me or Her Royal Highness."

"With any luck, you won't have to worry about that here." Levi stopped and looked around for a moment before continuing forward. "I forgot to ask you if you want help unpacking. I didn't give the staff permission to do that in case you had anything in your luggage that would reveal your identity."

"I already unpacked."

Levi stopped again and stared, only this time his attention was on her. "You already unpacked four suitcases?"

"I'm well practiced." Cassie had used the mundane chore to distract herself from the memories of the attack in Sereno. She didn't bother to mention that she had also spent an hour setting up her office in the spare bedroom and reviewing the latest technical data on the proposed drilling platform off the coast of Sereno.

She noticed a stone bench beneath a trellis covered in ivy. "That looks like the perfect place to hide away from the world."

"I like my favorite spot better. I can enjoy the gardens and the ocean."

"Will you show me?"

"Sure."

They continued down the sidewalk, and Levi took a right when two paths met. After a few meters, the trees on either side crowded the walk, the palms curtaining the sky.

"I would have loved having gardens like these when I was a kid. Hide-and-seek would have been so much fun."

"What is your home like?" Levi asked.

Cassie appreciated that he recognized the palace as a home instead of a landmark or a symbol of power. "English gardens, lots of open space. The south lawn now houses the new security office . . ." Her words trailed away. "I guess the enhancement wasn't as effective as my father expected."

"When was the new security office built?" Levi asked.

"Construction started nine months ago, but it wasn't completed until this past February."

"Do you know why your father decided to enhance security at the palace?"

"After what just happened, I think the answer is obvious."

"No. The shooting shows it was warranted," Levi corrected. "When people choose to make drastic changes to their security protocols, it's usually a result of a threat or the expectation that a decision will cause new opposition."

"So you want to know what change occurred nine months ago," Cassie said, now understanding his thought process.

"I think the problem would have been identified before that, probably at least a year. It could be much longer, as much as two or three years," Levi said. "It would have taken months for designs to be drawn up and construction crews cleared to work on the grounds."

"A lot of changes were happening around that time." Cassie did the mental math. Fifteen months ago, everything had been right in her world. Her mother had been happy and healthy, except for her recurring headaches. "My mother was diagnosed with cancer thirteen months ago. She passed away a few weeks later."

Levi stopped and took her hand. He waited for her to face him. "I'm sorry for your loss."

His sincerity touched her. She squeezed his hand. "Thank you."

"Tell me, did anything change in the power structure of your country when your mother got sick or after she died?"

"My sisters and I took on more duties."

"From what I understand, you took on the lion's share."

"Both of my sisters are still attending university. They have neither the time nor the experience to take on much beyond an occasional social role."

"Which put everything on you."

Cassie didn't deny it.

"Maybe the next couple weeks will give you some much-needed rest."

"You know, you're sounding a lot more like my boyfriend than my bodyguard."

"Sometimes it's possible to be both." He stepped off the main sidewalk onto a mulched path.

Cassie ducked beneath a palm leaf he held aside for her. When she straightened, she discovered they had emerged on the far side of the garden where a grassy hill overlooked the ocean. A cluster of trees shaded the single bench that faced the water. The lights lining the adjoining path filtered through the leaves, creating a soft glow.

"This is beautiful."

Levi motioned to the bench and waited for her to settle onto it before he sat beside her. "I love this spot. We're high enough to look over the sea wall but low enough that boaters can't easily see us."

"A perfect hideaway."

"A good place to find some peace anyway."

"Do you often need to find peace?" Cassie asked.

"Everyone does at one time or another," Levi said.

"Thank you for sharing this with me."

"My pleasure."

CHAPTER 6

LEVI LED THE WAY DOWN the dirt path leading to the stables. Cassie followed, her white button-up tucked into tan riding pants. She was supposed to be blending in, but at the moment, she hardly looked like a commoner. Levi suspected her boots alone cost the equivalent of a week's salary. He glanced down at the knee-length leather. Make that a month's salary.

"I thought you were going to teach me about security today," Cassie said.

"I am."

They stepped clear of the trees. A few horses grazed in the pasture to the right, and two horses were already saddled and tethered to the hitching post outside the stables. Not for the first time, Levi admired the long wooden structure. He knew firsthand it could easily house two dozen horses and had more square footage than most homes in the United States.

Cassie motioned toward the ring to her left, which currently had several jumps in place. "Are you planning on testing my riding ability?"

"No. That's set up for Prince Stefano's children. Paolo has been teaching them how to jump."

Her expression softened into a wistful smile. "That's sweet."

Paolo walked out of the stables. "There's the pretty lady."

Cassie's smile brightened. "Good morning, Paolo."

"It is now." Paolo took her hand and kissed the back of it.

"I didn't know you were such a charmer," Cassie said.

Levi put his arm around Cassie's shoulders. "Cassie, you can stop flirting with my friend."

"But he's so handsome."

"Ah, I knew I liked this one." Paolo gave a nod of approval.

"Did you see Patrice this morning?" Levi asked.

"Yes." Paolo nodded. "Everything is all arranged."

"Thank you." Levi nudged Cassie forward before she could ask any questions. "Shall we?"

"I guess we shall."

They both mounted their horses, and Levi started down the path that circled through the wooded area behind the chateau. Cassie took position to his right, her head held high, her posture straight.

"Where are we going?" she asked.

"We're checking the fence line of the chateau to make sure there hasn't been any tampering."

"Keeping the perimeter secure," Cassie summarized.

"Yes." Levi reined his horse to the right.

"How often do you do this?"

"It depends on the season and who is currently at the chateau." He reached a spot where cinder block and wrought iron created an inner barrier. Identical fencing ran along the outside of the property, and a high-voltage electrical fence ran between the two. "We rely on motion sensors and security cameras to detect intruders, but the fence is the first barrier to prevent anyone from penetrating the grounds."

"Why three fences?" Cassie asked. "If someone can get past the electrical fence, it wouldn't be a big deal for them to climb the inner wall."

Impressed that Cassie saw the nearly invisible electric fence, he said, "The inner and outer walls protect people from the high voltage. The royal family wanted to make sure that anyone injured from the electric fence knew they weren't supposed to be there."

"Do you worry Stefano's children might try to climb the fence?"

"They've all been taught of the dangers, not unlike teaching a child to look both ways before crossing the street," Levi said. He couldn't imagine having to address such issues as a parent, but then, he would never be royal. "Stefano and Alora never allow them to stray into the danger zone anyway."

"What happens if someone manages to cut off the electricity to the fence?"

"We have multiple backup generators for our security systems," Levi said. "To answer your original question, my men walk the perimeter at least once a day."

"I gather we're taking over that duty today."

"We are." They continued through the thick trees that lined the property edge. "Do you ride often?"

"Not since my mom passed away."

"Not enough time?" Levi asked.

Her head tilted slightly to the left, and her words were spoken as though well practiced. "Time is a luxury of which I rarely have an abundance these days."

"Do you have any pressing work that can't wait until tomorrow?"

"I need to review the engineering proposal for a new construction project."

"How long will that take?"

"A few more hours." Cassie breathed in the salt air. "If I work on it this afternoon, I can put together my comments and recommendations in time to get it to my father tomorrow."

"Good, because I have plans for us this morning."

"Something besides horseback riding?" Cassie asked.

"Yes."

"Are you going to tell me what they are?"

"No."

Cassie gave him a sideways glance. "Are you trying to be mysterious?"

The corner of Levi's lips twitched up. "No comment."

* * *

"A picnic." Delighted, Cassie reined in her horse and took in the picturesque setting. A red-and-white checkered blanket covered the grassy area beneath an ancient pine tree, the wide branches spreading over the peaceful setting. From where she currently sat, the Mediterranean spread out before her, the beach a short walk down the narrow path to her left.

"How did you manage this?" Cassie asked. "I've been with you all morning."

"Patrice put together the food, and Paolo rode out to set our picnic up for us." Levi pointed to a pack horse tethered a short distance away. "We'll take everything back with us so they don't have to come back to retrieve everything."

"They are incredibly kind."

"Yes, they are," Levi agreed. "It didn't hurt that they like you."

They both dismounted and tied their horses to a tree a few meters away from the picnic.

"I thought about taking you onto the cliffs," Levi said. "The view is incredible up there, but I figured you wouldn't enjoy that as much."

Cassie thought back to the night they met. "I must have looked terrified for you to pick up on my fear of heights so quickly."

"I recognized the signs. My sister is the same way. She used to sit in the center seat in the car so she couldn't see when we drove through the canyons."

"I don't blame her." Cassie stopped beside the picnic blanket.

"Let's see what Patrice packed for us. With any luck, she sent some of her fried chicken." Levi squatted beside the picnic hamper and flipped the lid. "We're in luck."

"Cold fried chicken," Cassie said. "That's not something I've tried before."

"What?" Levi looked up as though she had announced she was from another planet.

"Don't look so shocked. Picnics where I come from usually consist of shrimp cocktail, cucumber sandwiches, and fresh fruit."

"What about dessert?"

"The fruit is the dessert."

"You were a deprived child." Levi shook his head. "We're about to make up for that."

"I think you are the first person to ever call me deprived."

"Sit down. I'll show you what you've been missing."

Cassie sat on the edge of the blanket and proceeded to take her boots off. She placed them on the ground beside her and scooted closer to where Levi was laying out an assortment of food: fried chicken, sliced cheese, croissants, fat purple grapes, and thick brownies with fudge icing.

"Wow. Patrice outdid herself."

"You can see why I have enjoyed working here." Levi handed her a plastic plate, fork, and knife. "Here you go. Dig in."

Cassie used her fork to serve herself a chicken thigh and proceeded to add a sampling of the other food before her. One bite was all it took for her to roll her eyes heavenward. She chewed and savored.

"It's official. I have to steal Patrice away from Meridia."

"Those are fighting words." Levi shook his head. "If Patrice left, Garrett and Janessa would have a revolt on their hands."

"I wouldn't want to be responsible for starting a civil war." Cassie took another bite and pondered. "This chicken may be the best I've ever had. What do you think the chances are that Patrice would share her recipe?"

"If you ask her, she would probably teach you how to make it."

"Me? Cook?" Cassie shook her head. "Now that's taking foreign territory to a whole new level."

"I bet you could do it if you wanted to."

"Maybe. I've never really tried," Cassie admitted. "The chef at the palace isn't friendly to those who invade his kitchen."

"I can understand that. Patrice has been known to get territorial on occasion." Levi leaned back on one elbow. "I know you learned to ride horses when you were younger. What else did you do for fun?"

Cassie pondered the question: dance, piano, foreign language, archery, shooting, horseback riding, sailing, history, literature, tennis, golf, skiing, swimming. Lessons had dominated her childhood. "I always liked swimming, but I haven't been able to do that often since I was a kid."

"Why not?"

"A princess in a swimsuit? I might as well invite the paparazzi to throw me on the front page of their tabloids."

"We don't have any paparazzi here," Levi said. "At least not yet."

"True."

"What else besides swimming?"

Cassie ran through her various skills, weighing her enjoyment of each.

Before she formulated her answer, Levi added, "If you could walk out of your room and do anything you wanted, what would it be?"

"I like walking. Just walking."

"Walking," Levi repeated.

"The fall of my sophomore year of college, I got to spend a day in Tallinn, Estonia," Cassie said. "I was on my way to Helsinki for a trade summit, but for that one day, it was just me."

"And your security detail."

"Well, yes, but while I walked around the old-town part of the city, they let me pretend I was alone." She smiled at the memory. "I walked up to the old Russian Orthodox church, looked out at the Baltic Sea from a park above the city. I wandered through the parks and browsed the little shops. I loved it."

Levi's gaze intensified, and Cassie's cheeks grew warm.

"Do you have a couple hours to spare tomorrow?" Levi asked. "I think you would enjoy a trip into Bellamo."

"Is it safe for me to go into town?"

"I think so." Levi reached out and tugged gently on a lock of her hair. "I would suggest wearing a hat and your colored contacts though."

"Are you going to get into trouble for entertaining me instead of working?" Cassie asked.

"We'll both get our work done," Levi said. "We'll call this outing a lunch date."

"For someone who wasn't sure we could pass as boyfriend/girlfriend, you're sure getting into this charade."

Levi twirled her hair around his finger, their faces close. "To my surprise, I'm enjoying it."

Cassie's heart skittered. "I am too."

CHAPTER 7

AFTER ESCORTING CASSIE TO HER suite after their ride, Levi made his way to the security office. Franco sat in front of the bank of security monitors, images of various sections of the grounds visible.

"Anything concerning?" Levi asked.

"No activity except for the groundskeepers, you, and your girlfriend."

The reference to Cassie as his girlfriend illustrated that the gossip chain at the chateau was still alive and well. Rather than ask the source of Franco's information, he said, "I'll try to bring her up here to meet everyone when the shift changes."

"How long is she here for?"

"Not sure yet. At least a couple weeks."

"I guess her visit was a good reason to delay your departure," Franco said. "Any chance you're thinking about staying?"

Falling back on his latest cover story, Levi said, "My new job pushed back my start date by a month while they process the rest of my clearances, but I'll be leaving when they get everything sorted out."

"Too bad."

"You're stuck with me for the time being." Levi took a seat at the empty computer station beside Franco. "I spoke to King Eduardo earlier today. He asked that we keep an eye on the stability in the region."

"He's concerned after the assassination attempt in Sereno?"

"Yes, and understandably," Levi said. "I'd like to know who is behind it and make sure we don't have a threat heading our way."

"I'll start running some searches."

"I appreciate it." Levi leaned forward in his seat. "On to more important things. Have you found out what Patrice is making for dinner?"

"Not yet, but Brenna is supposed to text me when she finds out."

"Turning the household help into spies?" Levi asked, amused.

"What can I say? You taught me well."

* * *

Cassie reviewed her comparative analysis, not pleased with the results. Over the past few weeks, she had eliminated several of the companies who had vied for the rights to drill for oil and natural gas off the shore of Sereno, narrowing the contenders down to four. Of those four, one was a French company, one Greek, and the other two American.

If her father had his way, she would eliminate the American companies simply because of their country of origin. Though she didn't disagree with her father that they needed to limit foreign influence in their domestic affairs, no matter which company they selected, they would be entrusting the health and safety of their citizens and the protection of their environment to foreigners. Cassie's solution of maintaining strict government oversight wasn't popular with the companies or with parliament, but she refused to have an oil spill off her shores.

An incident like America's Deepwater Horizon could bankrupt her country overnight. She couldn't risk any company working in Sereno taking the kind of shortcuts that had caused that spill. The citizens of Sereno would be wary enough of a foreign company being entrusted with so much of their livelihood.

She picked up the French proposal again and started reading. She was ten pages in when someone knocked on her door.

Cassie startled, the pages dropping from her hand as she pressed her hand to her heart. She took a moment to let her pulse steady before she stood, then she straightened the pages she had dropped and turned them facedown.

She opened the door to find Levi standing in the hall.

"Do you have a minute?" he asked.

"Yes, of course." She stepped back and waved him inside. "I could use a break."

Levi glanced at the paperwork spread over the coffee and side tables, her laptop in the center of the mess. "Wind farms or oil rigs?"

"Oil rigs."

"You've got a huge task on your hands, deciding how to best balance energy needs and profit with environment."

"I've been feeling the weight of that decision today." She reclaimed her seat and motioned for him to sit. "What brings you by? It's not dinnertime yet. Is it?"

"Not for another hour." Levi sat across from her. "I wanted to know, what are the differences between you and King Alejandro on foreign policy?" Levi asked.

"You're talking about my father. Our views are very much the same."

"But not exactly the same." Levi retrieved a piece of paper and set it between them.

"I guess the main difference is that I'm more conservative on environmental impact issues."

"Like?"

Cassie motioned toward the balcony and the water beyond. "The Mediterranean has been overfished for years. I'm in favor of restricting the fishing within our territorial waters, and I've lobbied with several other nations to do the same."

"What else?"

"I've been pushing for my father to expand our airport and allow more airlines to come into our country to increase our tourism income."

"Neither of those would be reason for Americans to get involved. They don't fish this region, and lower prices in the tourism industry is in their favor." Levi tapped his pen on the blank paper in front of him. "You said you're the chairperson for the energy commission. Have you made any changes since taking over?"

"A few. Nothing major."

"Tell me about them."

She waved a hand in the air. "My main focus has been on developing our own energy sources so we aren't reliant on other countries."

"From what I understand, Sereno has been increasing its usage of solar power and has explored developing a wind farm off the coast," Levi said. "And I know you are reviewing bids for drilling rights in your territorial waters."

"You're well informed."

"It's my job to be informed."

Cassie debated a moment about whether to step onto the bridge of trust. "Have you heard of the Leviathan field?"

"Isn't that the natural gas field that Israel and Lebanon keep fighting over?"

"Yes. It's an enormous natural resource for the area."

"What does that have to do with Sereno?" Levi asked. "The Leviathan field is in the eastern Mediterranean. Your country is in the western Mediterranean."

"I commissioned a study last year to consider the possible location of a wind farm off our coast. Wind energy is greatly underutilized in the region, and if my calculations are correct, Sereno could become nearly self-sufficient within ten years."

"Makes sense," Levi said. "Avoid dependence on other countries, and your economy strengthens."

"Yes." Relieved that Levi understood the basic nuances of international relations, she forced herself to confide in him further. "It was during our study that we discovered a natural gas deposit in the Mediterranean floor."

"Which is why you're reviewing proposals right now."

"Yes, but with the exception of a few companies we have entered into confidential bidding agreements, the general public doesn't realize the potential of our discovery. It's quite substantial."

Levi's eyebrows lifted. "How substantial?"

"The Sereno field rivals the size of the Leviathan field." She drew a deep breath before offering the critical information. "Our initial estimates value it at 80 billion euros worth of harvestable oil and gas deposits."

"Eighty billion?" Levi repeated. "That would put Sereno on the map as one of the leading energy producers in the area."

"The wind farm alone would have been enough to make an impact, but by moving forward with it and partnering with an energy company for the drilling of oil and natural gas, Sereno will never have to worry about financial issues again."

"Assuming those financial gains are well managed," Levi said. "Venezuela is a prime example of what happens when an unstable government has control over such great wealth."

"The monarchy in Sereno has been in control since the 1600s. Every king from King Cesare in 1619 down to my father has ruled without any major revolts."

"Every king," Levi said.

"That's right."

"Every king," Levi repeated. "Not every queen."

"A queen has never ruled Sereno before," Cassie said. The weight of that fact pressed in on her. "I'll be the first."

"That's right. You'll be the first." Levi pushed out of his chair and crossed to the window. He turned back to face her. "What if this has nothing to do with economics and everything to do with who is in power?"

"You think someone has an issue with Sereno being ruled by a woman?"

"It's possible."

"I don't buy it." Cassie shook her head. "My youngest sister is eighteen. The citizens of Sereno have known for years that they would one day be ruled by a queen."

"What about cousins or any other extended family who would be next in line to the throne if you and your sisters were no longer able to rule?"

Cassie folded her arms across her chest. "If my sisters and I are assassinated?"

"Yes."

"Honestly, I'm not entirely sure. Rule would pass to another family, but my father lost touch with them before I was born."

"Don't you have any aunts, uncles, cousins?" Levi asked.

"My uncle Elliott, but he is my mother's brother. He isn't in line to rule. Neither are my cousins."

"How is it possible that your family has been in power for four hundred years and there are only three people in line for the throne?"

"The smallpox epidemic at the end of the 1800s devastated much of Sereno. Thousands of our citizens died, including almost all of the royal family," Cassie said. "Then in 1963, an earthquake hit in the Mediterranean. A massive mudslide wiped out an entire village. It was the same village where most of the royals resided."

"Your family sure has had a tough time of it."

"My grandfather especially. He was one of only three to survive the smallpox epidemic. When the mudslide occurred, only he, his wife, and his mother survived."

"So we know you don't have family members who can try to steal the crown from you and your sisters," Levi said. "Tell me about your uncle."

"Uncle Elliott serves on my father's advisory committee."

"What is his area of expertise?" Levi asked.

"He's my father's chief legal adviser and advises on foreign policy, specifically with North America."

Levi's eyes sharpened. "Does he have ties to North America?"

"He earned his MBA from Princeton, and he's the only member of the royal family who has lived in the United States, besides Crispan."

"Who's Crispan?"

"He's Elliott's oldest son. He also attended Princeton. After graduation, he went to work in Houston."

"Doing what?"

"He's a private consultant, working in the oil industry."

"Which means he could know about the extent of the wealth to be gained from the Sereno natural gas field."

"He's well aware of our findings," Cassie said. "My father and I asked him for recommendations of which companies to solicit bids from for drilling rights."

"Then he could be involved."

"I can't believe my own family would try to have me killed." Cassie's certainty hung in her words. "Crispan may be living in the US, but he is loyal to Sereno. He even suggested we consider several European companies rather than those from the US. Besides, what would he have to gain? My uncle and cousins benefit from their association with the royals. If something happened to my family, they would lose their positions."

"Unless they found a way to gain either power or wealth another way." Levi grabbed another notepad and slid it in front of her. "I need a lesson on your extended family. I want you to tell me everything about your uncle and cousins. Where they went to school, what their royal duties are, who they're close to, everything."

"This is going to take all night."

"Probably." Levi leaned forward and rested his elbows on his knees. "Might as well get started."

CHAPTER 8

A MORNING SWIM WITH NO paparazzi anywhere to be found. Cassie was certain she had died and gone to heaven. She stroked through the water and came to a stop at the side of the pool.

"You look like you're enjoying yourself." Levi set a tray on a wrought-iron table and picked up a thick towel from a lounge chair. "Ready for breakfast?"

"I am." She looked up at the blue sky. "What a gorgeous day."

"It is." Levi opened the towel and held it for her.

Cassie walked up the pool steps and took the towel. "Thank you."

"You're welcome." Levi remained standing until Cassie dried off and wrapped the towel around herself. After she sat on the chaise, he took the seat beside her and handed her a plate. "Patrice made blueberry scones this morning."

"That sounds good." Cassie lifted the cloth that covered the bread basket and selected a scone. She noted the fresh berries and sliced cantaloupe. "She sent fruit too."

"Patrice is a firm believer that breakfast is the most important meal of the day." Levi poured them each a glass of orange juice.

"Did you get any sleep last night?" Cassie asked. After talking about her mother's side of the family until eleven o'clock last night, she wasn't sure if Levi had stayed up later to keep digging into their backgrounds or if he had chosen sleep over work.

"I only stayed up another hour after I left your suite." Levi loaded up his plate. "I did want to ask about your cousin Crispan. You said he was involved in helping you identify potential oil companies to partner with."

"That's right."

"Do you think he had any help creating that list?"

"I don't know. I suppose it's possible," Cassie said. "Why?"

"Everything you told me checks out, and if I'm to trust that your family doesn't have any internal issues going on, then I have to wonder if anyone else might have inadvertently been given sensitive information about the oil contracts."

"Under normal circumstances, I would call him and ask," Cassie said. "I don't suppose that's possible while I'm staying here though, is it?"

"I might be able to set up a secure call through the US naval base. That shouldn't raise any red flags since Crispan is living in Houston."

"Are you sure you feel comfortable involving the Americans?"

"I have some contacts on base I know I can trust," Levi said. "If I ask for a favor, they won't demand to know the details."

"That's saying something," Cassie said. "It isn't often the military of one country will blindly do a favor for a foreigner."

"Yes, but I do have the advantage of working for a princess who is from their country."

"True." Cassie glanced at the sun. "With the time difference, it's the middle of the night in Houston."

"We can set up the call later this afternoon," Levi said. "I thought you might enjoy a ride into town today."

Cassie weighed her desire to explore with her lingering fear that came from knowing someone wanted her dead. "You're certain no one knows I'm here?"

"I'm certain," Levi assured her. "I think a couple hours away from the chateau will do you good, and it will only reinforce your cover story that you're here to see me."

"I suppose it would be good to keep everyone believing we're together."

"Is that a yes?"

"As long as you're bringing your gun with you, it's a yes."

"I always have my gun with me," Levi said. "Let's plan on leaving at two. We can have a late lunch in town."

"Perfect." Cassie looked up at the sun. "I think I might work by the pool today. It's too beautiful outside to close myself up in my rooms."

"You're a very smart woman."

"I'm glad you think so."

* * *

Levi looked over his latest reports, several of them from his CIA contacts. Cassie was right. From everything the analysts could see, her mother's side of the family was content with their supportive role to King Alejandro, and no one had uncovered any potential motives for any of them wanting Cassie dead.

With the eight-hour time difference between Meridia and Houston, the call to Crispan would have to wait until tonight, after he and Cassie got home. He experienced a tug at his emotions when he forced himself to face the fact that within weeks, home would once again be the United States. The mere thought of seeing Belinda again, of facing his greatest failure, left him hollow inside. He had loved her once, had even wondered if they might build a future together. All those feelings had changed over the months Belinda had recovered from the explosion and he had battled his own emotional demons.

Logically, he knew Belinda's decision to break protocol and go into the warehouse outside of Kiev had caused her injuries. What she didn't know was that Levi had killed two Russian operatives while trying to protect her. He had killed for the first time, and it had been her fault.

Coming to terms with Belinda's mistake and the results of it had taken time, but he had done it. He had even tried to explain to Belinda why he had distanced himself from her, but she hadn't wanted to hear it. She had spun the events in Kiev into an alternate reality.

Instead of her choosing to enter the warehouse before Levi had cleared the area, she believed he had told her everything was safe. She had convinced herself that Levi had stopped visiting her because he hadn't wanted to see the burns on her arms and neck or the reminder that they were his fault.

His phone rang, pulling him from the memories. Levi picked it up to find Janessa on the other end.

"Got a minute?" Janessa asked.

"Yeah. What's up?" Levi leaned back in his seat.

"I checked with King Eduard a few minutes ago. King Alejandro is still refusing help on analyzing their security issues the night of the shooting."

"I can't say I'm surprised," Levi said. "Neither one of us would be quick to let another foreign intelligence service view our internal security procedures."

"You're right, but I was hoping."

"That makes two of us."

"How is everything going with Princess Cassandra?" Janessa asked.

"We're making it work. I'm taking her into the village this afternoon," Levi said. "I think she's getting a little stir-crazy."

"Hey, you made it three days without leaving the grounds. That's not bad."

"When are you and Garrett getting back?"

"Either tomorrow or the next day. My father-in-law is taking advantage of having us at the palace."

"Wearing a lot of party dresses, are you?"

"Ha ha," Janessa said dryly. "I've been meeting with your replacement actually."

"It's about time a final decision was made," Levi said, even as he dreaded the changes that would follow his replacement's arrival. "When does he arrive?"

"She. Her name is Rachelle Bourgeau. She came over from Interpol around the same time Noelle and Jeremy started their training," Janessa said. "King Eduard likes the idea of having someone in your position who hasn't come up through the ranks of the royal guard."

"Keeping people who think outside the box, huh?"

"The king is a wise man."

"Does this mean I need to start cleaning out my office?" Levi asked.

"No need to deal with that yet. Rachelle can use one of the desks in the security office while you're still here," Janessa said. "I want you to have that extra privacy while Cassandra is at the chateau."

"I appreciate that."

"I figured you would. Also, Garrett wanted me to invite you and Cassandra to a dinner party on Saturday night," Janessa said. "It'll be a small affair, only twenty or so guests, mostly members of the ruling council."

"Thanks, but I doubt Cassandra is up for a public appearance at this point, especially since members of the ruling council are too likely to recognize her."

"Let her know she is welcome if she would like to come."

"I will."

"One more thing."

"What's that?" Levi asked.

"Since you're going into Bellamo, would you mind picking something up for me at the museum?"

"Sure. What do you need?"

"A painting," Janessa said. "While you're at it, you could give Cassandra a tour."

"I could, but I think I'll enlist the help of an expert."

"That would work too."

CHAPTER 9

CASSIE GRIPPED THE EDGE OF her seat as she and Levi drove toward the village of Bellamo. The plain sedan, her simple cotton dress, her colored contacts, her lightened hair—surely no one would realize she was Princess Cassandra of Sereno.

She glanced at Levi. "What do you have planned for us this afternoon?"

"There's a restaurant I thought you would enjoy. It has a great view of the water, and it's early enough that it isn't crowded yet."

"And the food?"

"You'll have to be the judge of that," Levi said. "Personally, I think it's a toss-up as to which is better, the food here or Patrice's cooking."

"Now I'm intrigued." They reached the top of a rise, the red-tiled rooftops littering the valley below. Cassie's grip on her seat loosened, and a pang of homesickness washed over her. "How quaint. It reminds me a bit of the village near the palace in Sereno."

Levi patted her hand. "We'll get you home soon, but for today, let's pretend you don't have a kingdom waiting for you."

"I'll try."

Levi pulled up beside a stone building, the wide patio beside it adorned with wrought-iron tables and padded chairs. A handful of customers sat beneath umbrellas, a waiter moving among them with a pitcher of water.

What would it be like, she wondered, to have the freedom and comfort to sit outside and enjoy the sun and the breeze?

Levi parked and circled to open her door. She put her hand in his and stood. They fell into step, the light breeze lifting her hair off her shoulders and teasing it around her face. The thought of how she would look in photos surfaced, immediately contradicting the scene before her. No paparazzi, no crowds, no attention whatsoever. Was this what normal felt like?

They reached the main entrance, and Levi released her hand. The sudden lack of warmth brought forward a new reality. The simple gesture of walking hand in hand had been so natural that Cassie hadn't realized Levi had maintained that connection between them until it was broken.

Levi escorted her through the double doors, taking her hand again as they approached the host standing at the podium.

"I have a reservation for Marin."

"Yes, sir." The bald man in his fifties picked up two menus. "Right this way."

If they couldn't sit outside, their table by the window was a good second choice. Levi pulled her chair out for her, and Cassie sat, her eyes still on the wide window and the view it provided: an open stretch of beach, gentle waves washing over the sand, a curve of land providing beauty and contrast.

Levi helped her scoot her chair in.

"Thank you."

"You're welcome."

The maître d' handed them both menus before he left them alone.

Cassie glanced at the menu and made her selection, her attention turning once again to her surroundings. Potted palms invited the outdoors inside and added a feeling of privacy from the nearby tables. Though a few other tables were occupied, it appeared most of the customers had opted to enjoy the beautiful weather.

"Do you know what you want?" Levi asked.

"Yes."

Levi signaled the waiter. After they ordered, Levi said, "I received a request from our hosts this morning."

"What request is that?" Cassie asked, noting how Levi didn't mention Garrett and Janessa's names in public.

"Two requests, actually," Levi amended. "First, we have been invited to join them for a dinner party on Saturday night."

"I'm not sure that's such a good idea."

"I know. I said you weren't interested in being in the spotlight at the moment."

"What was the other request?" Cassie asked.

"They have a painting they asked me to pick up at the gallery while we're in town," Levi said. "That is, if you don't mind."

"Would we be able to spend some time there?" Cassie asked. "It would be nice to enjoy art for a change without considering what wall it should go on or how much insurance to carry."

"I'm sure we can do that," Levi said. "I think you'll enjoy the current exhibit."

"What exhibit is that?"

"Shades of the Mediterranean. It features work from all over the region, including a few of Sereno's local artists."

"I had no idea."

"I think you'll enjoy seeing the beauty of Meridia and Sereno in the same place. It's quite a sight."

"I look forward to it."

The waiter arrived and set a plate of stuffed mushrooms in between them.

Cassie picked up her fork and lifted one onto her plate. She cut it in half and took a bite. "Mmm." She chewed, savoring. After she swallowed, she speared the other half. "Okay, this is seriously amazing."

"I know. Patrice has been trying to get this recipe for over a year."

"I can see why." Cassie lowered her voice. "Maybe she should get Garrett to issue a royal command."

"He thought about it, but instead, he lets Patrice hire this restaurant for some of the big events."

"They cater too?"

"Yes, and very well."

"Are they helping with the dinner on Saturday night?" Cassie asked.

"As a matter of fact, they are."

"In that case, maybe we do need to attend."

Levi took a mushroom for himself. "It's either that or raid the kitchen."

"I like the way you think."

* * *

Levi led Cassie into the main exhibit hall in the museum, where paintings lined the walls and sculptures adorned the open space in the center.

Cassie stopped in front of a slim column of wood that had been fashioned into a mermaid. "This detail is amazing."

Pierre, the museum director, emerged from an adjoining hallway. "Levi, good to see you." Pierre shook his hand. "I don't believe I've met your friend."

"Pierre, this is Cassie." Levi put his hand on her back, that brief contact that indicated their friendship was one of a romantic variety. "She's in town visiting me for a few weeks."

"So good to meet you." Pierre took Cassie's hand. Though he was old enough to be her father, Pierre lifted Cassie's hand to his lips. "Tell me, my dear, how did you ever get involved with this one? You are far too beautiful to adorn his arm."

"You are very kind." Cassie glanced at Levi, clearly amused. "He is rather handsome though, don't you think?"

"I won't contradict your opinion, but you have to admit he could use a bit more culture in his life." Pierre lowered his voice. "He returned a painting last week because he didn't like the frame."

"It wasn't just the frame," Levi countered. He didn't bother to add that while he found the piece hideous, the large size had created a significant difficulty for his staff to properly secure the valuable piece of artwork.

"Pollock has always been an acquired taste," Pierre said.

"If you say so." Levi waved a hand toward the nearby exhibit. "Since you're so concerned about my cultural education, though, perhaps you will spare some time to show Cassie and me around the museum today."

"I'd be happy to," Pierre said. "Are you here to pick up the Monet?"

"Yes."

"Let me inform my staff to prepare it for transport. Enjoy the new exhibit while you wait. I'll be back in a few minutes."

"Thank you, Pierre," Levi said.

As soon as he departed, Cassie wandered to the first painting in the display. "So you aren't an art connoisseur?"

"I like art. I just don't like ugly art."

"I can't disagree with you about that," Cassie said. "The palace decorator wanted to buy one of Willem de Kooning's paintings last year."

Levi cringed.

"I see you are familiar with his work."

"I've been around the royal family long enough to pick up a few things. A de Kooning wouldn't ever be one of them."

"I agree. The decorator wasn't very pleased with me, but my father was grateful when I showed him a picture of the piece that had nearly made it onto our wall."

"I can imagine." Levi wandered to the next painting, a seascape of the Amalfi Coast. "Now, this is something I wouldn't mind seeing on my wall every day."

"It's stunning." Cassie continued past him and pointed at another painting. "But I like this one better."

"Garrett has a piece by that artist. It's of the view from the chateau."

Cassie leaned forward and read the artist's name. "I think we have a piece by him in our library."

They wandered through the exhibit, discussing the various paintings, what they liked, what they didn't. Levi was pleased to find Cassie valued aesthetics over price tags.

Pierre returned as they reached the final painting. "Sorry about that. Now, let me show you our treasures."

Levi took Cassie's hand. "Lead the way."

CHAPTER 10

CASSIE HADN'T EXPECTED TO SPEND so long at the museum, and she certainly hadn't expected Levi to be so insightful as they went from one exhibit to another. Their tour of the museum had extended past regular business hours, and Cassie had enjoyed every minute—the paintings, the company, the sense of freedom, and even her basic privacy.

"You have done a wonderful job with this museum," Cassie told Pierre as they left the last display and walked toward the rear storage area.

"Thank you," Pierre said. "We are very proud of it."

"As you should be." Cassie and Levi followed Pierre past an armed guard to a storage room. Pierre stopped at a keypad, pressed his badge against the reader, and punched in a code. A moment later, the door clicked open.

"I appreciate your transporting this for me." Pierre stepped into the temperature-controlled room filled with crates.

"It's not a problem," Levi said. "It's good to change up the delivery methods to the chateau."

Cassie followed the two men inside and looked around. "I didn't expect you to have so much artwork back here."

"Most of it is part of the Mediterranean exhibit." Pierre waved a hand to encompass several crates to the right.

"I thought that's what we saw today," Cassie said.

"You saw the first series," Pierre corrected. "We'll change out the pieces over the next three weeks, ending with a complete display that will take up the three main exhibit halls."

"Sounds like a lot of work," Levi said.

"It is, but it's also giving the museum a great deal of attention. Some of these items haven't ever been displayed in public before."

"Really?" Cassie asked.

"Yes. We have artwork from all over the world, including the US, Sweden, Japan, and even South Africa."

"And all of these countries have artwork that represent the Mediterranean?" Levi asked skeptically.

"The beauty we enjoy is appreciated worldwide," Pierre said. "I'm particularly excited about two new pieces. One is a sculpture from Menorca that is owned by a private collector. The other is an exhibit on loan from Sereno."

"Which one is that?" Cassie asked.

"It's art of a different kind." Pierre's face lit up with anticipation. "You'll have to come back for the final exhibit to see it."

A pang of disappointment rose within her. "I'm afraid I won't still be in town by then."

"I'm sorry to hear that," Pierre said. "I'd show the piece to you, but it's stored in another location."

"You'll have to send me photos," Cassie said.

"I imagine we'll have quite the press coverage for this event. King Eduard is even planning to attend." Pierre put his hand on a protective case on his left. "This is the one for the chateau."

"Thanks." Levi lifted it and took a step toward the door.

An alarm rang out, the shrill sound blaring into the room.

Cassie covered her ears, her heart pounding as she was transported back in time. She was in Sereno, the alarm sounding, gunshots firing. She gasped when a hand gripped her arm.

Levi's voice broke through the memories. "Cassie, it's okay."

"What's . . . ?" she began but couldn't form a thought, much less a complete sentence.

The painting Levi had held a moment ago was again on the floor beside the door, and he now held a pistol.

"You two stay here." Levi pressed himself against the wall beside the entrance.

"You're leaving me?"

Levi looked at her now, and his voice remained calm. "This is the safest place you can be right now."

"He's right," Pierre said.

"But . . ."

Levi motioned to the door. "The threat is out there. It's my job to make sure it doesn't find you." He pulled a cell phone out of his pocket. "Here. Keep this. I'll call you when it's clear."

"How can you call me if I have your phone?"

"I have a spare." He handed her the cell. "Trust me. I won't let anything happen to you."

Cassie swallowed hard and nodded.

Levi turned to Pierre. "Secure the entrance until I get back."

Pierre moved opposite where Levi stood, concern evident on his face.

Levi lifted his gun, peeked into the hall, and, an instant later, disappeared from view.

The heavy door clanged shut, and Pierre pressed numbers on the security keypad.

Cassie stepped backward until she bumped into a crate as tall as she was and twice as wide.

"Careful." Pierre took her arm. "Here, come sit down." Pierre retrieved a metal folding chair and set it beside the wall. "Please sit."

Cassie lowered herself onto the chair, the metal cold against her bare legs. She smoothed her skirt beneath her to cover more of her thighs, her discomfort quickly lost beneath a new wave of panic. The space between the storage crates seemed to shrink, and her head pounded from the incessant noise of the alarm.

Levi said she was safe here, but her mind and body didn't believe the words.

Her breathing quickened. Her chest tightened.

They were locked inside. They were trapped.

* * *

Levi's gaze swept the hallway outside the secure storage room. The guard who had been present a moment before was noticeably absent, the entire area empty.

Levi confirmed he was alone before he pulled out his cell phone and called the gallery security office.

"It's Levi Marin. What's your status?"

"We have a security breach in the main exhibit area. A sensor alarm on the Renoir."

"Visual?" Levi asked.

"Video feed doesn't show any movement," he said. "Our guards are heading there now."

Which explained why the rear guard post had been abandoned.

"Send one of the guards to the secure storage room," Levi said.

"Yes, sir."

A guard arrived twenty seconds later.

"Stay here. Make sure no one gets near the storage room," Levi commanded.

"What are you going to do?"

"I'm checking out the exterior. Let the other guards know I'm here." Levi studied the back door and debated how long it would take him to unlock it. Even though he always carried a lockpick kit in his pocket, he decided to take the easy route today. "I need you to release the locks on the loading dock doors. As soon as I leave, secure the doors again."

The guard lifted his walkie-talkie and informed his coworkers of Levi's presence. He then used his badge and security code to unlock the back door.

Levi followed him to the back entrance, which was comprised of two wide steel doors that extended nearly to the ceiling. He waited for the guard to reclaim his position by the storage room. Then he pushed one of the exterior doors open a crack. He peered out to the left. Nothing. He switched doors, now scanning the driveway leading to the loading dock. A gray sedan occupied one of the four parking spaces beside the back door, a white coupe parked beside it.

Seeing both vehicles were unoccupied, he stepped outside, slowing long enough to snap a photo of the license plates with his cell phone.

He continued along the back wall until he reached the southwest corner of the building. Seeing the side wall was clear, he reversed course and proceeded to the other side of the building, finding nothing suspicious.

His gun at his side, he jogged to the front of the building. Again, nothing appeared out of place. He glanced through the glass doors of the entrance, able to see three guards congregated beside the main exhibit hall.

Trusting the guards to secure the interior, Levi moved into the parking lot and snapped photos of the dozen cars outside. Police sirens sounded, growing close enough to be heard over the wailing of the alarm.

Levi finished his task and pocketed his phone. Anticipating a potential confrontation with the local authorities, Levi holstered his weapon and retrieved his credentials from his pocket. He held his position by the main entrance, waiting calmly.

The first officer on scene climbed out of his car, immediately drawing his own weapon. "Hold it right there. Hands where I can see them."

Levi lifted his arms, his credentials visible in his right hand. "Take it easy. I'm on your side. Levi Marin. Royal guard."

While the first officer debated how to handle Levi's announcement, a second police car raced into the parking lot.

Captain Guillermo Reyes exited his vehicle. "Put your weapon away. He's one of us."

"Thanks, Captain," Levi said.

The young officer complied, holstering his weapon. "Sorry, sir."

"No problem." Levi waited for the two men to join him on the front walk. "I circled the perimeter and didn't see any movement. They said a sensor alarm went off. The guards are checking it out."

Guillermo rapped on the front door, and one of the guards approached to let them in. As soon as the door opened, the shrill ringing of alarms intensified.

"Status?" Guillermo asked.

"Nothing on the video feed, and we haven't found any sign of tampering," the guard said, raising his voice to be heard over the alarm. "Looks like a faulty sensor caused the problem."

"Can we get the alarm turned—" The captain cut off when the ringing stopped. "Man, that thing is loud."

"Do you have any other patrons still in the museum?" Levi asked.

"No. We cleared everyone out before Pierre accessed the storage room. It's standard policy to keep our secure areas closed while we are open to the public," the guard said. "We're checking all of the exhibits now, but so far, there's no sign of any intruders."

"Maybe it really was a faulty sensor," Captain Reyes said, "but I'd like to do a walk-through regardless."

"Do you mind if I help?" Levi asked.

"I'd appreciate it."

"Let me make a quick call first." Levi took his phone out and called Cassie.

"What's happening?" she asked as soon as she answered.

"Everything is fine. We think it was a bad sensor that set off the alarm, but I want you to stay with Pierre until we double-check the museum."

"Okay."

Levi heard the tremor in her voice and could only imagine the stress the past few minutes had put her under. "I'll be there as soon as I can."

"How long do you think you'll be?" Cassie asked.

"Fifteen minutes. Maybe twenty."

"Okay. I'll see you then."

Levi hung up and noticed Guillermo watching him.

"Everything all right?" the police captain asked.

"Yeah." Levi pocketed his phone. "I have my girlfriend here with me. She's with Pierre in secure storage."

"Can't ask for a better place to be if you need to hide out," Guillermo said. "Except maybe at the chateau."

"I look forward to getting her back there."

"Then let's get this search started."

"I'm right behind you."

CHAPTER 11

THE SILENCE IN THE STORAGE room rang every bit as loudly as the alarm had.

Cassie forced her fingers to relax on her cell and noticed Pierre staring at her with a look of expectation on his face. She nodded at the phone. "Levi said he thinks the alarm was triggered by a faulty sensor."

"Did he say where?" Pierre asked.

"No," Cassie said.

The relief she expected to see on Pierre's face didn't appear, his tension every bit as visible now as it had been when their ordeal had first begun.

"Why do you ask?"

"We tested all the sensors in the main hall the day before we opened the new exhibit," Pierre said.

"Maybe it was from one of the other displays."

"Maybe."

The skepticism in his voice did nothing to assuage Cassie's lingering fears. Had Levi and the guards really found the issue? Or was there another problem waiting to find them?

With some effort, she adopted her royal shield, hiding her own emotions behind a polished mask. Her voice only wavered a little when she asked, "Does this sort of thing happen often?"

"No. This is only the second time we've had a false alarm."

"What happened the first time?" Cassie asked.

"A construction worker sliced through one of our wired alarms when we expanded a couple years ago."

"I don't suppose you have any construction going on here at the moment."

"No, we don't." Pierre clasped his hands together. "I'm sorry. I don't mean to worry you. If anyone can get to the bottom of this, it's Levi."

"Have you known him long?" Cassie asked.

"Since he came to Bellamo. I guess it's been about two years now."

"I thought he had been here longer."

"No. He arrived about the same time Janessa did," Pierre said. "I got the impression the royal family wanted to increase security because they knew Prince Garrett was preparing to marry."

"I suppose that changing dynamic would create a new set of challenges."

"More than we ever could have imagined," Pierre said, a tinge of regret and sorrow hanging in his voice.

The door to the storage room vibrated when someone knocked on it from the outside.

"Who is it?" Pierre asked.

"It's me. Levi."

Cassie rose to her feet.

Pierre moved to the keypad by the door. He hit a button, and a screen on the wall lit up, revealing a view of the hall where Levi stood alone.

Pierre pressed his access card to the reader and punched in his code. The lock on the door clicked, and he pulled the door open.

Levi entered, his eyes landing on Cassie. "Are you two okay?"

She managed a nod, even though her insides were churning with emotions that demanded release.

"Where was the faulty sensor?" Pierre asked without preamble.

"On the Renoir—"

"In the main hall," Pierre finished for him.

"Yes. How did you know that?"

"This might have been a false alarm, but it was done deliberately." Pierre motioned Levi forward and closed them inside. Even though they were alone, Pierre lowered his voice. "I personally checked those alarms, and we included a backup system. If one sensor failed, another would have kicked in and sent a maintenance alarm to the security office."

"But that didn't happen," Levi said.

"No. Multiple sensors would have had to fail for the alarm to trigger, and they were all brand-new."

"Could you have gotten a bad batch of sensors?" Levi asked.

"We checked them multiple times," Pierre said. "The only way for this to have happened was for someone to force a power surge into the security grid."

"Could that have been done remotely?"

"No." Pierre shook his head. "It's a closed system."

"I suggest we have Captain Reyes run a check on all of your staff."

"Yes, and we need to check for tampering. Someone could have set some kind of timer to throw the alarm."

"True, but for what purpose?" Levi asked.

"I have absolutely no idea."

Levi glanced at his watch. "I hate to do this, but I need to get Cassie back to the chateau. Do you want me to go with you to meet with the captain before I leave?"

"No, I'll be fine." Pierre opened the door again and motioned to the crated painting. "Take this with you though. I'd prefer to lighten my inventory until we get everything sorted out."

"No problem."

"Go ahead and pull your car around back. I'll bring it out to you."

"Okay. We'll be right back." Levi took Cassie's hand and led her toward the front of the museum. "I am so sorry about this."

"You couldn't have known this was going to happen," Cassie said.

"Yeah, but the idea was to help you feel normal, not throw you into another tense situation." Levi led her outside, and instantly, Cassie looked around, her heartbeat racing, her palms sweating. She was no longer trapped in the storage room, but she was very much exposed in the open parking lot.

She quickened her step, relieved when she climbed into the car and Levi closed the door.

Levi circled to the back and parked beside the white sedan. "Do you want to wait here or come with me?"

Cassie didn't know how to answer. She didn't want to be alone, but she also didn't want to be outside where she would feel exposed again.

The door to the loading dock opened, and Pierre emerged, the crate in his hands.

Levi popped the trunk. Two minutes later, the painting was secure, and Levi was sitting beside her.

He started the engine. "Let's get you home."

Home. Cassie knew he referred to the chateau, but her thoughts went to her private quarters in the palace in Sereno. She wanted her home, but what would it take to get her there? And was she really any safer here in Meridia?

* * *

Levi passed the guards at the chateau entrance and parked the car near the front door. He didn't want Cassie to have to walk any farther than necessary to get inside. He turned off the engine. "I am so sorry about today."

"It wasn't your fault," Cassie said. "And I think you've apologized enough."

Levi turned in his seat to face her. The terrified woman he had left locked in the museum's secure storage room had disappeared, a remarkably calm princess now sitting in her place.

"Are you really okay, or are you wearing your princess mask again?"

Both elegant eyebrows lifted. "My princess mask?"

"Yeah, you know. That regal expression you adopt every time you need to meet new people or hide your feelings."

A flash of surprise surfaced, and her lips curved slightly. "I didn't realize you knew me so well."

"We've spent a lot of time together lately."

"That's true." She unclipped her seat belt. "I'm really okay, but the next time we go into the village, I get to make our plans."

"You'd be willing to go out again, even after what happened?" Levi asked.

"I have to admit I rather liked being out without an entourage following me," Cassie said.

"Did you have someplace in particular in mind for our next outing?" Levi asked.

"That ice-cream shop on the edge of town looked enticing."

"It is good." Levi looked up to see Martino approaching. "Let's continue this conversation inside."

Levi climbed out of the car, and Martino opened Cassie's door for her.

"I understand there was some excitement in town." Martino offered Cassie a hand.

"A little more than we expected." Cassie let Martino help her stand.

Levi popped the trunk. "The painting is back here."

"I'll take care of it," Martino said. "Do you want me to have Enrico park the car?"

"Yes, please." Levi waited for Martino to lift the wrapped painting out of its storage container before closing the trunk. "I'll get the door for you." Levi took Cassie by the elbow and guided her up the stairs a few steps ahead of Martino.

After they were inside, Martino set the painting down. "Patrice asked if you would both like to join her family for dinner tonight. She is testing a new recipe for the dinner party on Saturday."

"Are you up for that?" Levi asked Cassie.

"A chance to test Patrice's cooking?" Cassie nodded. "I'd love to. What time?"

Martino checked his watch. "Dinner is in twenty minutes."

"Tell her we'll be there." Levi motioned to the painting. "Do you need any help with that?"

"No, thank you." Martino lifted it again and headed down the hall.

"Are you sure you don't need some time to yourself?" Levi asked as soon as he left.

"Actually, I'd rather not be alone right now."

"In that case, should we go see if Patrice needs help in the kitchen?"

"Me? Help in the kitchen?"

Levi took her hand. "Come on. It'll be an adventure."

"Now I'm scared."

* * *

Cassie made the salad dressing all by herself. She even helped make the salad, if one could call washing the mixed greens and putting them into a bowl making a salad. Patrice hadn't trusted her with the fancy food processor that sliced the other vegetables, but mixing the dressing had been all her. She hadn't even messed it up.

Levi had been entrusted with preparing the garlic toast, a task he had apparently performed many times. The chaos and easy conversation in the kitchen had done wonders for Cassie's morale and had chased away the lingering uneasiness that had resulted from the false alarm.

Conversation at the dinner table with the Saldera family was very much like the previous week, lighthearted banter with an undertone of love and acceptance.

They were nearly finished clearing the table when Levi said, "Cassie, we'd better go make that phone call."

"I almost forgot about that." Cassie eyed the dishes stacked on the counter. "Patrice, did you want us to help with the dishes first?"

"No, you go. My men will help with the dishes tonight."

"Thank you for dinner," Cassie said. "It was wonderful."

"You are welcome."

Levi offered his thanks and led Cassie into the hall. He looked down at her with an expression that fell somewhere between pride and disbelief.

"What?"

"Princess Cassandra just offered to do the dishes."

"She also made the salad dressing."

"I'm not sure everyone will recognize you when you go back home."

"You could be right." She straightened her shoulders. "I think I rather liked helping in the kitchen."

"I know Patrice liked having you there." Levi headed for her suite. "Do you have your cousin's phone number?"

"Yes. I brought a physical list of phone numbers with me since I didn't bring my cell phone."

"Smart." When they reached her door, he opened it for her.

"Do we need to make the call on a special phone?"

"I have a secure cell phone we'll filter the call through." Levi closed the door and pulled a cell from his pocket. "Here you go."

"What do you want me to ask him?"

"We need the names of everyone he talked to about your list of oil companies."

"Okay." She retrieved Crispan's phone number from her address book and dialed. As soon as his voice came over the phone, a sense of home washed over her.

"Crispan, it's Cassie."

"Cassie! I've been so worried about you."

"I'm fine. Really."

"Are you back home?" Crispan asked.

"No, I'm staying with a friend," Cassie said. "I need to ask you a question though."

"Of course. What is it?"

"When we compiled our list of oil companies to solicit bids, did you discuss possibilities with anyone?"

"Nothing specific. Why?"

"What about in generalities?" Cassie asked.

"I talked to Steve Rozell, one of the consultants I work for."

"Anyone else?"

"Just the executives for the companies we decided to consider. Why?"

"We're trying to make sure the attack on the palace didn't have anything to do with the oil contracts," Cassie said. "Tell me what you talked to Rozell about."

"I just asked about companies he would recommend for offshore drilling. Again, nothing specific."

"What companies did he recommend?"

"North Coast Energy from Canada and Naizak Oil from Saudi Arabia."

"Neither of those even made it into our top picks."

"Yeah. I can't imagine him having any ties to what happened," Crispan said. "He's fifty-six years old, with a wife, three kids, and two grandbabies on the way."

Cassie put her hand over the phone and asked Levi, "Did you want me to ask anything else?"

Levi shook his head.

"Thanks for your help, Crispan."

"I wish I had more information for you," he said. "Stay safe."

"I will." Cassie said her goodbyes and hung up the phone. She replayed her conversation to Levi and added, "I'm afraid that was a dead end."

"I'll check out Steve Rozell in case there's anything your cousin doesn't know about him, but I agree that it doesn't sound likely he was involved."

"So we're back to square one."

"We're eliminating suspects," Levi corrected. "Eventually, there will only be one possibility left."

"I'd like to find that one now."

"I know." Levi pocketed the phone. "Come on. Let's go walk in the garden and forget about all this for a while."

"I'd like that."

CHAPTER 12

JULIEN LISTENED TO THE POLICE scanner, waiting as the seconds ticked by. His men should have started their first job ten minutes ago. In a matter of hours, he would have what he needed to topple the current monarchy in Sereno. Change was coming, and he was ready to take what was rightfully his.

Static preceded a voice on the scanner. A car accident on the bridge. A unit was dispatched and then silence once again. Nothing about a bank robbery. Julien blew out a breath. It was working, he assured himself.

He glanced at the television on the wall where the newscaster droned on about the weather. Nothing there either. His hands fisted, and he crossed to the window and stared outside. The forecasted rain had yet to arrive, but the clouds were hanging low in the sky. A good storm could benefit him and his men. What better way to wash away any evidence and slow down an investigation?

The mundane chatter on the scanner was interrupted by a new call. As if on cue, a siren wailed in the distance. Suspect descriptions were detailed, additional units were dispatched.

On the television, a banner for breaking news flashed across the bottom of the screen. Robbery at the National Bank. Now they were getting somewhere.

Behind him, raindrops against glass competed with the sound of the television. Julien smirked. This day was going to be perfect. Tomorrow, he would start his next phase of finding Sereno's princesses and setting things right in his world.

* * *

Levi stifled a yawn as he leaned back in his chair. He had spent all day in his office, only taking a quick break at lunchtime to check in with Cassie, who had been up to her ears in her own work.

She seemed to have powered through whatever anxiety she had experienced after yesterday's false alarm at the art gallery. He didn't know how she managed to be so resilient when facing so much stress in so little time. He couldn't help but admire that quality in her.

She hadn't asked about the investigation during their brief time together today, and Levi hadn't mentioned his efforts. She didn't need to know his suspicions until he could determine if they were even viable.

So far, he had two solid motives for someone wanting Cassie dead, but he had far too many suspects and not nearly enough evidence.

The idea that Cassie and her sisters would be targeted to prevent a woman from taking over the country was old-fashioned enough that he nearly dismissed it outright, but he knew from experience that in some cultures, men and women both resisted change.

In his mind, the more likely motive was tied to harvesting the oil in Sereno's waters. He had seen such a motivation in Meridia only eighteen months ago.

Ready for a break, Levi headed for the security office. He wasn't surprised to find Franco had reported early for his shift. Give the man a task and he always saw it through.

"How's it going?" Levi asked.

"Not too bad." He motioned to the laptop to his right. "I did notice something I thought you'd be interested in though."

"What's that?"

"You told us to keep an eye on volatility and possible terrorism in the region," Franco said. "Today, there was a string of bank robberies in the EU."

"Where?"

"Dublin, Paris, Zurich, Riga, Helsinki, Copenhagen, Barcelona, Rome, and Malmo."

"Nine bank robberies?" Levi asked. "All today?"

"Actually, it was nine cities, but there were twenty-three bank robberies in the space of three hours. Except for Malmo, Sweden, all of the cities had at least two."

"Similar MOs?"

"Almost identical," Franco confirmed. "Four gunmen and one driver at each. They went after cash and safe-deposit boxes."

"How much did they get?"

"The equivalent of 5 million euros, according to the initial reports, not including what they got out of the safe-deposit boxes."

"Did they catch any of them?" Levi asked.

"One was killed fleeing the first robbery in Zurich. They're assuming it was the same team because the second robbery only had three robbers."

"Twenty-three robberies and the authorities only stopped one man?"

"That's all we have under the official reports," Franco said.

"Reach out to Interpol. See if you can get us the surveillance feed for the robberies and more detailed information on what was stolen."

"They got at least 5 million euros. Doesn't that tell you everything you need to know?"

"No. If they robbed safe-deposit boxes at every bank, I want to know if anyone had boxes at more than one bank," Levi said.

"You think they were looking for something specific?"

"I don't know, but I want to find out."

"You got it." Franco reached for the phone.

"Also, see if you can get the name of the man who was killed."

"Already did. Nicholai Messi. He's got a rap sheet a mile long. Armed robbery is his forte."

"Known associates?" Levi asked.

"Interpol is working on it, but he looks like a hired gun. I'll let you know if I find anything else out."

"Thanks." Levi headed for the door. "Call me if you meet any resistance."

"Will do."

Levi left the room and dialed Janessa's brother, Jeremy, who was currently serving as an operative for Interpol.

"Levi. How is everything?"

"Hey, Jeremy. I need a favor," Levi said. "Did you hear about the string of bank robberies today?"

"Yeah. My wife and I are in Rome right now," he said, referring to Patrice's daughter, Noelle.

"Franco is contacting your headquarters to request video footage of the robberies. Any chance you can grease the wheels for us?"

"What are looking for?"

"Same thing you are. Commonalities." Without offering specifics, he added, "I have a private security matter I'm working on. I doubt it ties in, but the timing is pretty coincidental."

"Anyone I know?"

"No," Levi said, communicating in one word that his sister was not in danger.

"I'll do what I can."

"Thanks, Jeremy. Be safe, and give your wife my best."

"Will do."

Levi hung up, checked his watch, and dialed another number. The older man answered on the third ring. "Director? It's Levi Marin."

"Levi. It's not often I hear from you. I hope you aren't calling to beg out of your protection assignment."

"No, sir." Levi didn't mention that he had thought about doing precisely that when Janessa had told him about it. "Are you aware of the string of bank robberies this morning? Twenty-three hits in nine European cities within three hours?"

"It's up to twenty-three now?" Director Palmer asked. "Last I heard was nineteen."

"Hopefully, the numbers won't continue to climb," Levi said. "I don't know if we're working with Interpol yet on gathering intel, but I want to rule out the possibility that these robberies might be related to the assassination attempt in Sereno."

"I have a couple analysts looking into the possibility, but I'll make sure they give you access to the information."

"I appreciate it," Levi said. "Any new updates on the shooters in Sereno?"

"We've confirmed that the two who were killed served together in the army. One washed out of sniper training when he failed his psych eval. The other was given a dishonorable discharge after an altercation with his CO. He was accused of smuggling weapons when he was at Fort Bragg, but it was never proven."

"Any known associations with terrorist groups?"

"Nothing. So far, everything points to them being guns for hire rather than extremists working toward a cause."

"Profiteers."

"That's where the intel is pointing. Our analysts are searching now for a money trail that will tell us who hired them."

"Then we're still looking for a motive."

"I'm afraid so," Director Palmer said. "I have a meeting to go to, but I'll keep you in the loop."

"Do you want me to work directly with someone in the Europe Division?"

"No. I'm still limiting how many people know about your current cover. You report directly to me."

"If that's what you want," Levi said.

"It is. Good luck with the princess."

"Thanks, Director." Levi hung up and stood. Time to find Cassie. Maybe she would have some insight into how bank robberies could be tied to an assassination attempt, because he didn't have a clue.

* * *

Cassie set the file for the French company aside. One proposal eliminated, three more still in the running. In truth, any of the four would be acceptable, but the one from France had a record of safety violations in its current operations off the coast of Cyprus. With little else distinguishing one from the others, she had used that fact to remove it from consideration.

Of the final contenders, if she followed her father's line of thinking and removed the American companies, she had her winner: the company from Greece. But if country of origin wasn't considered, she was leaning toward a Houston-based company because of their exceptional safety ratings. The proposed agreement would also allow her family a significant amount of control over the location of the drilling platforms and the timing of production.

Four quick knocks sounded at her door.

"Come in."

Levi entered. "Do you have a minute?"

"Yes." Cassie stood. "Any news?"

"Yes and no." Levi lifted a manila folder into her view. "I had one of my men monitoring security concerns within the region. I don't know if any of this is connected to what happened in your country, but I wanted you to be aware of it."

Cassie took the folder from him. "What is it?"

"A series of bank robberies. Twenty-three in nine different cities," Levi said. "We're still gathering reports to figure out how much was stolen."

"Why would you think this would have something to do with someone trying to kill me?" Cassie asked.

"I don't know that it does, but the timing is suspicious," Levi said. "If someone is trying to disrupt the stability of the region, killing a royal and attacking the economic security in nine other countries could be part of a larger plan."

"You sound like you expect something else to happen."

"It's my job to expect something to happen."

"All of this national security is making my head hurt."

"Think of it as a puzzle," Levi said. "We want to see if these banks have anything in common and if they have any connection to Sereno."

"When you say it that way, it sounds so simple." She nodded toward her computer. "Kind of like comparing business proposals."

"Something like that."

"I'm happy to help if I can. Like you said, I can't learn about national security if I'm never exposed to anything that goes on behind the scenes."

"I don't think I said it quite like that, but close enough." Levi leaned forward and rested his elbows on his knees. "Would you mind eating in my office tonight? I thought we could have a working dinner."

"It sounds like I'm not the only one who has something to learn."

"What do you mean?"

"One thing my parents always insisted on was to protect dinnertime from all distractions," Cassie said. "Mom said everyone needs time to step away from the world, if only to regain perspective."

"In my job, that luxury isn't always available."

"I understand that, but is working through dinner going to undo any of those robberies?"

"No."

"Then maybe you should give my way a try." Cassie noticed his hesitation. "One hour. Give me that, and afterward, we can work together."

"Fine. If you insist."

"I do."

Levi stood and glanced out the french doors leading to her balcony. "It's nice out. Do you want to eat on the terrace?"

"I'd like that."

"Good. I'll meet you downstairs in an hour."

Cassie watched him go and debated whether she should look through the new information Levi had brought her or if she should pick up her work where she'd left off. Curiosity pushed her to open the new file.

One report after another detailed the location, basic robbery details, time, and description of suspects. Cassie had to read only three to recognize the glaring similarities. Deciding to organize the information the way she did best, she opened a new spreadsheet on her laptop and entered the details by column.

Little by little, new parallels surfaced. Levi was onto something. The timing of these robberies wasn't a coincidence.

CHAPTER 13

A BASKET OF ROLLS IN one hand and a carafe of water in the other, Levi approached the table where he and Cassie would dine tonight. When he had informed Patrice of his plans, the simple meal had turned into an affair of royal proportions. White linen now covered the wrought-iron table; the place settings of china and silver replaced the everyday dishes the staff typically used for their meals.

Levi had drawn the line at letting Patrice assign a maid to serve them. He didn't think he could handle dining with Cassie with Brenna hovering nearby, and he suspected she would have been the one given the duty of waiting on them had he agreed.

Patrice appeared in the doorway behind him, a covered serving dish in her hands. "You tell me if this gets cold, and I'll heat it up."

"Patrice, we'll be fine. You've already gone well above the call of duty."

"She's special, your Cassie."

"Yes, she is."

Patrice straightened a salad fork as though the fraction of an inch might make a difference in how the food tasted.

"Thank you, Patrice," he said, finding her attention to detail endearing. "I appreciate your going to all this trouble."

She patted his hand. "You enjoy your evening."

"Thanks. You too." Levi poured water into the crystal goblets on the table and sat to wait for his "date."

In the distance beyond the gardens, he could see two boats on the water, a sailboat and what appeared to be a small yacht. He wondered if Cassie had time for such pursuits when people weren't trying to kill her. He knew Garrett had to fight to make time for leisurely activities.

Admittedly, Janessa had been good for him in that regard. The two worked well as a team, and shouldering the burden of royalty together often allowed them to steal a few hours or even a few days to themselves when they needed it most.

Levi thought of Cassie's insistence on letting go of the day's stresses for a little while. He leaned back and stared out at the Mediterranean as the evening sunlight splashed over the waves and white foam rolled over the sand.

Clicking heels against stone broke into the soothing rhythm of water meeting land.

Levi stood as Cassie approached, his gaze lowering to the file she held. "I thought you said you didn't want to work through dinner."

"The bank robbers stole from safe-deposit boxes." Cassie held up the folder. "Every one of them."

"That's right." Levi pulled her chair out for her, amused that etiquette was so ingrained in her that even when she was upset, she still sat obediently.

Levi sat back down. "Do you have a theory as to why?"

"I can't be sure without talking to my father."

"Humor me with your best guess."

Cassie hesitated, and Levi could almost see her debating about how much she should reveal.

"I can't help if I only have half the facts."

"We're talking about national security here—my family's security."

Levi put his hand on hers and waited for her eyes to meet his. "You can trust me."

When she didn't speak, Levi pulled his hand away and picked up the bread basket. "Maybe we should eat dinner before we talk about this."

Cassie took a roll and put it on her plate. "It's not that I don't want to confide in you. I'm sworn to secrecy."

"Cassie, if you have suspicions that your family secrets have been violated, keeping them to yourself isn't going to help anyone except the criminals who already understand them."

Levi waited for Cassie to absorb the truth. He removed the lid from the serving dish.

"Prime rib?" she asked.

"With sautéed mushrooms and bleu cheese."

"Patrice outdid herself."

"Yes, she did." Levi served Cassie a piece before stabbing a piece of meat and placing it on his plate.

"Do you think you could arrange for me to talk to my father after dinner?" Cassie asked. "I know you don't want me calling him directly, but . . ."

"I think I can work something out."

"Good." Cassie picked up her fork. "Because I think my father should give you full access to what happened the night of the shooting."

Relief and a sense of anticipation bubbled inside him, but he didn't let his emotions show. "That would be helpful."

"And for the record, I do trust you."

* * *

Cassie stood behind Levi's desk while he fiddled with the settings on his internet server. A map appeared on the screen, a line zigzagging through cities all over the world.

"Okay, we're all set." Levi stood and offered his chair to her. "Put your father's phone number in there, and it will connect you."

"Are you sure no one will be able to trace the call?"

"As long as you aren't on for more than fifteen minutes, you'll be fine."

Cassie drew a deep breath and blew it out. She sat and punched in her father's private phone number. He answered on the second ring.

"Hello?"

"Papa, it's me."

"You shouldn't be calling me."

"It's okay. My friend made sure our call won't be intercepted, but I don't have much time," Cassie said. "Did you hear about the bank robberies today?"

"Are you talking about the robberies in Zurich?"

"That was only one city affected." Cassie didn't have to look at the list to remember the others. "Robberies also occurred in Malmo, Rome, Barcelona . . ." Silence hung over the line for a moment, and Cassie had no doubt her father was processing the information just as she had two hours ago. "Papa, every one of the thefts included cash and items from safe-deposit boxes."

"You know what they were after," he finally said. "Do you know if they were successful?"

"The only two they missed were the ones that are still privately held."

"You think someone working for the royal family is involved."

"It has to be someone with access." Cassie looked up at Levi. "I want to help with this."

"I don't want you putting yourself in further danger."

"You know as well as I that the only way to end this is to find out who is behind it," Cassie said. "I have someone here who can help, someone I trust."

"Who?" he demanded.

"The man protecting me," Cassie said. "He's from Meridia. His name is Levi Marin."

"Who is he?"

"He is head of security for the royal chateau."

"Is he there?" her father asked.

"Yes."

"Let me speak to him."

Cassie motioned for Levi to join her in front of the computer so he would be closer to the microphone.

"I'm here, Your Majesty," Levi said.

"And you think you can help us sort out our internal matters?"

"I would like the opportunity to try," Levi said. "King Eduard and his sons can give you a reference as to my ability and loyalty if you would like."

"Call me back in five minutes."

"Yes, Your Majesty." Levi disconnected the call and faced Cassie. "I guess he's doing my background check."

"Don't take offense. He doesn't know you."

"I'm not offended. I would be concerned if he didn't check me out before trusting me with government secrets."

"You have been doing this a long time, haven't you?" Cassie's eyes narrowed. "How old are you anyway?"

"Twenty-nine."

"That's awfully young to be in charge."

"I grew up in this business," Levi said. "My father was one of the best criminal investigators I know."

"You learned from him?"

"Not exactly."

"I don't understand." When Levi didn't expand on his answer, Cassie pushed for details. "You're asking my family to let you into our private affairs. The least you can do is let me understand where you come from."

Levi leaned back in his chair as though debating how much to say. "My father spent most of his career profiling the motivations of criminals. He used that knowledge to identify who committed a crime."

"And?"

"Let's just say I prefer to prevent crimes rather than react to them."

"Which is why you went into security instead of law enforcement," Cassie said. "Where is your father now?"

"He retired a few years ago."

"Do you talk to your family often?"

"A couple times a month. Texting is usually easier on all of us because our schedules rarely match up." Levi checked the time. "Slide over. I need to reestablish the connection."

The map maximized on the screen again, new lines appearing through new cities.

Exactly five minutes from the time Levi had hung up with her father, he initiated a new call. As soon as her father answered, Levi asked, "Sir, did you get the answers you were looking for?"

"Cassandra?"

"Yes, Papa."

"Give him everything he needs," King Alejandro said. "Mr. Marin, keep me informed, and keep my daughter safe."

"Yes, Your Majesty."

The call terminated from the king's end.

Cassie leaned back in Levi's chair, her eyebrows raised. "I didn't expect him to agree so quickly. King Eduard must think very highly of you."

"He does." Levi leaned against his desk. "Now that you have permission, tell me what I need to know. What was in those safe-deposit boxes?"

"A treasure map of sorts," Cassie said. "The keys to Sereno."

"I don't understand."

Cassie stood and paced across the room as she debated how to explain over four hundred years of history. "I'm not sure where to start."

"The beginning is always a good place." Levi crossed to the sofa and motioned for Cassie to sit.

She settled onto the couch and waited for him to sit beside her. "In the 1600s, Sereno was a hotbed for piracy. The king of Spain sent out two ship captains to take over Sereno and stabilize the region. If successful, one of them would be granted all rights to the island."

"How did he propose they would decide who would be the ruler if they both succeeded?"

"Whichever man married and produced the first heir would become king of Sereno. The other's family would get nothing beyond a land grant on the island."

"And your ancestor was the first to produce an heir."

"Yes, but it wasn't as simple as it sounds," Cassie said. "My ancestor produced a son a few months before his counterpart. The documentation was sent to the king, and my tenth great-grandfather was named king of Sereno."

"And?" Levi asked.

"A few days after receiving the official notice, the child died of a fever," Cassie said. "The man who had been named ruler no longer had an heir."

"But he had fulfilled the requirement to be named king."

"Yes. Luigi Escobar immediately protested the king's decision and insisted that the kingdom be granted to him instead, but the king of Spain had already granted the kingdom to my ancestor.

"In order to maintain peace, an agreement was made. My ancestor would remain in power, but if at any time a member of the Rossi family was not available to rule, the kingdom would transfer in its entirety to Escobar or his heirs."

"That's an interesting story, but what does that have to do with the bank robberies?"

"My ancestor was understandably concerned that if and when he fathered another child, Escobar's family would try to destroy any heirs to the throne in order to gain possession of Sereno."

"That would be a valid concern."

"Shortly after his wife became pregnant again, they attended a wedding in Spain for the king's youngest daughter. Luigi Escobar was also in attendance," Cassie said. "My ancestor was granted an audience with King Philip. He petitioned for the agreement to be dissolved to protect his unborn child, offering him gold and jewels in exchange for his help."

"I get the feeling he didn't agree."

"No, but he proposed another solution," Cassie said. "The agreement would be engraved into metal in sections and given to various royals and heads of state who were in attendance at the wedding. Escobar and my ancestor were also entrusted with a section to make sure neither side could hide its existence," Cassie explained.

"And what happens if your family ever dies out?"

"In order for Escobar or his descendants to take control of Sereno, the allies who were entrusted with a piece of the agreement would have to come together and verify that the death of the final royal heir had been of natural causes."

"And if it wasn't?"

"If any member of the Escobar family is ever convicted of involvement in the murder or attempted murder of a royal heir, the agreement becomes void."

"That's the piece of the agreement your family kept in its possession," Levi said.

"Yes."

"What would keep the other family from collecting the first twenty-three parts of the agreement and pretending that piece didn't exist?" Levi asked. "If your family was killed, no one would be the wiser."

"My ancestor thought of that too," Cassie said. "Besides maintaining possession of that piece of the agreement, we also kept a collection of gemstones that serve as a verification key."

"I'm not following."

"It's a safeguard of sorts. Gems of different sizes and shapes were imprinted into the metal. In order to claim the throne, the jewels would have to be retrieved from the royal vault and placed in the separate pieces of the agreement to verify that they were truly the originals," Cassie explained. "One of the stipulations of the agreement specifies that all twenty-four parts, along with the gems, must be presented to prove each is authentic."

"It was your family's way of ensuring someone couldn't create replicas of the various sections."

"Yes." Cassie nodded. "This requirement is known by the heads of state of the countries that safeguard the various sections of the agreement."

"You think the bank robbers were after the different sections of that agreement?"

"It's the only thing that makes sense."

"If that's truly the case, the person behind your assassination attempt is likely a descendant of Luigi Escobar."

"Yes, but it also would have to be someone who knows of the agreement and the nations involved. That isn't public knowledge," Cassie said.

"Yes, but surely Escobar would have passed that information down to his descendants so they would know how to claim Sereno in the event it ever became theirs."

"I would think so," Cassie said. "It's also possible a member of the extended family unearthed the details of the agreement."

"I think that's our next place to look."

"I'm tired of looking," Cassie said. "I'm ready to start finding."

"We'll work on that."

CHAPTER 14

Levi had to give it to her. Cassie was a trooper, and her education on her country was thorough. For the past hour, she had educated him on the European history surrounding the safekeeping of the founding agreement that created her island nation and made her family royal. After World War II, the four original safekeepers of the documents had expanded to nine, with the national banks becoming the vaults where the original metal engravings were held.

"Tell me what you know about the Escobar family." Levi retrieved two water bottles from the minifridge he kept in his office closet and handed one to Cassie. "I want to know who would benefit from the fall of your family."

"In the early 1960s, the man who would have been first in line for the throne behind my family made some bad business decisions and lost most of his family's fortune." Cassie set her water bottle on a coaster but didn't open it. "According to my father, my grandfather gave him some money to bail him out only to watch Jeremiah Escobar gamble it away."

"That couldn't have gone over well."

"No, it didn't. Still, my grandfather didn't yet have any children, and he didn't want to see the possible future royals in poverty. He bought the home the Escobar family lived in and allowed them to stay rent-free."

Levi lowered into the chair beside her. "That was very generous."

"I thought so, but Jeremiah's two sons didn't agree. With no income to support the lifestyle they had grown accustomed to, they demanded a stipend from the royal family."

"Your grandfather refused."

"Yes. The two sons saw the throne as theirs to be had and began stirring up discontent within the general population," Cassie said. "Our economy was still rebuilding after the earthquake and floods. The brothers accused my grandfather of hoarding the royal treasury instead of helping the citizens."

"What happened?"

"They knew if they tried to kill my grandfather, they would lose their claim. And then they found out my grandmother was pregnant."

"Which would put another obstacle between them and gaining control."

"Yes." Cassie motioned to her water bottle. "Do you have a glass?"

Levi rose and retrieved a glass from the shelf in his closet. Leave it to the royals to not know how to drink from the bottle. He twisted the cap off Cassie's water and poured liquid into her glass.

"Thank you."

"You're welcome." Levi sat again. "Tell me more."

"The oldest, Orson, had attended university in America. He had a friend who moved to Sereno and became the figurehead of the Avila revolt. He filled our citizens' heads with dreams of the American way."

"You're talking about Valentin Avila, the man who tried to assassinate your grandfather."

"Yes. Even though my grandfather couldn't prove the Escobar family's involvement, he exiled them from Sereno."

"And you don't know where they went?"

"Rumor had it that Orson went back to the United States," Cassie said. "The father and youngest son moved to Italy, but I don't know where they went from there."

"I would have thought someone would have kept track of them since they were still in line for the throne."

"My father was born a few weeks after the assassination attempt on my grandfather, and from all accounts, he had no interest in worrying about what would happen to the family who would only benefit from the extinction of his progeny."

"Understandable."

"Besides, at the time, they once again had a legitimate heir, and they hoped my grandmother would have more children."

"But that didn't happen?"

"She had a daughter who was stillborn but no other children beyond that."

"I'll get my staff working on tracking down the Escobar family."

"You have to keep the reasons confidential," Cassie said. "The secrecy of the succession agreement has protected my family for generations. With today's resources, if it became public, it would be far too easy for someone to try to create a political alliance with one of Escobar's descendants to destroy my family."

"I understand." Levi took her hand. "Like I said before, you can trust me."

She put her free hand over his. "Thank you."

The naturalness of the gesture made Levi want to forget that he was with her in an official capacity. He rose, breaking contact. "It's getting late. I should take you back to your room."

"I suppose I should get some sleep while I can."

Levi escorted her out of his office and up the back stairwell.

"What is our plan for tomorrow?" Cassie asked.

"We'll see what my security team uncovers on the Escobar family and find out what was stolen from the safe-deposit boxes."

"How long do you think it will take to find that out?"

"I don't know, but I think we should have more details by tomorrow afternoon," Levi said. "I'll try to meet you for breakfast in the morning, but if information is coming in, I may not see you until lunch."

"It's okay. I have plenty of work to keep myself occupied."

Levi opened the door for her. "I'll see you tomorrow."

"You'll let me know if you find anything out?" Cassie asked.

"I will." Levi remained in the hall until she disappeared inside. He returned to his office, his loyalty torn between his oath to his country and his promise to protect the Rossi family secrets. Hoping to find a balance between the two, he called the CIA director.

"Director, I need a favor."

"This is becoming a habit."

Levi sat in his chair and leaned back. "Yeah. Sorry about that."

"Don't apologize. What can I do for you?"

"I have a lead on the bank robberies," Levi said. "I hoped you might have a couple analysts who could do some backgrounds for me."

"Who are we looking for?"

"A father and two sons. Jeremiah, Orson, and Rinaldo Escobar," Levi said. "I'm sure Jeremiah passed away a long time ago, but I need to know about his sons and any children they might have had."

"Is that it?"

Levi hesitated. He couldn't give the source of his information, but one tidbit would help point the analysts in the right direction without betraying the confidence entrusted to him. "Have the analysts also look for ties to the Rossi family."

"You think the robberies are connected to the assassination attempt on Princess Cassandra?"

Levi chose his words carefully. "I want to eliminate the possibility."

"It's already three o'clock here. I'll talk to the chief of the Europe Division and have him get someone on this, but I doubt we'll have much for you before this time tomorrow."

"I'll take any help I can get."

"There is one more thing I need to talk to you about though," Director Palmer said. "We have new information about King Alejandro."

"I'm listening."

"You're going to want to sit down for this."

CHAPTER 15

CASSIE TOSSED AND TURNED ALL the night, her conversation with Levi replaying through her mind. The oddity of trusting someone she had known for only three days was strange enough, but her father's quick acceptance of him rattled her. What had King Eduard said to her dad that had caused him to invite Levi into their confidence?

By five o'clock, she gave up on sleep and headed for the shower. She let the warm water ease away the tension in her neck and shoulders, her mind opening to another uncomfortable fact.

She dried off and dressed, her thoughts racing as she dried her hair and put on her makeup.

For the Escobar family to take control of Sereno, an impartial investigation had to prove that the last living heir had died of natural causes. Her father was only fifty-six. Even if she had been killed and the assassins somehow found her sisters, her father could potentially live for another thirty or forty years.

Why now?

A memory of her father's personal physician leaving her father's suite a few days before the shooting pressed to the front of her mind. If her father was sick . . .

A rap against her door sounded four times in rapid succession. She recognized the sound now as being Levi's knock.

She pulled the door open to find him standing in the hall. "I thought you had to work this morning."

"I do, but I needed a break and thought you might be ready for some breakfast," Levi said. "Patrice is sending up a tray."

"Thank you." Cassie stepped aside. Her concerns about her father remained in the forefront of her thoughts. "I need a favor from you. I have to speak to my father again. Privately."

"I'm sorry, but that's too risky, especially after making two calls to him last night."

"I thought you masked the signal so it couldn't be traced."

"I did, but if anyone is monitoring his calls or electronic communications, they'll be waiting for us to contact him again," Levi explained. "My orders were very explicit that your safety is to remain my highest priority." Levi took her arm and guided her to the table.

She remained standing. "Levi, I need to talk to him."

"I know this isn't what you want to hear, but every time you talk to him, everything the two of you say increases the risk to both of you."

Her fears merged with her overwhelming feeling of helplessness. "You don't understand."

Levi took both of her arms now, holding her in place so they were facing each other. Compassion shone in his eyes. "Talk to me. Tell me what I don't understand."

Cassie pulled away and paced across the room to the balcony doors. She folded her arms across her chest and fought the tears trying to form. She knew better than to lose control of her emotions.

Levi's hand came down on her shoulder, and he turned her to face him. Without a word, he drew her into his embrace.

The gesture of comfort was so unexpected and so very much what she needed that her hands came up to his waist and she held on. An errant tear escaped, but she managed to blink the rest into submission.

"Shhh." Levi's hand caressed her hair before trailing down to rub her arm gently. For a minute, neither of them spoke. Finally, Levi pulled back enough to see her face. He lifted one hand and brushed away the single tear with the pad of his thumb. "It might help to tell me what has you so worried."

"I . . . I don't know. I might be jumping to conclusions, but . . ."

Levi took her hand and laced his fingers through hers. "Come sit down." He didn't lead her back to the table but rather to the love seat in the middle of the room.

Cassie sat, gathering her thoughts as Levi settled beside her. "I was thinking about everything I told you last night."

"And?"

"One element of the succession agreement keeps playing over in my mind," Cassie said. "For the Escobar family to take control, the last member of my family would have to die of natural causes."

"Yes, I remember you saying that."

"I have to ask the question, Why now?" Cassie said. "It's not like my sisters or I are about to have children of our own. None of us is even dating anyone, so why would someone choose now to try to kill me? Unless . . ." Cassie swallowed hard and pushed herself to speak her fears aloud. "Unless my father is dying."

Levi took her hand in his again. When she looked up, the truth reflected on his face. A sob welled up within her even as he spoke the words she had prayed never to hear again. "He has cancer. I'm afraid it's terminal."

"No." The word escaped her in a whisper, her hand lifting to cover her mouth.

"I only found out late last night," Levi said.

She blinked rapidly, but this time, she couldn't keep her emotions at bay.

Levi shifted closer, his arm reaching around her shoulders. She buried her face into his shoulder, the floodgates opening. Tears streamed down her face, and sobs shook her body.

"I'm so sorry," Levi whispered as he drew her closer.

Minutes ticked by as the storm raged, erupted, and finally faded into the last trickle of tears. She sat up and rubbed both hands over her cheeks. "I'm sorry."

"You have nothing to apologize for."

"I never cry in front of people." She swiped at her tears again. "I must be an absolute mess."

"You're beautiful," Levi countered.

The statement so simply delivered held more impact than a dozen flowery compliments. Surprised by the spurt of attraction at such a time, she focused once more on Levi's news. "Tell me what you know. Have the doctors said how long . . . ?" She couldn't finish the question.

Levi apparently didn't expect her to. "A year, give or take," he said. "My understanding is that he planned to have you step into his role after the first of the year."

"Eight months from now."

"Yes. That gives us some time to find out who knows about your father, and who in the Escobar family is trying to inherit your country."

"When do we start?"

"Breakfast first," Levi said. "A very wise woman told me that everyone needs to take a few minutes every day to spend with the people who are important to them. I thought I would take that advice this morning."

"A wise woman, huh?"

Levi stood and offered his hand. "Very wise."

* * *

Levi opened Cassie's door to find Brenna standing on the other side, a break-fast tray in her hands.

"Patrice asked me to bring this up for you."

Levi saw it now, the little flicker of attraction and disappointment in Brenna's eyes. He couldn't help but sympathize with her. He was beginning to understand what it felt like to experience an attraction for someone and know it would never be returned. It had taken every ounce of willpower not to kiss Cassie when he had held her moments ago.

Levi took the tray from her and gave Brenna a nod. "Thank you, Brenna. I appreciate it."

Brenna offered a timid smile. "You're welcome."

Levi closed the door and carried the tray to the table. Cassie remained on the window seat, staring out at the Mediterranean.

"Come eat," Levi said.

No response.

"Cassie." Levi crossed the room and put his hand on her shoulder. "You need to eat something."

"I'm fine."

Levi lowered himself onto the seat beside her, his hand trailing down her arm. He took her hand. "You aren't fine, and you need to keep your strength up," he insisted. "You aren't going to do your father any good if you starve yourself."

Her head turned, their eyes meeting. "Do you realize that you have ordered me around more than anyone I've ever met, excluding my immediate family?"

"Maybe you need to be ordered around every once in a while," Levi said. "Especially when you get so focused on others that you forget to take care of yourself."

She angled her head as she looked at him. "I thought you would be different."

"What do you mean?"

"Beyond the usual royal security force, I've had bodyguards before," Cassie said. "The kind that surround me and keep me protected from everyone and everything. You aren't like them."

She turned her hand over and linked her fingers through his. "Thank you for telling me about my father. You didn't have to do that."

"Yes, I did. You deserved to know."

"I agree." She leaned forward and kissed him. "Thank you."

The simple gesture sent the room spinning. Levi tightened his hold on her hand, and his eyes locked on hers. In that moment, he saw her. Cassie, the woman, not Cassandra, the princess.

His logic and discipline crumbled. His free hand reached up to cup the back of her neck. He leaned in, their faces close together, awareness lighting her eyes. He heard her quick intake of breath, felt her hand squeeze his.

Anticipation built painfully in his chest until he couldn't stand it any longer. He closed the remaining distance between them until his lips met hers. The spark of attraction he had experienced a moment ago exploded inside him. The possibility of what they could be together paled to the reality. She lifted both hands to his arms as though trying to keep her balance.

He shouldn't be doing this, but how could he refrain? Cassie's beauty, combined with her intellect, sharp wit, and devout loyalty to family and country were more than he could resist. Now that he had a sample of what she could do to him, he knew he was going to want more.

His fingers tightened on the back of Cassie's neck, kneading gently until he felt the worry and stress she carried there easing away.

He wanted her to forget everything in that moment except for the sensations they created together, but the warning in the back of his mind chimed like a foghorn in the distance.

A knock sounded at the door. They broke apart, Cassie's eyes wide, her hand lifting to her lips. A faint blush crept into her cheeks, a reaction Levi couldn't help but find endearing.

He put his hand on her knee and leaned in to kiss her cheek. "I'll see who it is."

Cassie stood as soon as he did. "I'd better freshen up."

Levi nodded as she rushed into her bedroom and closed the door.

CHAPTER 16

CASSIE DIDN'T HAVE TO LOOK in the mirror to know her cheeks were flushed, her lipstick faded. She pressed her fingers against her lips again. They still tingled from Levi's kiss. Then again, so did the rest of her body. That man was potent.

She touched up her makeup and applied a fresh coat of lipstick before she returned to her sitting room. Levi sat on the couch across from Garrett and Janessa.

The men stood.

Levi motioned to the new arrivals. "Garrett and Janessa stopped by to check on you."

"I hope you have been comfortable here," Garrett said.

"I have. Thank you," Cassie sat on the couch. "Everyone has been very kind."

"Janessa and I thought you might want to join us for dinner tonight." Garrett reclaimed his seat.

Cassie glanced at Levi, who now sat beside her. She caught the concern in his expression and turned her attention once more to Garrett. "I would love to, but wouldn't that draw attention to who I really am?"

"Does the staff still believe you are a new employee?" Janessa asked.

"Actually, we changed that up." Levi took Cassie's hand. "Meet Cassie, my new girlfriend."

"I didn't expect that," Janessa admitted.

"Sounds like we need to spend some time together," Garrett added. "I'd like to at least hear the latest of what has happened while we were gone. Has there been any progress on finding who was behind the assassination attempt?"

"They appear to be hired guns. No ties to any particular group yet," Levi said. "Our staff is following up on a few leads."

"I assume you heard about the string of bank robberies yesterday," Janessa said.

"Yes. We're looking into those as well in case there is a connection," Levi said.

"Let us know if you find anything." Garrett stood. "I have some calls to make."

"I should get some work done too," Janessa said. "Join us for dinner tonight, both of you. No one will think twice about us entertaining a valuable member of our staff and his girlfriend."

Though Cassie wasn't sure what to think about socializing with royals when she herself was pretending not to be one, she nodded. "I'd like that. Thank you."

"Let's plan on eight o'clock in the breakfast room."

"We'll see you then." Levi stood and walked them to the door. As soon as they left, Levi turned back to face her. "I need to check in with my staff. Would you like to come with me?"

Though part of her didn't want to be alone, she shook her head. "I think I'll stay here for now. Maybe I can distract myself with work."

"As soon as I get all my updates, I'll come back. It shouldn't be more than an hour."

"You don't have to babysit me," Cassie said. "I can manage on my own."

He crossed the room and sat beside her again. He dropped his hand on her knee, and his eyes met hers. "I know today hasn't been easy. I want to be here for you."

"As my bodyguard."

"I want to be here for you," Levi corrected before he stood. "I'll be back in an hour."

"Levi?"

"Yes?"

"Thank you."

"You're welcome."

* * *

Cassie dominated Levi's thoughts as he passed through the wide halls and headed toward his office. He hadn't meant to kiss her. But he had been thinking of doing exactly that since the day she arrived at the chateau.

In his head, he knew the situation between them couldn't go beyond the oasis they had created here in Meridia, but that hadn't kept him from losing the battle against his willpower. Had he not seen her at her most vulnerable, he might have been able to keep his distance. Maybe.

It was too late to go back now. Over the past few days, she had shown him glimpses of the real Cassie, a woman who, under normal circumstances, Levi would have actively pursued a relationship with. Of course, he hadn't lived in normal circumstances for years.

Since his breakup with Belinda, the few relationships he had attempted had all come during the weeks he had been Stateside, usually lasting less than two months before he would move on to the next assignment. Mexico, Italy, Venezuela, and now Meridia. If he lumped all of his days in the United States together since joining the Agency, he doubted he would reach a full year.

Seven years he had been working undercover for the CIA, and for the first time, he found himself thoroughly conflicted. The agency could be so much more helpful if they knew why the Escobar family was important to the country of Sereno, yet he couldn't bring himself to betray Cassie's confidence, even though that was what his duty demanded of him.

Levi dropped into the chair behind his desk and picked up the phone. He checked in with his security team to find all was well. Though he didn't expect anything new from the CIA, he checked his secure email anyway. Nothing.

He retrieved the summary of activity that had occurred near the chateau throughout the night. From what he could tell, Garrett and Janessa had returned home without incident and without the paparazzi. He wasn't sure how they had managed that, but he suspected Janessa's CIA skills may have come into play.

Satisfied that Cassie's presence would remain out of the public eye for the foreseeable future, he opened the latest report Janessa's brother, Jeremy, had compiled on the bank robberies. The Interpol reports offered more depth to the extent of the thefts. Though the detailed loss reports were still being collected, it didn't take long for Levi to see a distinct pattern. Every safe-deposit box that had been broken into had been cleaned out entirely, and in every case, either a row or a section had been robbed, but nothing beyond it.

As much as he hated to admit it, the evidence was consistent with the facts Cassie had shared with him.

A knock on his door caused him to look up. Janessa entered and closed the door behind her.

"I was wondering how long it would take you to make your way down here."

"I would have been here fifteen minutes ago, but I got caught talking to Patrice." She sat in the chair across from him.

"I should have known. You probably smelled the fresh croissants when you walked in the door."

"They're so good," Janessa said. "Patrice really is the best cook around."

"I agree, but I doubt that's what you came down here to discuss."

"You know me so well." Janessa crossed her legs at the ankles, a habit she had picked up since becoming a royal. "Jeremy said he sent you the latest updates on the robberies. What's going on with that?"

Levi hesitated a split second too long.

"Levi, don't go there."

"Go where?"

"Don't pull that 'you don't need to know' thing with me. I may not be Agency anymore, but as a member of the royal family, I obviously care deeply about matters affecting Europe," Janessa said. "And you of all people should know I can keep a confidence."

Levi didn't correct her assumption of why he was reluctant to share information. He leaned back in his chair. Janessa was right. She wasn't Agency anymore, and he couldn't think of anyone he trusted more fully. "Don't press me for details, but I think the robberies are connected to the assassination attempt in Sereno."

"Can you tell me why?"

"No."

Her eyes narrowed. "What's going on with you and Cassandra?"

"It's been a tough morning for her. She received some bad news from home."

"Nice evasion, but you didn't answer my question."

"Seems to me that we had a very similar conversation when you were pretending to be engaged to Garrett."

"And you were there for me when I needed you," Janessa reminded him. "Let me return the favor."

Levi debated a moment, but he couldn't bring himself to voice his feelings for Cassie aloud. He wasn't sure he could identify them himself. Instead, he tapped on the keyboard of his computer and retrieved the list of suspects he and Cassie had identified. "I asked Director Palmer to put some analysts on this, but if you want to help, I have a suspect list for the mastermind behind the robberies."

"Put me to work."

"Do you really have time to help?"

"Actually, yes. King Eduard asked me to set aside some of my other duties to help with the investigation into the assassination."

"Have you found anything?"

"I'm glad you asked." Janessa reached for her oversized purse and slid a file out. "Did you know that both of the assassins used to work for Pantheon?"

"What's Pantheon?"

"It's a private security firm. It just so happens that it provides security for a lot of oil companies."

"You know about the bidding war for the Sereno gas field."

"I do. I also know Cassandra is responsible for putting forward the recommendation of which company will be awarded the contract," Janessa said. "Since Cassandra took over the energy commission, King Alejandro has followed her recommendation every single time."

"Can you get me a list of oil companies that contract with Pantheon?"

"Jeremy is supposed to send it to me. As soon as I get it, I'll pass it along, assuming he doesn't send it to you too."

"Thanks."

Janessa stood, and Levi followed suit. A flash of amusement sparked in her eyes. "Don't think I missed the way you were looking at our guest."

"Sometimes you see too much."

"Part of my charm." Janessa flashed him a grin. "I'll talk to you later."

"That you will." Levi watched her go and sat at his desk again. He wasn't sure how Janessa had picked up on his attraction to Cassie, but he didn't need to reinforce whatever suspicions she had brewing in that head of hers.

Five minutes. He'd give Janessa that much of a head start before he went back to Cassie's room. Attraction or not, she was still his responsibility. He would keep her safe. If he could keep her safe and happy, so much the better.

CHAPTER 17

CASSIE STOOD ON HER BALCONY and watched the waves rolling over sand. Levi had checked in on her several times already, but she had spent the past three hours since lunch alone. The rhythm continued, the roar of the surf a constant background noise.

A lawn mower rumbled in the distance, and two groundskeepers spoke on the sidewalk below her window. Two more groundskeepers worked in the garden, pruning roses and planting new flowers near the swimming pool.

The simplicity of the scene made her long for the past when she didn't understand the evil in the world, when she still had her parents and didn't fully realize they wouldn't always be here.

A year from now, she would likely be an orphan, an orphan who would be expected to rule with the same grace and commitment as her father and grand-father before her. Could she even do the job she had been born to do? Would she survive long enough to find out? And if she did, would she be destined to rule alone, or would she someday find the opportunity to fall in love and marry?

Another weight pressed in on her. Being with Levi had unlocked those secret dreams of finding her own fairy-tale ending, of having a family of her own, but in truth, she barely knew him. Would he want to pursue a relationship with her once this ordeal was over? Could he stomach the constant scrutiny of the press and the lack of privacy?

A knock sounded at her door.

"Come in."

Levi entered and crossed the room to join her on the balcony. His hand lifted to her shoulder. "How are you doing?"

"I'm not sure." She waved toward the water. "I look out there and wonder what it's like to live a normal life. Then my mind starts going, and I know I'll never understand what that would be like."

"You're getting a glimpse of normal right now."

"I'm grateful for that." She leaned her right elbow on the railing and looked at him. "What is your normal like?"

"It's not much different than right now, except the time I'm with you would usually be spent in the security office," he said. "I received some information a few minutes ago about the gunmen in Sereno."

"What?"

"They both had ties to a security firm that contracts for various oil companies."

"What's the name of the firm?"

"Pantheon Security," Levi said. "I should have a list of the oil companies who use them shortly."

"And you want to compare that list to the firms I'm still considering."

"Yes. It might narrow down who would benefit from you being out of the picture."

"This sounds like you think the motive for trying to kill me was for profit," Cassie said. "The bank robberies point to someone trying to gain power. Which is it?"

"I don't know, but at this point, we can't rule anything out. We'll follow both leads and see where they take us."

"Every day we don't have answers is another day I'm away from my father. I don't know how many more days he has, but I would like to spend as many as I can with him."

"I understand." Levi held up a phone. "Are you up for calling your cousin again? I want to know if he's had any dealings with Pantheon."

Though emotionally exhausted, Cassie took the phone. "If you think it can help."

"It's a long shot, but . . ."

Cassie punched in the number, and Crispan answered on the second ring. After she greeted her cousin, Levi leaned close so he could hear both sides of the conversation.

"Crispan, I'm sorry to bother you, but I have another question for you. Can you tell me what you know about Pantheon Security? Have you ever used them before?"

"Once, but I won't again," Crispan answered without hesitation.

"Why?"

"I'm not sure how to put it into words," Crispan said. "When hiring a security firm, you are entrusting those people with your safety. It doesn't work when you don't trust the men and women carrying guns."

"No, it doesn't. What was it about them that made you uncomfortable?"

"Their employees are primarily ex-military, but they didn't possess the discipline I've come to expect from people with that background. I simply wasn't impressed."

"I see." Cassie turned to Levi, their faces close. She mouthed the words, "Anything else?"

Levi shook his head.

"Thanks for your help," Cassie said. She said her goodbyes and hung up. "So, Pantheon isn't the kind of company my family wants to deal with under any circumstances. Do you think the company was involved?"

"I'm not sure." Levi contemplated for a moment. "Do you think your father would be willing to join you here?"

Cassie shook her head. "He would never leave our country unless another family member was there to rule in his stead."

"Then maybe I need to see what is being done to enhance the security of your home."

Hope bloomed through the fragments of fear. "I think that's an excellent idea."

* * *

Levi lifted his hand and knocked on Cassie's door, feeling as though he were picking her up for a first date. In a way, he supposed he was. No longer was he her fake boyfriend, but he wasn't her real one either.

Throughout the day, the question had surfaced in his mind of whether she would even consider dating a commoner if her world wasn't turned upside down. He kept telling himself the kiss they had shared earlier had been simple and natural, something based on their mutual attraction. But what if it was more than that? What if it could be more than that?

The door swung open, and his breath caught. Cassie's hair hung over her shoulders in loose ringlets, her eyes expertly emphasized with makeup to give her a more mysterious look. Her lipstick was a shade darker than the pink dress she wore, which complemented her complexion.

Levi took her hand and brought it to his lips. "You're stunning."

"Thank you." Her cheeks flushed. "I don't look too royal, do I?"

"You look perfect."

The blush deepened. "Thank you."

Levi offered his arm, and she slipped her hand through the crook of his elbow.

Cassie glanced around the empty hallway. "Have you heard anything else about the matter we discussed earlier?"

"Not yet," he said. "Let's not worry about that for a few hours." His lips twitched into the beginning of a smile. "It's not often we get to double date with royalty."

"I suppose that's true." Amusement reflected in her eyes. "Kind of like how rare it is for you to take a night off."

"Touché." Levi escorted her downstairs into the kitchen, where Janessa stood beside Patrice, both women wearing aprons.

Janessa spotted them and waved toward the breakfast room. "Go ahead and sit down. Garrett should be here in a minute."

Levi watched Janessa load dinner rolls into a bread basket. The woman had been a royal for nearly a year, and she still couldn't resist lending a hand whenever she had the chance.

"Are you coming?" Levi bit back a smile. "Or are you trying to bribe Patrice to make you chocolate mousse again?"

Patrice chuckled. "You'll find out soon enough."

Levi guided Cassie into the breakfast room and pulled out a chair for her. He took the seat beside her but rose to his feet when Janessa entered a moment later sans apron, the bread basket in her hand. She set it down as Garrett walked in behind her.

Garrett put his hand on Janessa's waist in a gesture that was both natural and intimate. "I hope I didn't keep you waiting."

"Not at all," Levi said.

Garrett closed the door between the kitchen and breakfast room to ensure privacy, and everyone settled into their seats. "I haven't had time to read through the latest security reports," Garrett said. "Tell me what's happened the last few days."

Levi filled him in, leaving out Cassie's theory about the motive for the bank robberies.

"Then everything is pointing to money as being the motive," Janessa said.

"So far," Levi said. "Once we get the list of oil companies who employ Pantheon Security, Cassie will help me narrow down the possible suspects."

"Hopefully, only one of the finalists will be on the list," Cassie said.

"You said you'd have that tonight, right?" Janessa asked Levi. He caught the cryptic meaning that Janessa was giving rather than receiving information.

"Yes. I expect it will help the investigation tremendously," Levi said.

"Have you had the chance to discuss your theory with your father?" Garrett asked.

"They spoke briefly yesterday," Levi said.

Cassie looked at Garrett and Janessa. "Obviously you've heard the news."

The realization surfaced that Cassie believed he had learned of her father's illness from the Meridian royal family. His stomach clenched. He couldn't possibly give her the real source of his knowledge.

Janessa glanced from Cassie to Levi and back again. "I haven't heard anything specific. I'm sure you know a lot more than we do."

"I'm afraid not. Levi told me about his cancer, but he didn't have details either except—" Cassie broke off, clearly struggling to keep her voice from breaking.

Levi put his hand on hers. "Finding out her father is terminally ill has been understandably difficult."

"I can't begin to imagine," Janessa said.

"You have our deepest sympathies," Garrett added.

"Thank you."

"What can we do to assist your family?" Garrett asked.

"I think you have already done more than enough in assuring my safety."

"That was a good beginning," Janessa countered. "Levi, do you need any help with the investigation beyond the resources you currently have?"

"Actually, I would like access to the security team in Sereno," Levi said. "With her father's health declining, Cassie would greatly benefit from being able to return home."

"That's risky," Garrett said.

"If you knew you had a year or less to spend time with your father, wouldn't you want to take all the time you could?" Cassie asked.

"I would," Garrett said, "but I also know my father wouldn't want me to risk my life to do so."

"It sounds like our fathers are very similar in that regard," Cassie said.

"The burden of leadership." Garrett stretched his arm behind Janessa's chair and gave her shoulder a squeeze. "Ensuring the continuity of the royal family is every bit as important as balancing duty and love."

Cassie nodded but didn't respond.

Janessa put her hand on her husband's as though uniting them. "Levi, you want to be involved in upgrading their security?"

"I do." The thought of sending Cassie home without him pushed a new idea to the forefront, one that spilled out in his words before he thought to censor them. "With your permission, I want to go with her when she returns to Sereno to ensure her safety."

Levi sensed Cassie's surprise in the way her body stiffened slightly before she forced herself to relax. He put his hand on hers and gave it a squeeze, his focus still on Janessa and Garrett.

Garrett's direct gaze held an understanding Levi couldn't quite identify. "I believe we may be able to accommodate that request. How long do you think it will take to make the arrangements?"

"Two weeks. Maybe three," Levi said. "If we can keep Cassie's presence hidden until then, we might be able to sneak her back into Sereno without anyone knowing she is there."

"That's a good idea," Janessa said. "Let me know what we can do to help."

"I will."

The door swung open, and Patrice and Brenna entered carrying dinner plates. Chicken cordon bleu. Janessa's favorite. Shocker.

CHAPTER 18

CASSIE LISTENED TO LEVI AND Janessa discuss various ideas of how to best work with her country's royal guard, the ease of their conversation raising an uncomfortable red flag.

"Cassie, do you think your father will be open to some help?" Levi asked her.

"I honestly don't know."

"Garrett, maybe your father should approach him about it," Janessa suggested.

"That's a good idea." Garrett set down his dessert spoon and glanced at his watch. "I'll call him now."

Levi pushed back from the table. "Cassie, how about a walk in the gardens?"

Though she was mentally exhausted from the emotional roller coaster she had ridden all day, she nodded. "I would like that. Thank you."

Garrett stood. "We'll let you know when we have any news from your father."

"Thank you."

Levi escorted her outside onto the terrace. He put his hand on her elbow as they descended the wide stone steps. "Are you okay?"

"It's been a tough day."

"You've had more than your share of tough days lately. I hope we can put a stop to that." He guided her beneath an arched trellis laden with ivy.

"Did you mean what you said about coming with me?"

"Yes." He took her hand, his fingers lacing through hers. "Would that be okay with you?"

"You said when I first arrived that you were leaving here." Cassie leaned down and plucked a white poppy from the bed beside her. She twirled the stem between her thumb and finger. "Where would you have gone had you not been assigned to protect me?"

"I'm not sure."

"You aren't sure?" Her eyebrows drew together. "You were leaving in a couple weeks and didn't know where you were going?"

"In my profession, that happens sometimes."

The flower she held dropped to the ground. "What is your profession?"

"I've already told you. It's my job to keep people safe." Levi stopped and took her other hand so they were facing each other. "Why all the questions?"

She studied his face. He kept his eyes on her, his confusion evident. Had her uneasiness at dinner come from her inability to trust anyone outside her family? Or was Levi more than he appeared to be?

"The way you and Janessa were talking, it seemed like your duties extend far beyond personal protection duty."

"They do," Levi said. "My specialty is designing security plans to make sure people like you remain safe. That's why I offered to come to Sereno."

He ran his hands up her arms from wrists to elbows before taking her hands again. "I'd never forgive myself if you were hurt or worse and I could have done something to prevent it."

Whatever suspicions had been blooming during dinner withered away, a new flurry of emotions coming to the surface: attraction, simple and pure, dominated.

Cassie took a step toward him, cutting the distance between them in half. Pushing onto her toes, she kissed him, butterflies immediately taking flight in her stomach.

Levi's hands tightened on hers briefly before he pulled back and once again focused intently on her.

"You're trying to distract me," he said. "Tell me what upset you at dinner."

"Nothing." She leaned back on her heels. "Everything. I don't know."

"That's not much of an answer."

"Your announcement of coming to Sereno caught me off guard, and then I noticed the way you and Janessa work together. You act more like friends or coworkers than employer and employee."

"We are friends," Levi said. "And in a way, we are coworkers. Janessa is a talented linguist and has a keen sense of observation. On occasion, I have enlisted her help when I've needed someone to look at something with a fresh perspective."

"A royal helping with her own security. That's not common."

"Aren't you doing exactly that?" Levi asked.

"I suppose so." She angled her chin up. "Does that make us coworkers?"

"I'm not sure what we are." He released her hands and pulled her closer. "We'll have to work on defining that."

"You think so?"

He leaned down and pressed his lips against hers. "I do."

* * *

Alejandro fought against his impatience as the nurse disconnected the tubing from the medical port that facilitated his biweekly infusions. The decision to begin a new treatment regimen hadn't been an easy one, but traditional chemotherapy wasn't going to prolong his life long enough to justify the side effects that would impede his ability to rule. Dr. Lewis's alternative therapy impacted his weekly schedule, but except for the inconvenience of spending two hours in bed every other day, he had thus far been able to function fully.

His outer door opened and closed. "Your Majesty?" Elliott called out.

"In here."

The nurse completed her task, and Alejandro buttoned his shirt.

"I need a moment." Elliott held up the file in his hand. He waited for the nurse to gather her things and leave the room before continuing. "I have the list of safe-deposit boxes that were affected by the robbery."

Alejandro studied his brother-in-law. "And?"

"You and Cassie were right. It was our succession agreement that was targeted."

"How many?"

"Twenty-two," Elliott said.

"All of them except my family's piece and the one the Escobar family holds."

"That's correct." Elliott's fingers tightened on the file folder. "Whoever is behind this theft is in your inner circle or is part of the Escobar family."

"Or both." Alejandro selected a tie and draped it around his neck.

"You think someone from our family is conspiring against you?"

"No, but the timing of last weekend's attack is highly suspicious." Alejandro turned to face the mirror and proceeded to knot his tie. He wished he could cancel the dinner with his prime minister tonight, if for no other reason than to analyze this new information. "It has to be someone who knows I'm dying."

"Even your children don't know that."

"Which means our suspect list should be minimal."

"I'll have security start a deep background check on the medical staff."

"And the staff working in the residence."

"Of course," Elliott said. "What about the robberies? How much vulnerability does that create for the royal family?"

"There's only one reason for someone to steal the agreement," Alejandro said. "Someone in the Escobar family knows of its existence but doesn't have access to the details it entails."

"I don't understand."

"The procedures for the change of power is very specific. The rules of parliament to be enacted, the place it would occur, even what day of the week the petition can be submitted. These details were put in place to prevent a potential impostor from trying to lay claim to the Escobar family's rights."

"Then it might not be one of Escobar's heirs behind the thefts," Elliott said.

"Or it's a member of the Escobar family who hasn't been given the details."

"Perhaps it's time to look up the Escobars and find out where their families are now."

"See if you can locate them. I agree that it's time to make a call."

"Yes, Your Majesty." He bowed and left the room.

Alejandro slipped on his suit jacket and moved into the living room. He was debating whether to move the dinner with the prime minister from the dining room to his private quarters when his phone rang again. A bubble of panic surfaced when he saw King Eduard's name light his screen.

"King Eduard, is everything okay?"

"Yes, your daughter is fine," Eduard answered, giving Alejandro the most important information first. "She is, however, anxious to come home."

"That doesn't surprise me. My royal guard is working on increasing our security as we speak."

"I wondered if I might offer some assistance," Eduard said. "I know you are short-staffed after the shooting, and I have someone I've relied heavily on during our recent troubles. He's very good."

Though Alejandro's knee-jerk reaction was to reject the offer, Eduard was right. He was understaffed, and no matter how much he wanted all of his daughters home, he couldn't risk it until his security had been fully analyzed and enhanced. "What specifically did you have in mind?"

"I know this isn't an easy thing to share, but if you could let my man look at any video feed you have from the night of the shooting, as well as your security protocols, he can help determine where the weaknesses are and develop a plan to overcome them."

"I appreciate the offer, but that's asking a lot," Alejandro said. "We're talking about the security of my home."

"It took a bombing in Meridia to get me to agree to accept help," Eduard said. "I know it's difficult to invite outsiders into your confidence, but I also know that as a king and as a father, you want to protect your children as well as your country. Take some time to think about it. The offer is available if you need it."

"Thank you. Please send my daughter my love."

"Of course."

Alejandro hung up. Sharing his security protocols with a foreign entity went against every instinct, yet he couldn't deny the truth. Someone had already breached his home, and he couldn't risk bringing any of his daughters home until he could ensure their safety.

One way or another, changes needed to be made. Darius's concern that an inside source might exist within the palace walls caused him to pick up his phone. Whether he liked it or not, he needed someone from the outside to help him protect his daughters. He only hoped the man Eduard spoke of was up to the task.

CHAPTER 19

JULIEN LAID THE ENGRAVINGS ON the velvet cloth covering the carpet in front of the fireplace. The secret to gaining power was here. Now he needed to understand it.

If his father would have taken the time to explain, he wouldn't have needed to go to such extremes to learn what the ancient agreement said.

He read the first three lines, the words outlining the story that had been handed down through the generations of his family. His mother may not have known much beyond vague stories, but it had been enough to plant the seeds of where his destiny lay.

He continued reading, stopping twice to look up the meaning of a word. He hadn't realized how much the Spanish language had changed over the past four hundred years.

He read through the rest of the agreement, noting the incomplete sections. Two more pieces of the puzzle and he would have it all. Then again, if his mother had relayed the family stories correctly, he already knew what the missing sections contained.

His phone chimed, indicating a new message. His hand tightened on it when he saw the text Pratt had sent. *Apartment in Malmo compromised. Surveillance team across the street.*

Did someone know Julien was involved? Or were the authorities searching for someone else in his family? No matter. He had handed the keys over to Pratt months ago when Julien had decided to erase all traces of his connection to his family.

Julien texted Pratt back. *Looks like you're staying with me for the foreseeable future. Make sure you aren't followed.*

Understood.

Julien set his phone aside and focused on the agreement again. He read through it a second time, noting the procedures in place for him to ascend to the throne when the time came. He stumbled over one word and backed up to reread the sentence.

A new thought surfaced. Julien moved to his bookshelf and retrieved the book that contained the governing documents for Sereno. For the next hour, he scoured the constitution and the various amendments. It wasn't until he reached the changes made after his family was exiled that he found what he was looking for.

A slow smile crossed his face. Apparently, his family's belief that they couldn't be involved in a royal assassination wasn't entirely true. If he was correct, he was perfectly justified in taking matters into his own hands.

* * *

Levi kept Cassie's hand in his as they ascended the spiral staircase to the guest quarters. Their conversation in the garden replayed through his mind, and he mentally kicked himself for letting his guard down. He knew better than to let his friendship with Janessa show, and yet, when they had all been sitting together, he had seen Cassie as part of the team, not as an assignment with a beginning and an end.

He wondered if it would have been easier had they stuck with his original plan to have her pose as a security officer, but he was also having a hard time regretting where their relationship had gone. Thoughts of a future together threaded through his mind only to be pushed aside into a messy knot that had ceased to follow reason.

"Thanks for walking me back to my room," Cassie said, interrupting his thoughts.

"My pleasure." He kissed her good night, her hold on his heart tightening with the simple contact. "I'll see you tomorrow."

Reality crashed over him. Cassie was a princess. He was an intelligence operative from a country she didn't trust. His next thought was that those details didn't matter. He needed to focus on the here and now without letting his nationality and social status get in the way.

Then, reminding himself he had a job to do, he went to the security office, where he found Franco at his desk.

"You're working late," Levi said.

"Still trying to get the updates on the bank robberies," Franco said. "I emailed you the latest a few minutes ago."

Levi sat at an open computer. He reviewed the intel reports Franco had sent, his frustration rising. He had yet to gain an inventory of what had been stolen from the various safe-deposit boxes.

"Franco, doesn't Interpol have anything else on the safe-deposit boxes?" Levi asked.

"Not yet. They have to interview all of the people who rented them to find out what was taken, and even then, the police have to rely on what the customers say."

"Get me a list of who rented those boxes," Levi said. "Interpol has to have that much by now. It's been two days."

"I'll make a call."

"Thanks." Levi waved at another stack of files beside Franco. "Anything new on the investigation in Sereno?"

"Sereno's captain of the guard had the same concern about an inside source at the palace helping plan the attack."

"And?"

"The only person who red-flagged was Leon Cordova, but he was killed the night of the assassination attempt," Franco said.

"No one else on the suspect list?"

"No one they're talking about." Franco picked up the open file beside his computer. "I did get the report back on the extended family members of the late queen of Sereno."

"Anything of interest?"

"Only that the queen's nephew is working for an oil company in Houston," Franco said. "I thought that was a bit odd since King Alejandro leans anti-American."

"I looked into him as well," Levi said, "but I couldn't find any motivation for him to want Princess Cassandra dead."

"That's consistent with what our analysts found. The company he works for is based out of the UK, and phone records show he has an ongoing relationship with his parents, uncle, and siblings."

"Any spike or decrease in communications between them in the past eighteen months?"

"Only in the month the queen died. Other than that, everything appears to have held steady."

Comforted that his analysis agreed with the CIA's, Levi asked, "Anything else?"

"Not yet. I'll let you know when I get that list from Interpol."

"Thanks." Levi stood. "I'm going to see if I can dig up anything else on the Escobar family. I'll be in my office if you need me." He left the room. As soon as he was in the privacy of his office, he logged in to his secure email and checked for any new analyst reports from the CIA. Two topped his inbox.

He opened the first, an analysis of Cassie's uncle and cousins. The contents added more detail than what Franco had given him, but the bottom line remained the same: the relationships between the royal family and the in-laws appeared to be warm and beneficial to all.

The second report, this one on the Escobar family, gave less information than the first. It also raised Levi's suspicions. Cassie said her family had lost track of the family that could ultimately take over Sereno. Did she know that shortly after Rinaldo Escobar died three years ago, his only son had disappeared from sight? His home had been sold, his bank accounts closed, and his cell phone turned off.

Levi's first thought was that the man had been killed, his assets seized by someone. As he read further, he came to the same conclusion as the author of the report. The signature on the sales agreement for the house appeared genuine, and Raymond Escobar had reportedly appeared in person to close out his bank accounts. Either the man had decided to disappear from sight, or someone had pressured him into doing so. The question was, where was Raymond now? And why had he gone into hiding?

A new email popped up, this one from Janessa. It contained the list of oil companies Pantheon served.

Levi printed the list and walked back to Cassie's room. He knocked on the door, surprised it took a full minute for her to answer. When she did, her hair was tied back in a messy ponytail, her face free of makeup. Instead of the dress she had worn to dinner, she was now dressed in a pair of black silk pajamas, a matching robe tied hastily at her waist.

"Did you forget something?"

Levi struggled to find his voice. "Do you know you're every bit as beautiful without makeup on as you are with it?"

Disbelief showed on her face, along with a blush. "Thank you, but I don't think you came back to tell me that."

"No. That was just a bonus." Levi held up the papers in his hands. "May I come in for a minute?"

She tightened the belt at her waist and pulled the door open wider. As soon as he passed through, she closed the door again. "What's that?"

"The list of oil companies that employ Pantheon. I need you to tell me if any of them are on your list of finalists for the oil deal in Sereno."

Cassie took the list from him and scanned through it. Levi noticed the two times she paused, once on the first page and once on the second.

"Which ones?" Levi asked.

"Vector Oil from the United States."

"And?"

She looked up as though surprised he knew there was more than one. "Satori Oil and Gas."

"From Greece."

"Yes."

Levi considered the two options. "If the gas and oil drilling rights are the motive behind the assassination attempt, either company could be behind it. How do they rate against their competition?"

"They are in the top three. The only other company in the running is also from the US."

"If the assassins had been successful and you hadn't survived the attack, your father would most likely have awarded it to Satori."

"Yes, I believe so."

"Then that's the one we need to concentrate on," Levi said.

"Doesn't it seem odd to you that a company from Greece would hire assassins from the United States?" Cassie crossed to the love seat and sat.

"Not at all." Levi sat beside her. "If an American had killed his daughter, there's no way your father would have awarded the drilling rights to an American company, regardless of how good the proposal was."

"You're right."

"When we first talked about the proposals, you said there was a fourth company. Did you already eliminate it?"

"Yes."

"Can you tell me which one it was?" Levi asked. "I'd like to make sure no one from that company was involved."

"But it's not on this list."

"Yes, but it pays to make sure someone wasn't hiring these mercenaries as a way to throw us on a false trail."

Cassie's eyebrows lifted. "You're very thorough."

"I try."

"The one I eliminated is Kronos Oil."

"What country does it operate out of?" Levi asked.

"France."

"I'll look into it." He stood.

"Thanks."

Levi crossed the room, forcing himself to walk away from the beautiful princess dressed in silk. "See you in the morning."

She followed him to the door and leaned in to give him a good-night kiss. "Yes, you will."

* * *

Levi scanned Captain Reyes's report on the false alarm at the museum. Faulty sensors. Two of them. Levi wasn't buying it. Thankfully, neither was the captain. Unfortunately, none of the employees at the museum had flagged as suspects, and the license plates Levi had photographed all belonged to someone who had had a reason to be there.

He glanced at his cell phone to check the time. Eleven twenty. He needed sleep, but he also needed answers. He was wavering on which need would win out when his phone rang.

He picked it up to find Director Palmer on the line. He hit the talk button. "This is Levi."

"Do you have a minute?" Director Palmer asked.

"Yeah. What's up?"

"We have a lead on our gunmen," Director Palmer said. "Finance found a spike in fees being paid from Satori Oil to Pantheon over the past six months. The amount is small enough to fly under the radar, but when you add them all together, it's nearly $400,000."

"Can they link it to our gunmen?"

"One of them, anyway," he said. "They're working on the other one."

"Let me know what you find out," Levi said, then added, "Any luck finding the Escobars?"

"The oldest son, Rinaldo Escobar, passed away three years ago, and Orson died two years before that," Director Palmer said. "We're following up on any children they might have had, but nothing definitive yet. I'll give you an update at the end of the day."

"Thanks."

"There is one more thing."

"What's that?" Levi asked.

"Our tech guys developed a new spyware program. I want you to embed it on Princess Cassandra's laptop."

"What? Why?"

"Levi, you know as well as I do that Sereno isn't always friendly to the United States. Gaining access to the communications of their next head of state could be invaluable in protecting our interests in the region and in identifying any future threats."

"Sereno is a small island country with no military to speak of."

"And it's about to control a significant piece of the oil trade in the area," Director Palmer said. "The program is in your email. The easiest way to load it would be to drop it from an email account."

Levi's gut twisted into knots. This was his job. Spying was what he did for a living. So why did the thought of performing the simple task send ripples of anxiety through him.

"What about detection?"

"That's the tricky part. You'll need to identify what kind of defensive programming she has on her computer to see if you can load the spyware without detection."

"Great."

"We'll touch base tomorrow."

The line went dead, and Levi circled his desk and sat down. He opened his email and saw the spyware program the director mentioned.

He worked through several scenarios in his head, ultimately choosing a simple solution. He created a new email account and added the spyware to it, even as he fought against the knowledge that if he followed through, he would be betraying Cassie's trust.

Levi considered a tracking program he and Janessa had adapted a few months after she'd become a royal. Following instinct, he added that program too.

He stood and took a moment to erase the last few minutes from his mind. He would go to bed and pretend none of this had happened. The conversation with Director Palmer didn't exist.

CHAPTER 20

CASSIE HAD HARDLY SLEPT. THOUGHTS of returning home consumed her, along with what might happen when she dared face the dangers that would accompany that action.

She had managed to doze for a few hours, the result of sheer mental exhaustion, but three o'clock came around and her mind had decided rest was no longer an option. By four, she gave up on trying to get back to sleep.

She showered and dressed for the day, opting for casual wear that would allow her to maintain the appearance of a commoner. Her instinct was to sit down in her makeshift office and work, if only to create her own list of suspects, but when she looked out her window and saw the fingers of light on the horizon, a new plan emerged.

She unearthed a pen and notebook from her briefcase, slipped on her shoes, and left her room. The chateau was quiet when she descended the stairs and passed through the main parlor. She took a moment to look outside to make sure she was alone before she opened the door. *Alone.* What a concept. She could count on one hand how many times in the past few months she had been granted that privilege outside of her private quarters.

Cassie glanced at the gardens. She was tempted to find a quiet bench to enjoy the early-morning hour, but when she took in the spectacular view before her, she opted to sit at the small table on the terrace. From her elevated view, the gardens provided a backdrop of color, light shining through the leaves, dew glistening. The first rays of light caught on the waves, the horizon aglow in pink and purple.

She settled into a chair and stared at the natural beauty. Something like peace washed over her. For the first time since her ordeal began, she contemplated how abnormal her life truly had become. Ironically, her time with Levi gave her a sense of normalcy she had always craved and had never understood.

A door opened, and it wasn't until Janessa spoke that Cassie's brain registered she was no longer alone.

"Good morning," Janessa said.

"Good morning."

Cassie noticed Janessa's hesitation, as though the American wasn't sure if she should leave Cassie alone or join her. Cassie waved at the seat beside her. "Please, sit down. I was enjoying the stunning view."

"I love the mornings here." Janessa took the seat across from Cassie, both women's chairs angled toward the horizon.

"I can see why." Cassie glanced at her watch. 5:55 a.m. Remembering that the American was also now a princess, she asked, "Are you always an early riser, or do you have duties getting you up this morning?"

"Both," Janessa said. "I think the hardest part of being a royal is the evening engagements that always seem to stretch out far too long."

"I know what you mean. It completely messes with your sleep schedule."

"That it does." Janessa's posture relaxed slightly. "What do you have planned for today?"

"I think I'm helping Levi with some research." Cassie studied Janessa a moment. Like herself, Janessa had opted for casual attire this morning, and her long red hair flowed freely over her shoulders. Taking a tentative step toward friendship, Cassie asked, "Do you think I'm crazy for wanting to go back home?"

"If my father were sick, I'd do anything I could to be with him," Janessa said without hesitation. "I'm sorry you have to jump through so many security hurdles to give yourself that gift."

"Thank you." Remembering Janessa had endured her own share of security issues, Cassie asked, "How did you and Garrett deal with the stress of knowing someone was trying to kill you?"

"We worked with Levi," Janessa said. "He's very good at what he does."

"I have to admit I've never dealt much with security before."

"When you have the right people working for you, ideally you don't have to think about it," Janessa said. "Good security is like a warm blanket. It sits unnoticed for months on end, but when that cold winter night comes, it gives you the comfort you need."

"Unless it doesn't work."

"Levi will review the video feed and the security plans to identify how your palace security was breached." Janessa reached out in what appeared to be an instinctive gesture and laid her hand on Cassie's arm. "You can trust Levi with your life. Garrett and I have, and we're still here to talk about it."

Cassie looked down at the hand on her arm. Janessa withdrew it and the warmth with it. Not willing to let the tentative bonds of friendship fade, Cassie asked, "Can I ask you a personal question?"

"Of course."

"How long did it take you to get past the nightmares?"

"A while," Janessa said, and Cassie couldn't help but admire the other woman's honesty. "I had Garrett to help me through them, and he had me."

"I envy you that."

The door opened behind Janessa, and Levi walked outside. Janessa glanced at him before lowering her voice. "I don't think you have anything to envy." Janessa started to rise.

Cassie surprised herself when she reached out and put her hand on Janessa's arm. "Thank you."

Janessa covered Cassie's hand with hers. "You're welcome. You two enjoy your morning."

"Thanks," Cassie said. "You too."

* * *

Levi watched the exchange between the two women, warmed by the way Cassie had let her guard down with Janessa, if only for a moment. As soon as Janessa went inside, Levi took her vacated seat. "What was that about?"

"Nothing really," Cassie said. "You're up early."

"From the looks of things, I slept in compared to you. How long have you been up?"

"A while. I couldn't sleep." Cassie looked around the empty terrace before focusing on him. "I keep thinking about what you said about the oil contracts. For the life of me, I can't tie that in with the bank robberies."

"Maybe they aren't connected."

"You don't believe that."

"No, but it isn't outside the realm of possibilities," Levi said. "I have some people searching for Jeremiah Escobar's descendants. If we're right about Satori Oil being behind the assassination attempt, that narrows down the pieces of the puzzle we're trying to connect."

"True." She let out a sigh. "What are our plans for today?"

"King Eduard already reached out to your father to offer my assistance in enhancing your family's security," Levi said. "If King Alejandro agrees, we can start working on the necessary enhancements so you can go home."

"If my father agrees, will you have to go to Sereno right away?"

Levi had asked himself that same question repeatedly since last night. Under normal circumstances he would have been the first to request the assignment, but the thought of leaving Cassie in someone else's care unnerved him enough that he was already considering other alternatives. "I have a former employee I trust. He's with Interpol now. I thought I would reach out and see if he and his partner can oversee the security enhancements." Levi didn't mention that Jeremy's partner was also his wife and Patrice's daughter.

Cassie visibly relaxed. "I wasn't crazy about the idea of being handed off to someone else while I'm here."

"The new chief of security for the chateau arrives this afternoon from the palace," Levi said. "That will open up my schedule so we can work together on your home's security."

"How do you feel about being replaced here?"

"It's bittersweet," Levi said. "The people here are like family. I don't know that I'll ever find an assignment I will enjoy as much."

"Then why are you leaving?"

"Orders."

"I would think that as well respected as you are by the royal family that King Eduard would let you stay if you wanted."

Levi didn't correct her assumption that his reassignment had originated from the royals in Meridia. "It isn't always that simple."

"It should be."

"I won't disagree with you." He glanced out at the lightening sky. "It's beautiful out this morning. Would you like to eat breakfast out here?"

"I'd like that."

"I'll be right back." Levi rose. "Are you comfortable out here by yourself?"

"Surprisingly, yes." She angled her head as though in deep thought. "Thank you for helping me feel safe again."

His shoulders lifted. "That's my job."

"Right." Her voice chilled. "Your job."

Levi sat back down. "Don't start that."

"Start what?"

"That 'everyone only wants to be my friend because they have to' thing." He reached across the table and took her hand. "I don't know what will happen when you go back, but I don't want you to ever think that what we've shared together happened because I was paid to protect you."

"But you are being paid to protect me."

"You're here and you're safe because I'm good at my job," Levi said. "Whatever this is between us has nothing to do with orders or a paycheck."

The terrace door opened, and Brenna emerged with a breakfast tray. "Patrice asked me to bring this to you."

"Thank you, Brenna." Levi stood and waited for her to set the tray down. "Tell Patrice thank you for us."

"I will." Brenna disappeared back inside, and Levi reclaimed his seat.

"How did Patrice know we were out here?" Cassie asked.

"I'm sure this is Janessa's doing." Levi picked up the bread basket and held it out to her. She hesitated briefly before she took a croissant.

Cassie tore off a piece but didn't eat it. "I'm sorry. I shouldn't have assumed . . ."

"That this is a relationship of convenience?" Levi finished for her.

"Something like that." She took a bite, chewing slowly as though trying to gather her thoughts. She swallowed and focused on him again. "It's hard knowing our time together is limited. If you're successful in finding who is threatening me and my family, you won't have any reason to be with me anymore."

"I have plenty of reasons to be with you," Levi countered. "I don't know what it will look like when we get past this, but I'd like to think we can see each other even when you're safe and your security enhancements are complete."

"I'd like that too."

Levi squeezed her hand. "Then we'll make it happen."

CHAPTER 21

WE'LL MAKE IT HAPPEN. LEVI's words repeated through her mind as they worked side by side in his office. Levi had abandoned his desk, choosing instead to use his laptop beside her at his worktable.

As though by unspoken agreement, they had adopted a professional air while they worked. No more touches on her hand or shoulder, no more talk about what might happen in their future. Cassie tried to keep that question out of her thoughts, remembering that living to see her future was her first priority.

"I have the list of primary stockholders in Satori," Cassie said. "Do you want me to email it to you?"

"Yeah, but let me set up a dummy email account for you to use on our secure server," he said. "I don't want any electronic signatures to connect us."

"Okay."

Levi motioned to her computer. "May I?"

"Sure." Cassie angled her computer toward him.

Levi started tapping on her keyboard, opening a window to access a secure server. The thought that she had allowed him access to everything on her computer flared for a moment. She reminded herself that she trusted Levi. He hadn't done anything since meeting her except try to help her.

"Can you hand me that pad of paper over there?" Levi pointed at the legal pad by her left elbow.

"Sure." She reached for it and handed it to him.

He finished tapping something on her keyboard and took it from her. "This is the email address I'm giving you. You can use whatever password you want, but I'll need you to tell me what you pick so I can access it as well."

"Why?"

"Because you aren't going to email me. You'll put anything you want me to have in a draft email," Levi said. "If it isn't sent, there won't be a record. When we're done transferring information, we simply delete the email and no one is the wiser."

"Clever."

"It works anyway." A knock sounded on the door, and Levi called out, "Come in."

Janessa entered. "I spoke with King Eduard. King Alejandro agreed to let you revise their security plan."

"Excellent." Levi stood when Janessa held out a file. "What's this?"

"The crime scene photos after the shooting and the current images of the palace grounds in Sereno."

"Thanks." Levi tucked the file on the far side of his laptop. "What about security footage?"

"It's in your email."

"Perfect."

"Garrett also wanted me to remind you that tomorrow night we're hosting the French ambassador. He thought you both might want to join us."

"I don't know if that's a good idea," Levi said. "Sereno has a lot of dealings with France. I don't think it's worth the risk in case someone recognizes Cassie."

"I figured you would say that, but Garrett wanted me to offer."

"It was a kind gesture," Cassie said. "Please thank him for me."

"I will." Janessa took a step toward the door. "I'd better get going. I'm off to the museum to discuss the upcoming gala."

"Good luck," Levi said. He waited until she left the room before he sat back down. "Now, where were we?"

"We were looking for the people who are keeping me from being able to wear pretty dresses."

Levi's eyebrows lifted. "You like wearing pretty dresses?"

"Actually, I do."

"Hmmm." Levi slid her computer back toward her. "We'll have to see what we can do about that."

"Let me revise that statement," Cassie said. "I like dressing up when I don't have to worry about anyone shooting me."

"Noted."

* * *

Levi had done it. Sort of.

The firewalls installed on Cassie's laptop would have immediately detected the spyware, but he had taken the precaution of loading his location app that would run in the background undetected. That brief moment when Cassie had looked away to retrieve his notepad had been all the time he had needed to add it.

Levi should have been disappointed that he had failed to fully complete an assignment given him, but his sense of duty couldn't quite overcome the idea that he would be betraying Cassie by following through. He could justify the tracking program. After all, he would be the only one who could access it to find her computer if she or it disappeared. With his plan to stay with her through this security threat, he doubted he would ever need to use the tracker, but he preferred to take precautions when possible.

A phone call from Franco had given him a handy excuse to pull him away from his office and to provide him time to come to terms with his actions of the past hour. He should have been able to compartmentalize his work life and his relationship with Cassie, but the lines were blurring, and he didn't know what to do about it.

His phone rang, a blocked number indicated on his screen. He answered with a simple hello.

"Levi, Director Palmer asked me to call you," a woman said.

Levi took a moment to replay the words in his mind and recognize the voice. He tensed. "Belinda. I didn't realize the director had brought you in on this case."

"Only in a limited fashion. I have the latest information on Raymond Escobar."

"What do you have?"

"We tracked him as far as Italy. We'll look through various transportation methods to figure out where he went from there."

"I appreciate it." Levi only had to close his eyes to visualize the woman Belinda had been before the accident, to remember her before she had tripped a booby trap that had resulted in an explosion that left burn marks on her neck and arms. "Was there anything else?"

"Actually, yes." Silence hummed over the phone. "I wanted to say I'm sorry."

"You're sorry?" Levi repeated, dumbfounded. "If you hadn't come with me to Kiev, you never would have gotten hurt."

"If I hadn't gone inside the warehouse before it was clear, I wouldn't have gotten hurt," Belinda corrected. "I know I blamed you, but it wasn't your fault."

"Why the sudden change?" Levi asked. "The last time we spoke, you didn't want to talk about anything having to do with the accident."

"I know, but I finally forced myself to look at the files," Belinda said. "You tried to tell me the truth, and I didn't want to hear it."

Suspicion bloomed. "Have you been talking to Janessa?"

"Actually, I have. I asked her to be one of my bridesmaids."

"You're getting married?"

"I am."

A weight lifted off Levi's shoulders. "Congratulations. I'm happy for you."

"Thanks. I'd better get going, but if we find anything else on Escobar, I'll pass it along to the director. He seems pretty invested in your current assignment."

"He has been. It's kind of odd, actually, after having so little contact with him the last year."

"He didn't tell me what he has planned for you, but I got the impression it was something that would help both of your careers," Belinda said. "Good luck."

"Thanks." Levi said his goodbyes, Belinda's words lingering in his mind. What did the director have in mind for him that would affect both of their careers? Was it something that would pull him away from Cassie? Or was the director hoping to exploit the friendship he and Cassie shared?

Levi's heart sank. It didn't matter what the director had in store for him. Either way, the lies that existed between him and Cassie would prevent him from ever being able to build the future that had firmly invaded his dreams.

* * *

Cassie's heart lifted at the mere sight of Levi. What was wrong with her?

Levi's earlier words about the future scrambled inside her like a hundred puzzle pieces looking for a home. She wanted time to find out what he would be like when he wasn't on protection duty, for him to see her in her natural environment. She wanted him to meet her father and sisters, but mostly, she wanted to know what she and Levi could become.

She waved a hand toward the food on the table. "Lunch arrived right after you left."

His gaze dropped to her empty plate. "You didn't have to wait for me."

"I knew you would be back soon." She lifted the cover off a dish. "Patrice sent us chicken-and-mushroom crepes."

"Sounds good." Levi sat beside her.

"Is everything okay?"

"Yeah. Why?"

"I don't know. You seemed distracted."

"I got some unexpected news from home a few minutes ago."

"What kind of news?" Cassie asked.

"My ex-girlfriend is getting married," Levi said.

A flare of jealousy surfaced, but Cassie fought against it. "Were you together long?"

"A little over a year." Levi picked up a spatula and lifted her plate. He transferred a crepe onto the plate and proceeded to serve himself.

"Tell me about her," Cassie said. "Why did you break up?"

Levi took a bite, and Cassie suspected he was delaying his answer. He chewed, taking his time before swallowing. "We used to work together. She had an accident, and she blamed me for it. We were never the same after that."

"Was the accident your fault?"

"No, it wasn't. And she knows that now."

"That's good, right?"

"Yeah, it is," Levi said. "I hadn't realized how much it bothered me that she blamed me all this time. It's nice to have that chapter closed." Levi scooped up another bite with his fork and nodded at Cassie's computer. "Any progress while I was gone?"

"Not really." She poured herself a glass of water from the carafe on the table. "I feel like I'm going in circles."

"Maybe we should go for a walk after lunch," Levi suggested. "It would be good to clear our heads."

"I'd like that." She took a bite, savoring the mixture of crepe, chicken, mushroom, and cream sauce. They ate in silence for several minutes, and Cassie looked at Levi again. "Are you sure you're okay?"

"Fine." Again, he put his hand on hers as though to reassure her. "Just a lot on my mind."

"I hope that changes for you soon."

"Me too."

CHAPTER 22

LEVI PACED ACROSS HIS DARK bedroom, moonlight spilling onto the carpeted floor. He had managed to make it through dinner with Cassie, but every time he thought of what he had done, what he had almost done, he wanted nothing more than to put some distance between them. He had feigned a work emergency after dessert to give him that distance as well as time to regain some clarity.

He considered what her reaction would be if she learned he was CIA. Another wave of regret and apprehension crashed over him.

Cassie had left his office an hour ago, taking her laptop with her. Levi thought of their plans to meet for a walk in the garden and hoped he could chase away the worst of the guilt before then. He wanted Cassie to trust him. He needed her to trust him.

He forwarded the latest list of suspects to Director Palmer, and his phone rang a few minutes later.

"Levi, I think we may have found the missing link," Director Palmer said without preamble.

"What do you have?" Levi asked.

"After being exiled from Sereno, Jeremiah Escobar immigrated to Italy with his wife and son, Rinaldo."

"We already knew that."

"Yes, but we found Rinaldo had a son."

"I saw that in the analysis you sent me."

"We're tracking down all known associates of the son, Raymond. We found an immigration record from three years ago in Sweden for one of Raymond Escobar's former business partners, a man named Julien Bartolli. We aren't sure what the connection is between the two men, but Julien has been working as a financial consultant."

"Let me guess. Pantheon is one of his clients."

"You got it," Director Palmer said. "What's the status with Princess Cassandra?"

"I gained access to her computer, but the firewalls were too advanced for me to plant the spyware."

"Too bad."

"I don't think it's necessary anyway," Levi said. "She's been very forthcoming with information so far."

"Don't get fooled by her youth and her pretty face," Director Palmer warned. "From everything we know about her, she is a brilliant strategist. She isn't going to reveal anything more than what gains her an advantage."

Levi's first instinct was that Director Palmer didn't know Cassie the way he did. His second thought was to doubt himself. Was Cassie playing him? Was she simply using him to regain her sense of security, using him to do the legwork to protect herself, her family, and her country? Levi had witnessed her intelligence firsthand as they'd worked together, and the Agency analysts had spent much more time studying her than he had.

He shook those thoughts from his head. The analysts might know Princess Cassandra, but they didn't know Cassie. "Where is Julien Bartolli now?"

"He has been living in Malmo. I dispatched a surveillance team. I'll let you know if they manage to pick him up."

"Thanks. I appreciate it."

"I'll talk to you tomorrow."

Levi hung up the phone. He crossed to the window. From his room, he could see the front gate. To his left, he could see a sliver of the gardens and the darkness where the Mediterranean Sea met land.

He saw the flow of a blue dress before he identified Cassie as the woman walking in the garden, her hair pulled back in a loose braid. He shouldn't have been able to identify her from this distance, but her regal posture left him with no doubt it was her. He also couldn't help but note that she had gone for her walk without him.

He let Director Palmer's warning repeat in his mind, a hollow sensation settling deep within him.

Cassie turned to her left before disappearing from view. He caught a flash of blue when she passed beneath one of the garden lights. It took only a moment for him to figure out where she was going.

He knew he should keep his distance and somehow find a way to regain control of his emotions, but his heart didn't agree.

With some effort, he pushed aside the fact that he had invaded Cassie's privacy earlier. He mentally filed his CIA persona away and headed for the door. Time to forget about loyalties for one night and to trust his heart.

* * *

Cassie couldn't put a finger on what had changed. Levi had put up a wall between them, a glass wall, but a wall nonetheless. This wasn't like the professionalism she had experienced when working beside him earlier today. He had distanced himself. He was in plain sight but different somehow.

Cassie didn't know what had caused the change, and she didn't like it.

She reached the spot Levi had shown her. His favorite spot.

Her chest tightened as she thought of the man and the many complexities in their evolving relationship. She had believed him this morning when he had talked about making it work between them in the future. She wasn't naive enough to assume that meant they would get a happily ever after, but she had hoped to explore the possibility. Now she wondered if she would ever see him again once this threat against Sereno was over.

He was changing jobs soon. So was she.

The truth of that fact swept over her, along with the reasons she would soon become the first female ruler of Sereno.

The turmoil of grief swept over her. She lowered herself onto the bench and let the first tears fall. Her father was dying. Her king was dying.

How many more days would they have together? Would they spend his last days as father and daughter? Or would necessity force her to focus on learning how to rule Sereno?

She swiped at her eyes and sniffled.

"Here."

Cassie startled and looked up. Levi stood beside her, handkerchief in hand. Her cheeks flushed in embarrassment, but she accepted the offering.

Levi sat beside her. "Thinking about your dad?"

She nodded. She used the handkerchief to wipe her eyes, struck by the oddity that Levi had produced one so readily. "I didn't realize you were the type to carry a handkerchief."

"I work at a royal residence. It became a necessity a long time ago."

"Do you often come across weepy females?"

"More often than I care to admit," Levi said. "Besides, Patrice told me years ago it was my duty to carry one."

The mention of the cook's name brought a smile to her lips. "Sometimes I think she's the one running the chateau."

"Oh, she is, and we all know it."

"Even Garrett?"

"Especially Garrett," Levi said. "She threatened to put him on dish duty only last week when he forgot to tell her about a change of plans."

"Sounds pretty harsh for a minor miscommunication."

"That minor miscommunication was Garrett forgetting to tell Patrice about a state dinner."

"Not so minor, then."

"No."

"Are you going to tell me what's been bothering you today?" Cassie asked.

"Nothing is bothering me."

Cassie shifted away from him so she could see his face. "I know better than that. This morning you were talking about how to make time to see each other when all of these threats are behind me, and tonight at dinner, you couldn't wait to get away from me."

"I wasn't trying to get away from you. I had a lot of work to do."

She considered Levi's long hours and their constant time together. "I suppose you probably wanted time to yourself too."

"It wasn't that." Levi stared out at the water. "I work in a profession that is filled with questions. I'm always preparing for the future, no matter how scary it might be. It's difficult to do my job well when I'm emotionally involved with the person I'm protecting."

Cassie didn't know whether to delight in his comment that he was emotionally involved with her or fear a coming change between them. "How have you handled this sort of situation in the past?"

"I've never had to, at least not with someone I was tasked to protect," Levi said. "I guess protecting Janessa is the closest I've ever come to being attached to someone I was assigned to help."

A flare of jealousy surfaced. "How is it that you and Janessa became so close?"

"I told you before. We work together sometimes," Levi said. "She and Garrett probably know me better than anyone outside my family."

"I envy you that friendship."

"You can have that too."

"It's not easy in my position."

"Nothing worth having is ever easy." He laced his fingers with hers.

She looked down at the connection between them. "I suppose you're right."

CHAPTER 23

LEVI WAS GRATEFUL THE SURVEILLANCE tapes of the Sereno attack didn't arrive until after he had said good night to Cassie. The violence of what had happened during the assassination attempt wasn't something he wanted her to relive anytime soon.

The display of violence was bad enough, but what disturbed Levi more than anything was the methodical way the assassins had gone about their task. Deliberate, controlled, with no show of emotion. They were well prepared, the attack well planned, and they knew exactly where their target would be when they arrived.

That last fact repeated through his mind. He agreed with the security forces that Cassandra had been the target. If he were to guess, her sisters would be next if the next attempt succeeded. Levi had no doubt there would be a next attempt. The question was, When and where?

The precision of the assassins' timing raised the possibility of an insider from the palace leaking information, but an interception of communication was also within the realm of possibilities. Had the downed guard been the source, or was someone else working within the walls of the palace in Sereno?

Levi spent two hours replaying the surveillance tapes and then got up early the next morning and watched them twice more. Every viewing brought him to the same conclusion. The timing was perfect. The assassins knew when Cassie would pass by the entrance within seconds of her arrival.

After Levi showered and dressed for the day, he went in search of Cassie. When his knock on her door went unanswered, he wasn't surprised to find her sitting downstairs on the terrace.

Breakfast was spread out before her: a basket of rolls, a bowl of cut canta-loupe, and a platter of meat and cheese.

Cassie spotted him and waved to the seat beside her. "Have you eaten yet?"

"No." Levi glanced around the terrace to find it deserted except for the two of them.

"Patrice sent plenty for me to share."

Because he needed to assure himself that Cassie was alive and well, Levi leaned down and greeted her with a kiss. Her hand came up to rest on his arm as though holding him in place.

"Good morning," Levi said.

She smiled. "Good morning."

"How long have you been up?" Levi took his seat and scooped some cantaloupe onto his plate.

"You asked me that yesterday," she said. "This is starting to become a habit."

"Is the answer the same as yesterday?"

"I managed to sleep until six, so a little better," Cassie said. "How about you?"

"I've been up for a while. I had some work I needed to do." He saw her expectant look. Avoiding the inevitable, he took a bite of his fruit and chewed slowly while he organized his thoughts. "I need to talk to you about the night of the shooting."

The smile on her face faded, and she set her fork down.

"I know this isn't an easy subject, but what I want you to relive is the ten or fifteen minutes before the unexpected guests arrived."

She took a deep breath and let it out slowly as though trying to clear her mind and settle her emotions. "I went to my father's private quarters." A weak smile appeared, and Levi didn't miss the wistful look on her face. "Dad needed help with his tie. He never could properly manage a bow tie on his own."

"Was anyone else there?"

"No, not until Theo arrived to escort us to dinner." Cassie picked up a roll and broke it in half.

"Did you have a scheduled time to arrive?"

"The invitations said seven. My father always makes his entrance later, usually half an hour or so."

"Did he have a specific time designated for that night?"

"Not exactly. The typical routine is for Theo to inform us when the guests have arrived and are ready to receive us," Cassie said. "After that happens, security prepares for us to move from the residential side of the palace to the dining hall."

"How does security prepare?"

"The front gate is closed, and additional guards are stationed at the main entrance."

Levi took a bite of cantaloupe and mentally compared the chateau's security protocols to what Cassie described. "Where do the extra guards come from?"

"I'm not sure."

"Is this procedure followed at every formal dinner?" Levi asked.

"As far as I know, yes." She buttered her roll and took a bite.

"Then anyone who knows about the security shifts could have used this as a signal on when to attack."

Her food once again forgotten, Cassie's eyes met his. "You think the assassins used our own security protocols against us?"

"It was either that or someone inside the palace signaled them."

"I can't believe any of our staff would betray my family that way."

Levi thought over the timing of the attack again. Had Cassie been a few steps farther down the hall, she wouldn't still be breathing. "Did anything happen from the time Theo arrived until you reached the entrance that slowed your progress down the hall?"

"No. Why?"

"The attackers' plan was very precise. You were within seconds of being exactly where they wanted you when they broke through the door," Levi said. "They either were told when you would be there or someone had managed to time your progress at a previous event."

"The only people who would have access to that knowledge would be our security staff," Cassie said. "And most of the people who did know the timing were killed or injured during the attack."

"I'd like to do a deep background on everyone with access regardless," Levi said. A new thought occurred. "Do the guards at the gate log when your guests arrive?"

"I believe so."

"That would be something else to explore," Levi said. "Someone could have deliberately arrived late at a previous engagement to evaluate how security is handled. If the extra guards at the main entrance are from outside, they would have been able to time the guard shift."

"Guests arriving late is not common," Cassie said. "That should be a relatively short list."

"Assuming your father agrees to let my friends from Interpol help, they'll get that for us," Levi said.

"You haven't heard from King Eduard yet?"

"No, but I imagine your father wants to check out the operatives I want to work there before he approves everything."

"Of that I have no doubt."

* * *

Cassie blinked, trying to fight the dryness that came from staring at a computer screen for too long. Levi had left shortly after breakfast to meet with his replacement. In his absence, she had reevaluated the final three candidates for the drilling rights in Sereno.

The weeks of comparisons, the spreadsheets and safety measures, the equipment and logistical requirements. All of the things that had to be considered were finally behind her. She had made her decision. She had chosen a winner. At least, she had chosen a potential winner. Once she and Levi could confirm that the company didn't have any ties to the assassination attempt, she could move forward with awarding the contract.

She wasn't going to think about her father's reaction when he learned which company she had chosen. Instead, she was determined to take some time to enjoy the satisfaction of knowing she had completed her task.

With a celebration in mind, Cassie powered off her laptop and headed for the kitchen. With any luck, she would be able to sweet-talk Patrice into helping her pack a picnic lunch to enjoy on the beach.

She took the long way so she could pass by Levi's office in case he had time to join her. She found him in the hall beside his office door, an attractive blonde standing with him. The woman was nearly as tall as Levi and appeared to also be in her late twenties.

"Cassie, this is Rachelle Bourgeau. She's my replacement here."

Cassie extended her hand. "Good to meet you."

"You too," Rachelle said.

"Where are you headed?" Levi asked.

"I was thinking about a picnic on the beach."

"Mind if I join you?"

"I was hoping you would have time," Cassie said.

"I'll leave you to your lunch," Rachelle said. "It was nice meeting you, Cassie."

"You too."

Levi slid his arm around Cassie's waist, and they started down the hall. "How have you spent your morning?"

"Working."

"Sounds like we're both due for a break," Levi said.

"I agree."

Fifteen minutes later, Cassie slipped off her sandals when they reached the beach. Levi carried the picnic basket in one hand and a blanket tucked beneath his other arm.

"Is this okay?" Levi asked, pointing at the stretch of sand halfway between the seawall and the rising tide.

"It's perfect."

Levi spread out the blanket and set the basket down. He then crossed to the shed situated beneath the stairs leading to the chateau and returned a moment later with a beach umbrella that he placed at the corner of the blanket. "Thought you might want some shade."

"Thank you." Cassie opened the basket and handed a plate to Levi.

Levi sat beside her and set out the food. "Did you get a lot of work done this morning?"

"I did. In fact, I have an idea that might help reduce the threat against me."

"I'm listening."

"I selected the company I want to award the drilling contract to," Cassie said. "That is, assuming you can confirm they weren't involved in the shooting."

"I'm still working on determining who is behind the attack, but all evidence points to Satori. We can see where a payment was made to the shooters."

"And the American firms?"

"My staff hasn't found any flags for either of them," Levi said. "We're still looking into Vector Oil, but so far, the only firm where we can trace unexplained payments to Pantheon was Satori."

"Then I have a winner."

Levi took her hand and gave it a squeeze. "Congratulations."

"Thanks."

"Does awarding the contract have anything to do with your idea?"

"It does," Cassie said. "It seems to me that once the announcement of the winner is made, winning the drilling rights will no longer be a motivation to come after me."

"That's true." Levi popped a grape in his mouth.

"Do you think it would be a good idea to dispense with that possible motive?"

"Yes and no."

"Explain."

"Yes, I think it would greatly reduce potential threats against you, especially if we're right about who is behind the assassination attempt."

"And no?" Cassie asked.

"No, because I worry your security in Sereno will see that as the only possible motive and won't consider that another threat might still be out there."

"What do you suggest I do?"

"I think you should move forward with your plans. I'll do what I can to work with your security forces to make sure they know this may not be over."

A sense of satisfaction swept through her. "I can complete the contracts by the end of the day, but I will need to contact the company to arrange a meeting."

"Is a meeting necessary?" Levi asked. "Can't everything be handled through video conference and courier?"

"Everything except for the announcement, but it would take significantly longer to do it that way," Cassie said. "Besides, I doubt you want to deal with trying to hide the electronic signal for video chats that would last for hours."

"True," Levi said. "Tell me what the announcement will entail."

"Not only will the decision need to be publicized in order for the competition to know who won the contract, but it is also an unprecedented opportunity to put my country on the world stage. Tourism is a growing industry in Sereno and very important to our citizens and our economy."

"Can your father handle the press side of things?"

Cassie tried to envision the possibility. "You probably know my father is not warm toward the United States," Cassie said.

"I am aware."

"The winner of the contract is an American company. I don't see my father being comfortable standing in front of the press and explaining why he has set aside his prejudice for profit."

"But he's not. You are."

"That's right, which is why I need to be the one to make the announcement," Cassie said. "I am the next ruler of Sereno. Opening the doorway to an improved relationship with the United States could go a long way, not only by ensuring the oil and gas harvesting will be done at the standard I have set but also for paving the way for more American tourists to visit our country."

"So you don't share your father's sentiment about Americans."

"I didn't say that, but I will admit that knowing Janessa a little better has proven that all Americans aren't what my father has painted them to be."

"What is your father's objection to the United States?"

"From what I understand, the tensions started during my grandfather's reign," Cassie said, her back straightening a little as she thought of the stories her grandparents and parents had shared. "The United States wanted a military base in the Mediterranean, and Sereno offered the strategic position they desired."

"I don't understand why that would matter. Sereno was opposed to Meridia allowing the US Navy to build their base here in Bellamo."

"At the time, my grandfather recognized the benefits. With only a small military of our own, the alliance would offer Sereno protection and also bring a constant flow of consumers into our towns."

"What happened?" Levi asked.

"The agreement was made, and a date was set for the formal announcement and the official signing. In the meantime, the Americans negotiating with my grandfather gained permission to begin clearing the land."

"Before the official agreement was signed?"

"You see where the problem started," Cassie said. "My grandfather was told signing the papers was a mere formality, and the Americans paid for the labor and equipment to be brought in. Tourism started picking up, and everything was running smoothly."

"And then?"

"And then four days before the agreement was to be signed at the White House, the US president was shot and killed."

"Kennedy."

"That's right." Cassie took a sip of her water. "The vice president never approved of Sereno as a site for a military installation. Within a week, he pulled out of the agreement, leaving a cleared field, hundreds of displaced citizens, and equipment the navy no longer had use for and didn't care to remove."

"I can see how that would leave a bitter taste in your grandfather's mouth."

"Grandfather always took ownership of his mistake in allowing construction to begin before the official agreement was in place. The strain might have eased with time had it not been for the American investors who came in and tried to buy the land for pennies compared to what it was worth."

"Obviously your grandfather didn't agree."

"No, but the economic ramifications of having that land idle nearly bankrupted our family and our country," Cassie said. "New homes had to be built for the citizens the construction had displaced, a cost the United States had promised to incur, and the land that previously provided a significant portion of our farming industry was no longer occupied. It was hard for everyone in Sereno."

"This is a piece of history I never learned about."

"And yet, it is a defining piece of Sereno's history," Cassie said. "My grandfather took a huge risk and developed that abandoned property. He borrowed heavily from our European allies and built a new city."

"Porto Blu."

"Yes," Cassie said. "My grandfather turned the potential devastation of our country into one of the most popular tourism spots in the Mediterranean."

"I understand it's now also the home for several tech companies."

"Yes, and if I have my way, it will soon host the energy companies that will support the drilling efforts."

"Sounds like your family is good at turning negatives into positives."

"We try." Cassie looked out at the water, enjoying the peaceful view. A sailboat passed by, the white sail catching the wind. She turned her attention back to Levi. "So, back to the original issue. How do I work through this contract without putting myself at risk, and where do we hold the press conference?"

"How long do you think it will take to go through the final negotiations?"

"If I could meet in person, a week, maybe two."

"In that case, I think it's time to extend an invitation to your winning company to visit Meridia."

"Have the company's representative come here?"

"Yes." Levi nodded. "Give me the name of the person you expect to deal with, and I'll run a deep background check. If all goes well, you can start your meetings by Tuesday."

"Thank you."

Levi plucked another grape. "Now, for more important topics. Want to go riding this afternoon?"

"I would love to." Cassie leaned back on her elbow. "I thought tomorrow I might convince you to take me back into the village. It's supposed to be the perfect weather for a Sunday drive."

"I think that can be arranged."

"I was hoping you would say that."

CHAPTER 24

LEVI CHECKED HIS MESSAGES, FRUSTRATED he had yet to hear anything from Interpol about the contents of the safe-deposit boxes that had been robbed. He was ready to go to the various banks himself to shake the information loose. The robbery had happened three days ago, and still, he was being stonewalled.

Cassie had retreated to her suite to prepare the invitation for the winning oil company. Another twenty minutes and they could both leave their work behind for a little while and remember there was life outside the chateau walls.

Franco knocked on his office door and entered.

"What's up?" Levi asked.

Franco held up a thick file. "I have the inventory lists from the safe-deposit boxes."

"Finally." Levi reached out his hand. He flipped through the first few inventory lists, disappointed when he didn't see a common name at the different banks. "This may take a while."

"Good luck," Franco said.

"Thanks." Levi waited until Franco disappeared back the way he had come before he laid the reports from the various banks out on his worktable. He scanned each one, hoping for an obvious commonality, but like his counterparts at Interpol, he didn't see one.

Cassie walked through the door. "Are you ready to go riding?"

"I was, but the inventory reports just came in. I'm not sure I'll have time now."

Cassie crossed to where he stood and looked down at the papers scattered on the table. "Did you find anything?"

"Not yet. I may have to use your method of plugging everything into a spreadsheet to sort it all out."

Cassie picked up the paper closest to her and read it. She set it down and proceeded to do the same with the next one and the one after that. Cassie continued around the table and read three more.

Cassie looked up and tapped a finger against the report she currently held. "The succession agreement was the target."

"How can you tell? I didn't see anything to do with your family listed in the inventories I looked at."

"You didn't know what you were looking for." Cassie handed him the page she held and pointed at the sixth line down. "Start here, and read the next three lines."

"Box 246, diamond bracelet, two thousand dollars in bonds, stock certificates from a dozen companies."

"Next."

"Box 247. This is all legal documents."

"Next?"

"Box 249." Levi started to read the inventory of what was stolen before his mind caught up with the anomaly. "The number skipped."

"Yes. I think you'll see the same thing on all of these. Or at least on twenty-two of them."

"Why would that be?"

"When governments reserve safe-deposit boxes for their use, it's usually to protect something they don't want in an inventory somewhere," Cassie said. "Because of that, their holdings aren't reported to anyone."

"Even when there's a theft?"

"Even then. The point of contact for the box rental would be informed, along with a government representative, but that's it." Cassie motioned to the pages she had already read. "All of these skip a box number."

Levi grabbed two highlighters from his desk drawer. "Want to help me mark the ones that are missing?"

"Sure." She took one of the highlighters from him and sat at the table. "Now that we know my country's succession agreement was the target, what do we do next?"

"That's largely up to your family. My options are limited if I can't bring Interpol and our local intelligence agency into the circle of need-to-know."

"I know, but I don't think there's any way my father would agree to share such private information."

"In that case, we increase our efforts in the search for possible heirs to the throne."

"Do you think it's possible this had anything to do with the shooting?"

"Right now, the only commonality between the two is Sereno. It's hard to say if your family is having really bad luck or if someone is coming after you in two simultaneous attacks."

"You think they are connected."

"Yes, I do."

* * *

Cassie walked in silence beside Levi as they emerged outside and headed for the stables. Her excitement about awarding the drilling rights had dissipated as soon as she'd seen the new evidence Levi had received about the robberies. The idea to eliminate the threat against her had given her hope. The theft of the succession agreement raised so many questions and left her wondering if it would ever be safe for her to return home.

"You're quiet all of a sudden," Levi said.

"I was just thinking." She looked out at the lovely gardens and the Mediterranean glistening beneath the afternoon sun. "I've enjoyed my time here so much more than I ever would have imagined, but I miss my family."

"I know, and I'm sure the information we were looking at wasn't quite what we were hoping for."

"No, it wasn't, but like you said before, it's better to know there could still be another threat out there, so we don't let our guard down prematurely."

"I'd prefer you not let your guard down at all," Levi said.

"Do you think I can at least find a new normal that will let me feel like I'm not always surrounded by guards?" Cassie asked.

"It'll happen," Levi said. "We've been through this more times than I'd like to admit here in Meridia, but the royal family has found a happy medium between having security in place and still being able to live their lives as they choose."

"I want that for me and my sisters," Cassie said. "You asked me once what the differences were between me and my father, and I think that's the one thing I would most like to change about how my government operates."

"What? The security protocols?"

"Yes. I want my family to be able to interact with the citizens of our country without always feeling like we have to hide behind ten-foot walls." Cassie glanced at him. "Do you think that's even possible?"

"It's possible. It takes time and planning, but it's possible."

"Then it's a possibility I want to explore," Cassie said.

"First, let's get through these investigations. I want the known threats eliminated before you decide to start shaking hands with your subjects."

"That sounds reasonable enough." They reached the stable yard. "I guess for now, I'll have to enjoy the illusion of freedom you've given me here in Meridia."

"Come on." Levi offered his hand. "Let's make the most of it."

Cassie put her hand in his. "I'm ready when you are."

* * *

Levi rode beside Cassie and wondered why it had taken him so long to decide to go horseback riding while checking the perimeter. He could have been doing this for the past two years instead of entrusting his staff to always tend to this task.

His shirt rippled in the breeze, and he glanced at Cassie riding beside him. Her understanding of security protocols had greatly expanded since her arrival, and Levi suspected she could do the perimeter check on her own if it wasn't for the section of fence that overlooked the cliffs. Every time they started up the hill, she veered off and took a parallel path that didn't trigger her fear of heights.

They reached that spot, and he urged his horse up the hill until he reached the peak, and then he took a moment to evaluate the water traffic on the Mediterranean below: a few sailboats, a handful of motor craft, and a tanker passing in the distance. He noted a sailboat hovering on the edge of the chateau's restricted waters. Levi sent Franco a text to make sure the security office was monitoring it.

Levi continued to follow the fence until he rejoined Cassie. "You really need to come up with me sometime to see the view. You don't have to go close to the edge."

"I'm good," Cassie said.

Levi didn't press. Their horses fell into step, his eyes still on the fence line. A mound of fresh dirt caught his eye. He reined in his horse.

Cassie stopped beside him. "Is something wrong?"

Levi pointed. "Do you see that?"

"It looks like a gopher hole."

"We shouldn't have gophers in here," Levi said. "We have low-level electrical currents running through the ground beneath the fence to prevent animals from burrowing under the wall."

"Then what could cause that?"

"I'm not sure." Levi pulled his phone from his pocket and dialed. "Franco, I need you to send someone to check out the exterior fence by marker twenty-three. I see fresh dirt inside the wall."

"You got it."

An alarm sounded through the phone.

Levi straightened in his saddle. "What's that?"

"We have a sensor alarm, marker twenty-one."

"Call you back." Levi pocketed his phone and turned to Cassie. "Come on. We have to go."

"What's wrong?" Cassie asked, her concern evident.

"We're heading back to the stables. Let's go." Levi reached out and smacked her horse's rump to send the gelding into motion. As soon as Cassie's mount started forward, Levi urged his own horse into a gallop. Together they raced across the open field, down the trail that cut through the woods, and into the stable yard.

"Paolo!" Levi yelled. He reined his horse to a rapid stop, dismounted, and drew his weapon.

Cassie swung down from the saddle as Paolo emerged from the stables.

Paolo's gaze landed on Levi's gun. "What's wrong?"

"Security breach. Take Cassie into the loft and cover me," Levi ordered. "Cassie, go inside."

Cassie hurried through the open double doors, escaping to the relative safety of the large wooden structure.

Paolo grabbed the reins of both horses. "I'll tie them up inside."

"Thanks." Levi scanned the area for movement and called Franco again. "Status?"

"We had a spike in the electrical current for the fence but no interruptions."

Levi stepped into the stables and closed both doors. "Call in our off-duty guards. I want sentries posted along the interior wall."

"Rachelle already activated them. She's on her way with Henri to check out the area."

Oddly unsettled to know he wasn't in charge, Levi said, "Keep me posted."

"I will." He glanced at the ladder to the loft, and Cassie was still on the third rung. Paolo stood beside her, a rifle in hand. "Sorry, Cassie. I wasn't thinking. Come back down."

Tentatively, she lowered her feet until she reached the ground.

"Paolo, go up there and tell me if you see any movement. I'll have Cassie stay in the tack room."

Paolo nodded his assent and began his climb.

"What about you?" Cassie asked.

"I'm staying here with you, but I want to be able to see the entrances." Levi opened the door to the tack room, the only windowless section of the stables.

Cassie passed inside, and Levi gripped his gun. Something had set off that alarm, and all he could do was wait to make sure that whatever it was didn't get to Cassie.

CHAPTER 25

CASSIE LEANED AGAINST THE WALL beside the door, her heart racing. She drew in a deep breath and let it out slowly. Levi was only a few feet away. He was staying with her.

The planked wooden walls blocked the sunlight, but from the swath of light coming through the crack in the door, Cassie could see the rows of sawhorses holding saddles. Bridles and lead ropes hung on the walls, and a set of shelves in the corner held saddle pads.

She breathed in the scent of leather and horses and willed her heartbeat to slow.

Several minutes passed before she thought to listen for movement outside.

A horse in one of the nearby stalls nickered, and she could hear another outside in the pasture.

"Paolo, anything?" Levi called out.

"Nothing. I don't see anyone but our guards."

"That's a good sign," Levi said. "Cassie, are you doing okay in there?"

"I'm okay." She heard his phone ring, followed by his simple greeting.

"Marin." A brief pause. "Post guards on the terrace and by the path to the stables. I want extra security while I bring Cassie back to the chateau." Another pause. "Keep the sentries in place until I talk to Rachelle."

Levi hung up and pushed the tack-room door open wider. "Come on. I'm going to take you back to the chateau."

Cassie's heartbeat quickened again, but she forced herself to join him in the main area of the stables. "What about Paolo?"

"Paolo, can you cover us until we get back to the chateau?"

"I'm watching you," he said. "Keep that pretty lady of yours safe."

"I will. Thanks." His gun still in hand, Levi motioned her forward. "Stay on my left side."

"Are you sure about this?"

"Yes," Levi said. "The motion sensors haven't gone off anywhere besides the exterior wall, but we're taking extra precautions just in case my team missed something."

Another false alarm. Cassie hoped that was really all it was. She drew another deep breath. "Okay. I'm ready."

Levi opened the barn door, looked around, and once again motioned Cassie forward.

Cassie peeked outside before she left the safety of the structure. She walked at a quicker-than-normal pace down the dirt path that led to the chateau, with Levi matching her step for step.

She didn't think about what might be hiding in the trees as they passed through a wooded area. At least, she tried not to think about it. They reached the open space on the edge of the garden, the terrace doors now fifty meters away. When they left the shade of the trees, she wasn't sure what she disliked more, the thick woods or the open space where everyone could see her.

She noted the guards posted along the terrace, but her focus was primarily on which door was closest.

Levi led her into the one leading into the reception hall, and she breathed a sigh of relief as soon as the door closed behind her.

Levi holstered his weapon and turned her to face him. "Are you sure you're okay?"

"I can't say I'm a fan of these false alarms."

"I don't blame you." He took her hand. "Let's go to the security office and find out what's going on."

They walked upstairs, and Levi opened the door to reveal a long office, a bank of television screens on one wall, and a guard sitting at a desk facing them. Rachelle stood behind another desk. She looked up when they entered. "Levi, I hoped that was you."

"What have you got?"

"I walked the exterior fence line personally. It looks to me like someone was trying to tunnel something underneath it."

"The fresh dirt we saw didn't look like it was from anything with much size. I would have mistaken it for a gopher hole had I not known better," Levi said.

She waved at one of the monitors on the wall. "Take a look at this."

Levi moved deeper into the room, and Cassie followed.

Rachelle played an image of the street view near where they had seen the fresh dirt. A car passed the camera and disappeared from view.

"Is that your suspect vehicle?"

"It passed the first camera but didn't pass the next one for fifteen minutes," Rachelle said. "The license plate was also covered in mud."

"Sounds suspicious," Levi said. "Play it again for me, only slow it down."

Rachelle complied.

Cassie stared at the image, the car now moving at a snail's pace across the screen. Something on the dashboard caught the sunlight, a glare reflecting in the image.

"That make and model of the car is common enough that it isn't going to be easy to trace without the license plate number," Levi said.

"Can you play it again?" Cassie asked. "Only freeze it right before the glare."

Rachelle's eyebrows lifted, but once again, she backed up the image and started it a third time.

Cassie watched the car come into view and anticipated the spot she noticed the item on the dash. "There."

Rachelle froze the image.

"Can you blow this up?" Cassie asked.

She zoomed in. "A camera."

"Looks like paparazzi," Levi said. "One of them was probably trying to cut the electrical current to the main electric fence so they could sneak onto the grounds tonight." He put his hand on Cassie's shoulder. "That's good work."

Her cheeks grew warm under the unexpected compliment. "Thanks."

"Franco, pull up our list of paparazzi in the area," Rachelle said. "Let's see if we can ID this guy."

"Yes, ma'am."

"We'll get out of your way." Levi nudged Cassie toward the door.

"Cassie, thanks for your help," Rachelle said.

"You're welcome." She followed Levi into the hall. "Well, that was a bit more exciting than expected."

"Sorry about that," Levi said. "Anything I can do to make this up to you?"

"You did mention the caterers were helping out with tonight's dinner," Cassie said. "Think they might have stuffed mushrooms?"

"Since Janessa likes them as much as you do, I guarantee it."

"What are the chances you can sneak some out of the kitchen for us?"

"I think my chances are excellent." He started down the hall. "When I break in somewhere, I don't get caught."

CHAPTER 26

LEVI COULDN'T BELIEVE HE HAD been so careless. He stared at his laptop, the image of him with Cassie on the beach filling the screen. His back had been to the water when the photo had been taken, but Cassie's face had clearly been visible, both before and after he'd kissed her.

He had checked for boats in the water when they had walked down to the beach and not seen any. Shortly after a sailboat had passed into view, they had packed up and gone back to the chateau. Apparently, someone on that boat had had one heck of a zoom lens on his camera.

Now he had to wonder if the paparazzi were at the chateau yesterday looking for a story about the Meridian royals or if they were looking for Cassie. He stared at the headline, afraid it might be the latter.

The caption was simple and exactly what he didn't want to see: *Princess Cassandra visits Meridian Royals. Has she found her prince?*

Guilt washed over him. He knew better than to get so emotionally attached to an assignment. He also should have foreseen the potential risk in going to the beach with her, but when she had issued the invitation, his desire to spend time with her, to make her happy, had overshadowed all reason.

A piece of his heart chipped away as he faced the truth: in order to protect her, he might very well need to put up the emotional walls between them that would take away everything that was most precious to him.

Levi took a deep breath and blew it out. He tried to pretend he had control over his emotions when he picked up his office phone and dialed the security office.

"Rachelle."

"Did you see the news?" Levi asked with more sharpness than he intended.

"It was hard to miss," Rachelle said. "I thought your girlfriend looked familiar, but I didn't realize she was a princess."

Levi absorbed the pang that speared through him at her use of the word *girlfriend*. "Have the paparazzi already shown up?"

"They're lined up along the south gate," Rachelle said. "We had a perimeter breach along the cliffs, and a boat came into the chateau's private waters."

"Were they both intercepted?"

"Yes. No one was apprehended, but someone has been pushing the boundaries. At least Prince Garrett and Princess Janessa don't have any pressing engagements in the village today."

"That's good." Levi went through his mental checklist of how to best heighten security. "I assume you heard about the attempt on Cassandra's life a couple weeks ago."

"I did. I already sent extra guards out to do a perimeter check this morning, and we're keeping an eye on the motion sensors and security cameras," Rachelle said. "Everything's been quiet for the past couple hours."

"Do you need an extra set of eyes?"

"That's okay. I already reworked the schedule so we'll have enough staff," Rachelle said.

"Good. That'll let me work on some other security issues."

"One more thing I thought you should know. We picked up the paparazzo who was outside the chateau yesterday."

"Who was it?"

"His name is Oscar Laxmi."

"Does he have any connection to Sereno?"

"Not that we can tell, but this is the first time he's been picked up here in Meridia," Rachelle said. "He said he's been living in Italy, but that's all we got out of him. In fact, this is the first time he's ever been picked up with anything to do with infringing on someone's privacy."

"Is he still in custody?"

"He's being released in an hour and will be escorted to the airport. Prince Garrett said he would inform King Alejandro of the man's identity in case he tries to follow Cassandra home when she leaves here."

"Thanks."

"I'll keep you updated."

"I appreciate it." Levi hung up the phone and saw Janessa in the doorway to his office. He stood and waved her inside. "Janessa, I'm so sorry. Cassie and I left the beach as soon as I saw a boat coming into photography range. Obviously, I didn't move fast enough."

Janessa walked in and closed the door. "Levi, everyone can get distracted now and then, especially when you spend so much time with someone you find interesting and attractive."

"I know better."

"So did I." Janessa sat in the chair across from him and waited for him to reclaim his seat. "That didn't keep me from falling for Garrett, nor did knowing I was human take away the guilt when an assassin almost succeeded in killing him."

"You aren't helping," Levi muttered.

"I'm about to."

"How are you planning to do that?"

"I'm going to give you advice I wish I would have been given when I was protecting Garrett."

"And what is that?"

"Don't fight your feelings for Cassie. Learn to work with them. Learn to work with her."

"Janessa, this is different from when you were protecting Garrett," Levi insisted. "You were pretending to be his fiancée. Now that we've been seen together, my presence invites extra attention at a time when she should have been kept invisible."

"You managed to keep her invisible for over a week," Janessa said. "You know our security will hold up against outside threats."

"Our security force is trained to identify threats. They aren't military. Even though they are well trained, if someone sends in a special-forces squad like they did in Sereno, we'll lose lives."

"I agree. That's why I asked King Eduard to lend us some extra assistance."

"What kind of assistance?"

"One of our special-ops teams that trained with the Navy SEALs last year is stationed here in Bellamo," Janessa said. "They are going to provide extra security outside our gates for the next two weeks."

"They need to be cleared."

"Rachelle is already working on it, but they won't be coming onto the grounds unless a threat occurs," Janessa said. "No one will even know they're here."

"This is one time I don't mind a little extra protection, especially if it makes Cassie feel like she can keep living her current normal."

"I understand completely." Janessa reached across the desk and put her hand on his. "Rachelle will keep things under control. You focus on helping Cassie get home."

Levi mulled over the issues laid out before him, weighing the risks with Janessa's advice. "What do you think it would take for me to get Director Palmer to lend Alan to me for a month or so?"

"Alan Niesler?" Janessa asked, referring to their CIA buddy who worked with a K-9 partner.

"Yeah. Max is the best bomb-detection dog I've ever seen, and the possibility of an inside source at the palace in Sereno worries me," Levi said. "I'd like to know someone I'm working with."

"Normally, I'd say it's a good idea, but Alan doesn't speak Italian well enough to pass for a native. I'm afraid he would be recognized as an American," Janessa said.

"You're right. I hadn't thought about that."

"The good news is that King Alejandro has agreed to let Jeremy and Noelle help with his security," Janessa said. "I spoke to Jeremy this morning. He and Noelle are on their way to the palace in Sereno. They'll arrive this afternoon."

"That's great. Thank you."

"He'll give you a call when they get settled," Janessa said.

A knock sounded on the door.

"Come in," Levi called out.

Cassie pushed the door open and walked in, then noticed Janessa. "I hope I'm not interrupting."

"Not at all. I was just leaving." Janessa stood. "Levi, don't forget what I said."

Levi didn't say anything, but he doubted Janessa expected him to respond.

Cassie moved farther into the room as soon as Janessa left. "Are you sure I didn't interrupt?"

"I'm sure." Levi waved at his computer. "I have something you need to see though."

"What?" She looked down when he angled his laptop toward her. She sighed. "They found me."

"I'm so sorry. I should have known better than to let you down on the beach."

"It's not your fault." A flash of vulnerability appeared on her face, but her voice remained calm and even. "Do I need to leave?"

"No. Rachelle is enhancing the security here at the chateau," Levi said. "I think it's safer to keep you here than to try to move you."

"I trust your judgment." To Levi's surprise, she kept her eyes on the image. "It's a good picture of us."

"You sound like you like being in the news."

"No, not at all, but it's a necessary part of my life." She waved dismissively at the image. "This will blow over soon enough. I'm sorry that it has caused your staff unnecessary work though."

"It's part of the job, but with the paparazzi camped outside the chateau, our plans to go into the village will have to be canceled."

"That's too bad, but hopefully they'll get bored within a few days," she said. "If all goes well, the announcement of the drilling contract will take priority over my social life."

Levi wasn't sure whether he should be impressed by how easily she adjusted to the news or if he should be insulted that he was one of countless stories that would quickly fade into obscurity.

"Have you started on the plans for the palace in Sereno?" Cassie asked.

"I have a couple ideas, but I'll know more when my friends arrive."

"When is that supposed to happen?"

"Today."

"You don't waste any time."

"With your location now public, I don't have any time to waste." He saw the concern light her eyes again, realizing now that her calm facade was just that: a facade. The concern was there and so was the fear.

He debated briefly if now was the time to step away from her and their growing friendship, but that glimpse of vulnerability prevented him from taking the step. He circled his desk and slipped his arms around her. "I'll keep you safe."

"How much will that photo hurt your career?"

"My name isn't mentioned, and I doubt it will be," Levi said, realizing how lucky he was that the images shared didn't show a clear view of his face. "For now, let me show you my ideas for enhancing your father's security."

"I'd like that."

* * *

Julien hung up the phone and slammed it onto his desk. Incompetents. Couldn't anyone do anything right?

The tabloids had succeeded in locating Princess Cassandra, and yet no one seemed to be able to penetrate the chateau walls. How hard could it be? The chateau wasn't even the primary residence of the king of Meridia. Surely there had to be a way inside.

Pratt knocked on his office door. "Did you already hear from Oscar?"

"I heard he got questioned by the authorities. He's already on his way to Rome. Apparently, he's not welcome in Meridia any longer."

"He's lucky they didn't arrest him."

"They did, but he got off easy and only had to pay a fine." Julien spread out photos Oscar had emailed him from his surveillance this morning. "What about sending someone in on the beach?"

"We tested that possibility yesterday. The royal navy must be using some kind of sonar because every time a boat gets close to shore, it gets intercepted within a few minutes."

"What about from the woods over here?" Julien tapped on a photo that showed the spot where the beach ended and rocks and trees began.

"Oscar tried to get through there too. He said he didn't even make it onto the grounds before a guard chased him off."

"He's lucky they only fined him," Julien muttered.

"I hate to say it, but I think our best chance is to wait until the princess goes back to Sereno."

"They'll be ready for us next time." To prove his point, Julien slid the photos aside and dumped out another set, these taken from the video feed of one of his would-be assassins. "Look at how many guards were in the entryway. And that was without them knowing we were coming."

A figure kneeling over a fallen guard caught his eye. Julien picked the photo up for a closer look. "I don't believe it."

"What?"

"I think you're right. We should plan our next move in Sereno." He tapped his finger against the photo. "This time, we'll have two items of business to take care of instead of one."

CHAPTER 27

LEVI COULDN'T STOP THINKING ABOUT her. Having Cassie sitting two feet away wasn't going to solve that problem any time soon. Since the moment he'd kissed her, he'd been trying to convince himself that a relationship between them was impossible.

It *was* impossible: he was a CIA operative. She was a princess from a country that didn't like Americans, a princess who still thought he was from Meridia and not the United States. Yet, as he watched her sitting across the table from him, he could only see her as a woman. An intelligent, interesting, attractive woman. He might have been able to resist those three qualities if he hadn't glimpsed her strength that surfaced along with the pockets of vulnerability she tried so hard to hide.

Was it knowing he was one of the few who had seen that side of her that drew him in? Or the protective instincts she drew out of him? Or perhaps it was the whole package.

They had spent their morning working in her suite, their lunch order expected to be delivered within the next few minutes.

Cassie lifted her hand and ran her fingers through her hair in a gesture he now recognized as one she did only when she was away from the public eye. She leaned back in her chair and asked, "Any luck with finding Jeremiah Escobar's descendants?"

"Not yet. How are you doing on the oil company employees?"

"It's slow work, but I think I can get it done today."

His phone rang, and he picked it up; it was Director Palmer. He hit the talk button. "Marin."

"Do you have a minute?" the director asked.

"I'll be right there," Levi said in Italian, answering a different question deliberately so the director would know he wasn't alone.

"Call me back as soon as you can."

"Okay. I'll see you in a minute." Levi hung up and stood. "I'm sorry, but I've got to go to the security office."

A flash of concern illuminated her features. "Is everything okay?"

"Yeah. I won't be long."

"No alarms going off or anything, right?"

"No alarms. I promise." He put his hand on her shoulder. "I'll be back in a few minutes."

"Okay."

Levi left Cassie's suite and made his way to his office. As soon as he walked inside, he closed the door and called Director Palmer.

"Can you talk now?" Director Palmer asked in lieu of a greeting.

"Yeah. What's up?" Levi asked.

"We received a tip from Interpol. The attempt on Princess Cassandra's life wasn't the only crime that occurred at the palace in Sereno," he said. "A robbery occurred as well."

"What was stolen?"

"Loose gemstones. Six of them."

"Six gemstones," Levi repeated. "That's it?"

"I know. I found the report odd too. The gems taken were a diamond, sapphire, emerald, garnet, amber, and topaz," Director Palmer said. "With all of the priceless valuables in the palace, I would have thought the inventory of missing items would have been more extensive or that at least some of the crown jewels would be missing."

"That was my thought too," Levi said, an uncomfortable sensation creeping up his spine. "The gems must have been important for them to be reported."

"That's why I wanted you to know about it. If you can get any insight out of the princess, let me know."

"I will," Levi said as he tried to believe his own words.

He finished his call and headed back to Cassie's suite, where he knocked and pushed the door open.

"Everything okay?" Cassie asked from her spot at the table.

"More or less." Levi sat across from her. "I received a report of a theft from your home. Six loose gemstones were stolen."

"Six?" Cassie asked. "Was there a description of them?"

Levi listed them.

"All of those are among the gems in our founding jewels, but there are twenty-four, not six."

"Can you think of any other gems that would be of enough significance for your father to enlist the help of Interpol?"

"Interpol is involved?"

"That's where I got the information."

"I have to think the missing gems are the ones that are used as the key for our succession agreement, but I don't know why someone would steal six and not take the rest."

"Unless they couldn't find the rest."

"As far as I know, they were all stored together in the royal vault."

"Maybe your father chose to secure some somewhere else," Levi said. "You did mention he increased security last year."

"True, but if he separated the gems, he didn't tell me."

"You said they act as the verification code for the agreement. What benefit would they be beyond their street value to someone?"

"Nothing that I can think of." Cassie nudged her laptop aside. "The Escobar family knows what the agreement says."

"But they do need the gems as well as the twenty-four pieces of the agreement to take power if your family could no longer rule," Levi pointed out.

"Yes, that's true, but the more I think about it, the more it doesn't make sense," Cassie said. "If my family was wiped out, the other countries would produce the various pieces of the agreement. Why go to the trouble of stealing them?"

"I have no idea."

Cassie ran her fingers through her hair. "I really wish we could get to the point that we didn't keep adding to our list of questions."

"Me too."

* * *

Cassie sat beside Levi, his computer in front of them. He clicked his cordless mouse on the worktable. "We should be good now."

"Who are we teleconferencing with again?"

"A couple of friends from Interpol," Levi said.

Cassie watched his screen while they waited for the secure video call to connect. When it did, Cassie saw the familiar painting behind the couple on the screen, a painting that hung in one of the guest suites in her home in Prima.

"Levi, good to see you," the man said. Though he spoke in Italian, she detected a slight accent.

"Good to see you too." Levi nodded at Cassie. "Jeremy, Noelle, this is Princess Cassandra."

"Good to meet you, Your Highness," Noelle said.

"You as well."

"Have you done an initial assessment?" Levi asked, breaking up the formalities.

"We haven't been given access yet to the secure areas of the palace, but we have walked the perimeter and evaluated several other structures on the property."

Cassie listened to Jeremy and Noelle discuss various security concerns with Levi. Until the attack two weeks ago, the gates and the presence of the guards had given her the illusion of safety. Hearing this discussion, she realized that was all it was: an illusion.

"When are you supposed to gain access to the rest of the palace?" Levi asked, interrupting her thoughts.

"Someone named Paciano is supposed to meet with us this afternoon," Noelle said. "He is one of the senior members of the royal guard."

Levi looked at Cassie for confirmation. Embarrassed that she didn't know her security staff by name, she shrugged.

Levi leaned closer. "Do you not know Paciano?"

"I'm not sure," Cassie whispered. "I don't know everyone's name."

"Paciano did give us a summary report about late arrivals to events at the palace," Noelle said. "We're running everyone through Interpol, but we haven't had any hits."

Levi straightened and focused on the screen again. "I'd like an update by tomorrow."

"I'll drop my notes in an email for you tonight, and we can discuss the most immediate issues tomorrow," Jeremy said.

"Sounds good. Thank you." Levi ended the call and angled his chair to face her. "Should I be worried that your father assigned someone to assist us that you don't even know?"

Her heart sank. She didn't want to admit her callousness toward her own servants, but she also didn't want Levi's suspicions to get in the way of her returning home. "No. If anything, you should be disappointed that I know so few of my staff members' names."

His eyebrows drew together. "What do you mean?"

She drew a deep breath. How to explain? "I've lived my whole life with people always standing nearby, watching my every move. It didn't matter that I craved privacy," Cassie said. "This is the first time in my life I've received the simple gift of being able to go for a walk without an entourage or finding my own way to the kitchen without guards trailing behind me."

"What does that have to do with knowing your staff?"

"I know my staff. I don't know their names." Another deep breath. "I found if I didn't take the time to learn about them, I could pretend they weren't there."

Levi stared at her a moment as though recalling a memory. "So if I had come to work for you in your family home, you never would have noticed me."

"Honestly, I don't know," Cassie said. "I probably would have noticed you, but I would have tried not to."

"I see."

"I don't think you do," Cassie said. "Please understand how different my life has been from yours. Until arriving here, I didn't know it was possible to find any sense of normalcy while also being a royal."

"And now?"

"Now I want what Garrett and Janessa have."

"Their relationship with their staff isn't something you can create on a whim," Levi said. "You can't go from not caring about the people serving you to expecting them to invite you into their lives."

"Please don't judge me for who I was. I look back now, and I cringe when I think of how I chose to ignore the people who were so dedicated to protecting me," Cassie said. "I hate that people were injured and killed because of me, and I didn't even know their names."

"Do you want to know their names?"

"I do," Cassie said, "but not only the ones who were injured. I want to know everyone who works at the palace. I want to create the kind of environment I've witnessed here at the chateau."

"Like?" Levi asked.

Cassie sensed curiosity in the question rather than judgment. "I love that Patrice runs this place, that she is a second mother to Garrett and is so thoughtful to everyone. She was every bit as kind to me when she thought I was a commoner as I imagine she would be now that she knows I'm a royal."

"Assuming she knows," Levi said. "She's never liked the gossip magazines."

"That doesn't surprise me," Cassie said. "Patrice is one of a kind. I wish I could clone her and take her back with me to Sereno."

"I imagine you could convince her to come for a visit," Levi said. "Assuming a royal is allowed to entertain a mere servant."

"Levi, don't do that."

"Do what? Put class between us?" Levi asked. "You already did."

"Maybe when we first met, but I haven't pulled the royal card since I got here." Cassie pushed back from his worktable and stood. "Why are you acting like this?"

Levi pushed out of his seat, his gaze meeting hers. "I promised to keep you safe, but I don't need to get pulled through social media only to be touted as the commoner who spent a few weeks with a princess."

"The paparazzi don't even know your name."

"Not yet." Levi's jaw clenched, and he took a moment before he spoke again. "As soon as we arrive in Sereno, you can bet someone will ferret it out."

Cassie read between lines she hadn't known existed between them. "Are you saying you don't want to be with me anymore because I'm royal and you're not?"

"That pretty much sums it up." He closed his laptop. "It's easier to end things now before our lives get too complicated."

"I never realized you were afraid of complicated." She took a step back. Levi's face was masked as though he had no care for her or anyone else. Though her pride demanded she turn and leave, her heart dominated. Tears threatened, but she blinked them back. "I'm sorry that's the case, Levi. I truly have enjoyed every minute we've spent together, and I care for you more than words can express."

She made it nearly to the door before Levi spoke. "Wait, Cassie."

He rushed across the room and pushed on the door to keep her from opening it.

"Let me pass."

"No." His fingers curled around her arm, and he tugged so she would turn to face him. Regret appeared in his eyes before the apology came out in his words. "I'm sorry. It's my fault you were found here. I've let my feelings for you distract me, and I don't know if I could live with myself if something happened to you."

"The photo wasn't your fault. If anything, it was mine. I know how persistent the paparazzi can be. With Garrett and Janessa home, I should have known better, but I wanted to keep the illusion of normal going for as long as I could."

"But you do know this is all make-believe."

"It doesn't have to be," Cassie said, surprising herself. "What if you came to Sereno and stayed? Would you ever consider working in my country instead of Meridia?"

"I don't know," Levi said at length. "It's a lot to think about."

"Will you though?"

Several seconds passed. "Yeah, I will."

CHAPTER 28

LEVI DIDN'T RECOGNIZE HIS NEW routine until he was four days into it. Breakfast with Cassie in the morning, work with Rachelle until noon, lunch with Cassie, design security plans with Cassie in the afternoon, dinner with Cassie, followed by a walk in the gardens. Occasionally, he and Cassie would spend time with Garrett and Janessa in the evenings, but his favorite moments were those they spent alone.

Levi couldn't miss the recurring theme in his activities: Cassie. Even his time working with Rachelle was largely devoted to clearing Keith Maloney, the CEO of Axion, to ensure Cassie's safety. Maloney would arrive tomorrow, along with his lead attorney and his accountant.

The paparazzi's discovery of Cassie's location had complicated the routine for the chateau's security staff, but Rachelle seemed to be taking it all in stride. Seeing her efficiency firsthand took away some of the guilt he had been harboring about leaving the chateau. Logically, he knew he wasn't the only person capable of protecting the royal family in Meridia, but that hadn't kept him from feeling like he was abandoning Garrett and Janessa somehow.

With his growing confidence in Rachelle, he couldn't help but think about Cassie's suggestion that he come to work in Sereno. He left the security office and headed for his own. His office. Within days, he would need to clean out his personal belongings and turn the space over to Rachelle.

His phone rang. When he saw Director Palmer's name, he hurried his steps, waiting until he closed his office door before he answered. "Hello, Director."

"I haven't heard from you in a few days. How is the situation with the princess?"

"Good. She actually offered me a job a few days ago."

"A job?"

"Working with the security force in Sereno."

"That's interesting."

"I thought so," Levi said. "As for my real job, the security plans for Sereno are moving along. Jeremy Rogers has already started implementing several enhancements."

"Glad to hear he has been there to help. He's a good man."

Jeremy had worked for the CIA before switching to Interpol.

"I hope you don't mind me pulling him in," Levi said.

"It was a smart move. In fact, he might make a good intermediary to push information back to me once you go to Sereno."

"Why? With my secure cell phone, our calls won't be intercepted."

"No reason to chance it. We may never get another opportunity to insert an agent so close to the royal family in Sereno again."

"Yes, but since the assignment will only last until the threat is neutralized, is it really necessary to take such precautions?"

"It is because I hope you will be there much longer than two weeks."

"What?"

"You just told me the princess offered you a job. Levi, we couldn't have asked for a better opportunity to drop in our laps," Director Palmer said. "An invitation for one of our operatives to work intimately with the royal family, and in a security capacity, no less. You'll be able to feed us everything we could possibly need to know about the region."

"You're assigning me to Sereno for my next post?" Hope took flight within him only to be tempered by reality. He could live close to Cassie, but he would forever be torn between what was in her best interest and what the Central Intelligence Agency needed to know.

"That's right. I want you to go undercover working for the royal family."

"You want me to spy on Princess Cassandra and her family," Levi corrected.

"Is that a problem?" Director Palmer asked. "This is what you've been doing in Meridia for the past two years."

"No, I've been working with the Meridian royal family to protect the interests of both countries," Levi said. "It's been a while since I've done undercover work without my host knowing who I really am."

"I suppose that's true, but in essence, your job will be the same. Learn everything you can and feed us everything we need to know to ensure stability within the region. How soon will you leave for Sereno?"

"Between a week and ten days." Levi started to mention the contract negotiations that would soon be underway but then focused on the practical. "I have a few more details I need to put in place before I'm willing to take Princess Cassandra back to Sereno."

"Keep me informed."

"Yes, sir." Levi hung up, a new weight settling over him. The knowledge that Cassie's father harbored a grudge against the United States had settled deep into his subconscious, and Levi had managed to ignore it until now. He didn't want to think about what Cassie would think if she knew his true nationality, nor had he wanted to contemplate what would happen once Cassie and her family were finally safe.

The possibility of working for her security force gave him hope that they would be able to continue seeing each other, but what kind of relationship would they have if it was built on lies? And would he even be able to date her if he was in the employ of her country's security service?

A cloud of despair settled over him. Cassie might be the central focus of his life right now, but they were living in a dream world. Soon they would enter her reality, and he suspected that he would quickly become a fading memory as far as the princess was concerned.

Could he function in his new assignment in Sereno knowing he would see Cassie every day? He knew how royals worked. He wasn't in her class, and he had no doubt her countrymen would point that out to her if their relationship became public. More importantly, how could he continue a relationship with her when he would forever be torn between his feelings for her and his duty to his country?

He pushed those thoughts away, struggling to tuck them into the corner of his mind. He was with Cassie now. He needed to enjoy their time together while it lasted.

* * *

Cassie paced the library, her stomach tying itself in knots. Levi had informed her that Keith Maloney had arrived fifteen minutes ago. As she and Levi had previously discussed, she would use the chateau library to meet the man who could very soon be her country's new partner.

So many things were changing both for her and her country. An impending turnover in leadership, a new industry that would greatly improve the economy, and the possibility that Levi would come to Sereno with her to stay.

The earlier strain between them had faded. Ironically, Levi's attempt to put distance between them had done the opposite and had drawn them closer.

The realization that her safety meant more to him than his own happiness had endeared him to her in a way she couldn't describe.

She let her thoughts linger on Levi for a moment and, by doing so, found a new sense of calm. She didn't know what it was about him that made her feel both safe and cherished, but she couldn't imagine her future anymore without him in it. It was hard enough to think of how much would change when she returned to Sereno and ultimately took over for her father.

She looked around the library. Like in her own home, the artwork featured a combination of modern and classic. A Monet on one wall, a local seascape above the fireplace. A new conference table in the center of the room and an antique occasional table in the corner. Full bookshelves lined the wall and gave the room warmth to what would otherwise look like a classy conference room.

Cassie had seated herself on one side of the oval table where four copies of the proposed contract lay on the glossy surface: one folder in front of her and the other three arranged at the seats across from her.

She was ready. She hoped she was ready.

Cassie placed a hand on her stomach in an attempt to settle her racing emotions. Looking through business proposals was one thing, but conducting negotiations on her own was quite another. The draft of the contracts had been written by her attorneys weeks ago in anticipation of this day, but this first meeting was all on her.

Footsteps approached, and she turned to see Levi escort three people inside, two men and a woman.

"Princess Cassandra, may I present Keith Maloney, the chief executive officer of Axion Oil," Levi said.

Cassie extended her hand to Keith. "I am so pleased to meet you. Thank you for agreeing to meet me here."

"It's my pleasure." Keith glanced around the room. "This is the first time I've been invited to a royal home."

"If all goes well, I doubt it will be the last," Cassie said.

"This is Alexis Garcia, my attorney, and Richard Nasser, my accountant."

"It's a pleasure to meet you both." Cassie waved toward the table. "Please sit down."

Levi circled behind her chair and pulled it out for her.

"Thank you." Cassie sat.

"I will be outside if you need me," Levi said as soon as her guests had joined her at the table.

"Thank you, Levi."

He nodded, a look of encouragement on his face.

The door closed, and Cassie opened her proposal. "If you will turn to page four, we can get started."

The three executives from Axion complied, and Cassie straightened her shoulders. She could do this, she assured herself. And when she completed her task, she would be one step closer to going home.

* * *

Even though his conversation with Director Palmer had occurred days ago, Levi still hadn't managed to reconcile his feelings for Cassie and the promise of a new assignment in her home country. As though appearing from the turmoil swirling within him, she entered his office. His confusion deepened.

He glanced at the clock. Six thirty. Almost time for dinner.

"You look very serious this evening." Cassie crossed the room and leaned over his desk to kiss him in greeting. "Are you at a good stopping place? I hoped you could join us for dinner."

"Us?" Levi asked, struggling to allow himself to be the person Cassie believed him to be.

"Me, Garrett, and Janessa," Cassie clarified.

"What about your guests?"

"They're planning a conference call with their board of directors tonight," Cassie said. "Patrice is sending dinner to the conference room for them."

Levi closed the file he had been reviewing and stood. "Did your meetings go well?"

"Very well." Cassie smiled, her face alight with confidence she had rarely exhibited since her arrival. "We have a few points to iron out, but I think the company will be a good match for us."

"Will your father forgive you for bringing in an American company?"

Some of her enthusiasm faded. "He doesn't have much choice."

"I'm sorry. I shouldn't have mentioned him." Levi skirted around his desk. "I know you've worried about his prejudice against Americans though."

"I do worry about it, but it isn't something I can control," Cassie said. "My father entrusted this decision to me, and I'm making it."

"I'm sure he will appreciate all the time you've put into this project," Levi said.

"I think he'll be more excited about reducing the threats against the family," Cassie said. "My sisters and I should be home with him."

"It's going to be a while before security will be ready to have all of you in one place, but we'll get there."

"At times like these, I wish I weren't royal. My sisters aren't going to be any happier than I was to find out our father is fighting a terminal illness and didn't tell us."

"Like you, I'm sure they'll understand," Levi said. "I look forward to getting to know them."

Cassie's expression brightened. "Does this mean you're staying with me in Sereno?"

"Is the invitation still open?"

"Of course. I wish we could talk to my father about what position would suit you best, but I don't imagine that's possible until after we arrive."

"No," Levi said. "For now, maybe we should stick with our current cover."

Her eyebrows rose. "You do realize that if you play the part of my boyfriend in Sereno, you'll be hounded by the press."

"I have no intention of parading myself out in public for them to see," Levi said.

"I hate to tell you this, but the press is a lot more intrusive at the palace than what I've dealt with here."

Levi cringed inwardly at the thought of landing in the tabloids. He had watched Janessa navigate those murky waters enough times to prefer avoidance if at all possible. "The only people who need to know I'm your boyfriend are your guards."

"Any new arrival will be noticed."

"Not when your security team is in the process of increasing its staff."

"True." Cassie linked her fingers with his. "I just don't want you to be upset when you get linked to me in the press. The longer we're together, the more likely it is to happen."

Levi replayed his earlier comment. Had he really referred to himself as her boyfriend? Had their fake relationship somehow evolved into a real one?

"How long do you want us to be together?" Levi asked, needing clarification as he struggled against Director Palmer's directive.

"It's scary to admit, but I don't want this to end."

Levi cupped her elbows to hold her in place, his gaze capturing hers. "Neither do I." The moment the words were spoken, Levi recognized the truth of them. He might be a CIA operative, but right here, right now, he was simply Levi Marin, the man who was falling for a princess.

He leaned down and captured her mouth with his, the kiss seeping through him. No matter what Director Palmer might think, Cassie could never be an assignment. Levi was falling for her, and he suspected that she was quickly becoming the woman he could love for a lifetime.

CHAPTER 29

CASSIE READ THROUGH EVERY WORD of the final agreement, her heart pounding in her chest. This was it. The moment she signed her name, Axion Oil would have the drilling rights in Sereno's territorial waters, and her country would benefit from the jobs that would soon be created.

Cassie fought to keep her public armor in place and picked up her pen with a steady hand. She signed her name and slid the contract across the table. She repeated the process with the duplicate original.

Keith followed her lead, flipping pages to verify the latest negotiation points were included before he signed.

As soon as his signature was in place, he stood. He handed one agreement to his attorney and the second original back to Cassie. "Your Highness, I look forward to working with you. Thank you for this opportunity."

Cassie accepted the offered contract and rose to her feet. "Thank you. I look forward to seeing you in Sereno."

"I will see you there." Keith excused himself, his attorney and his accountant following him out of the room.

Cassie looked down at the contract in her hand. She had done it. The decision was made, the contracts were in place, and she was going home. More importantly, Levi was coming with her.

Cassie tucked the contract into a file inside her soft-sided briefcase and headed for Levi's office. She found his door closed. When she raised her hand to knock, she heard his voice, but it was barely audible.

She lowered her hand, waiting to see if she heard any other voices to determine if he was in a meeting or speaking on the phone. Levi's voice went silent for a moment before he started speaking again. Recognizing now he was on the phone, she knocked.

Levi's words carried through the door as he approached. "Hold on a minute." As soon as the door swung open, he switched from English to Italian and said, "I'll have to call you back."

"I'm sorry to interrupt."

"It's fine. How did everything go today?"

"The contracts are signed."

"Congratulations." Levi pulled her into a hug. "That's fantastic."

"Thanks." She stepped back so she could see Levi clearly. "How soon do you think we can leave for Sereno?"

"The initial security improvements are already in place at the palace," Levi said. "How long will it take you to pack?"

"An hour."

"It'll take me a little longer than that to arrange our flight." Levi glanced at his watch. "Let's plan to leave here at ten."

She checked her own watch; it was a little after four. "Ten tomorrow morning?"

"Ten o'clock tonight," Levi said.

"You do realize that will put us in Sereno in the middle of the night, right?"

"I do. My friends from Interpol have been coming and going to the palace at odd times for days to set a precedence," Levi explained. "They'll pick us up from the airport so no one knows you have arrived."

"I like your confidence, but someone will know."

"Eventually, but not before we have you safely inside the palace gates."

Her last moments in the palace surfaced. "Will it be safe inside the palace gates?"

"Yes, it will." Levi took her hands. "I'll be right there with you to make sure it stays that way."

"I guess I'd better go pack."

Levi released her and picked up his phone. "I'll let Garrett know we're leaving tonight. I'm sure he'll want to have dinner with us one last time."

"I'd like that." Cassie crossed to the door and opened it. Behind her, Levi greeted Garrett in Italian and began his explanation of their plans.

Cassie was halfway down the hall before Levi's previous conversation caught up with her. Levi had switched to Italian when he'd seen her, but she had clearly heard him speaking in English when she'd approached the door.

Questions flooded her mind. Who had he been speaking to? Had he tried to hide his ability to speak English from her? And if so, why?

* * *

Levi didn't know how Cassie could pack in an hour. He'd started packing two days ago, and it had still taken him over three hours to complete his task. Of course, he was packing two years of his life, not three weeks.

Dinner with Janessa and Garrett had given him a much-needed break and the time to remember the few things he had forgotten. What was it about phone chargers? He always seemed to leave his plugged in somewhere out of sight when he traveled.

He hauled his suitcases to the van waiting outside, where Cassie's bags were already stored neatly in the back.

Enrico took one of his bags and loaded it for him, leaving the second for Levi.

"How many more bags?"

"Two." Levi wasn't sure how to feel about having as many suitcases as Cassie. Though, the remaining two cases housed his weapons. One held his rifle and the other his spare sidearm. Since he and Cassie would be taking King Eduard's private jet to Sereno, Levi's primary weapon remained holstered at his waist.

"I can send Martino to get them."

"That's okay. I'll get them," Levi said. "Have you seen Cassie?"

"She's in the kitchen saying goodbye to Patrice."

"Probably trying to get her recipe for fried chicken."

"I may have heard some mention of a bribe when I walked through."

Levi's lips twitched into the beginnings of a smile. "I'll be right back." He went back to his living quarters and took another look around. Ignoring the tug on his heartstrings, he picked up the silver cases that housed his weapons and turned his back on the cozy living room and the view out his window.

Levi detoured to the kitchen and found Cassie hugging Patrice and Janessa in turn. "Cassie, are you ready?" he asked.

"Yes." She picked up two pastry boxes.

"What's in there?"

"Some snacks for us and some muffins for Patrice's daughter," Cassie said. "You should have told me Patrice had family in Sereno."

Levi wasn't sure how Patrice found out Noelle was in Sereno. As far as he knew, the Saldera family still didn't know of their daughter's association with Interpol. "I was going to tell you when we got there."

"You give my girl a hug for me," Patrice said.

"I will," Cassie promised. "I look forward to meeting her."

Patrice reached for Levi and gave him a hug. "You take care of yourself. Come back soon."

Unexpectedly emotional, Levi swallowed before he managed to speak. "I'll do what I can."

Janessa moved to the door. "I'll walk you out."

They left the kitchen and made their way outside.

Cassie turned to face Janessa when they reached the van. "Janessa, thank you again for your hospitality."

"You're very welcome," Janessa said. "I hope you will visit again soon."

"I'd like that."

Levi opened the passenger door and waited for Cassie to climb in. As soon as she was securely inside, Enrico handed Levi a set of car keys.

"Renzo and I will follow you to the airport so we can retrieve the van," Enrico said.

"Thanks."

Enrico walked to the car parked behind the van, with one of his younger drivers waiting in it.

Janessa stepped closer. "Jeremy called a few minutes ago to let me know the first shipment of motion detectors arrived this morning. He also brought in one of Interpol's bomb-detection dogs. They're doing a sweep now."

"Good to know," Levi said. "The last thing I want is to find a bomb waiting for Cassie when she arrives."

"Jeremy said they've already cleared the palace," Janessa said. "It will take some time to do a complete search of the grounds, but the immediate area should be done before you get there."

"I appreciate knowing that is taken care of."

"Be safe."

"You too." Levi gave Janessa a hug. "Don't get too royal on me."

"I'll do my best." She flashed a smile. "But just so you know, I may have used my royalness to score you those scones you like so much."

"Patrice made blueberry scones?"

"She did."

"That does it. I think you rank as my best friend again."

"Don't you forget it." Janessa gave him another quick hug. "Let me know if there's anything I can do to help with Cassie."

"Thanks." Levi fisted his hand around the car keys and circled to the driver's seat. He climbed in and felt Cassie's gaze on him. "You ready to go home?"

"I'm ready to see my father."

"Then let's make it happen." Levi slid the key into the ignition and started the engine. A second later, he put the van in gear, and they were on their way.

CHAPTER 30

CASSIE LOOKED OUT THE WINDOW of the plane. The glimmer of lights sparkled beneath them like beacons breaking up the darkness. Even though she couldn't see the coastline of her island nation at night, she recognized the bright beam of the lighthouse that stood beside the bay a few miles from the airport.

The light shone out into the dark harbor, a signal to sailors of the dangers that lurked nearby. She hoped she would be one to find safety tonight, but really, she didn't know what to expect. Would the announcement of the contract with Axion protect her and her family, or was there still another danger that had yet to be identified?

Cassie gripped her armrests. Someone had tried to kill her the last time she'd been in Sereno. Would someone try again?

The plane descended, finally touching down on the tarmac of the airport her country's small military used. Cassie's grip tightened.

"Are you okay?" Levi asked.

"I'm fine."

He leaned closer and lowered his voice, even though they were still alone in the passenger cabin. "You don't have to hide your feelings from me."

She turned her head, her gaze focusing on the dark brown of Levi's eyes. He was right. If she wanted a real relationship, she couldn't afford to hide behind her shield as she did with everyone else. "I'm scared," she admitted.

"I know." He took her hand. "I'm here for you though, and so are my friends."

The plane came to a stop. Only a couple minutes passed before the pilot emerged from the cockpit and opened the door.

"Ready?" Levi asked.

"Do you want an honest answer?"

"I know the honest answer," he said. "Let's go anyway. I want to get you home."

Cassie stood. She collected the pastry boxes and waited while Levi retrieved the silver case he had brought into the main cabin with him. He led the way outside, blocking the entrance for a moment as though making sure it really was safe for her to exit. After a moment, he nodded to her and motioned her forward.

She stepped onto the aircraft stairs and looked out at an SUV parked at the bottom, a woman in her twenties standing beside it. A man who appeared to also be in his midtwenties carried suitcases to the back of the SUV and loaded them inside.

Levi escorted her to where the woman waited. Though she expected him to introduce his friend, Levi simply opened the back door for Cassie, who slid inside. Levi closed the door, and the tinted windows hid her from view.

She looked behind her, where Levi and his friends were loading more luggage. After a couple minutes, the door opposite where she sat opened and Levi climbed in.

The couple took their positions in the front seat, the woman behind the wheel.

"Princess Cassandra, these are my friends, Noelle and Jeremy Rogers."

"Nice to meet you in person," Noelle said.

"I believe this is for you." Cassie passed the pastry box from Patrice between the two front seats.

"Is this from Patrice?" Jeremy asked.

"It is."

"We're going to eat well today," Jeremy said.

Noelle put the car in drive and started forward.

"Are you going to share?" Levi asked Jeremy, who now held the box protectively.

"You have your own box," Cassie said.

"Yeah, but that was for on the plane."

"You didn't eat anything on the plane," Cassie reminded him.

Levi jerked a thumb toward the front seat. "They didn't know that."

Noelle slowed at the security gate long enough to wave to the guard. "It was a nice try, Levi."

Levi put his hand on Cassie's knee. "Cassie, you need to work on keeping secrets."

"You didn't tell me there was a secret to keep," Cassie said, amused.

Jeremy peeked at the pastries he now held. "Muffins and croissants? Oh, man." He looked at his wife. "I really love your mom."

"The feeling is mutual." Noelle glanced in the rearview mirror. "We'll be to the palace in fifteen minutes. Are we still keeping Princess Cassandra's presence a secret from the household staff?"

"For now," Levi said.

"What about the royal guard?" Jeremy asked.

"What is the latest on the background checks?"

"Only one name flagged. Leon Cordova."

"I understand he was one of the casualties the night of the shooting," Levi said.

"That's right," Jeremy said.

"Wouldn't that mean he wasn't involved?" Cassie asked.

"Either that, or the people he was working for made sure he didn't live to tell about it," Levi said. "We'll keep digging to see if we can determine which one. Regardless, any time I'm not with you, I want one of my friends nearby."

"I doubt you'll let me out of your sight except when I'm sleeping," Cassie said.

"You have a point."

"Does my father know I've arrived?" Cassie asked Jeremy and Noelle.

"Not yet," Jeremy said. "We knew he would be asleep by the time you arrived and thought it best to let you see him in the morning."

Disappointment crested, but she pushed against it. They were right. Her father needed his strength, and a middle-of-the-night conference wasn't in anyone's best interest.

Noelle made the last turn toward the palace, and Cassie's heartbeat quickened in anticipation. She was really home. Tonight, she would sleep in her own bed, and in a few hours, she would see her father and finally be able to talk to him face-to-face.

* * *

Levi's first thought when he saw the Sereno palace was that he had arrived at Disneyland. His second impression brought with it a sense of dread. While aesthetically pleasing, the palace had been built on a small bluff overlooking the Mediterranean, and the buildings of the neighboring city encroached it on two sides.

From the security lights spilling over the wrought-iron fence that surrounded the palace grounds, Levi could barely make out the coastline. "What's on the far side of the palace?" Levi asked.

"It's family land. We own everything from the coast to the top of North Mountain," Cassie said.

"Duck down," Jeremy said from the front seat. "A few paparazzi have been known to stake out the entrance."

"Even this time of night?" Levi asked.

"Especially this time of night."

Levi and Cassie both leaned down so they weren't visible as they approached the palace gates. The car slowed almost to a stop before increasing speed again. It wasn't until they parked in the garage that Jeremy said, "Okay, we're all clear."

Levi straightened and took in the well-lit garage. He counted six cars to his left. His view to his right was obscured by another SUV.

"Wait here for a minute," Levi told Cassie. He climbed out of the car as Jeremy did the same. "Is there a clear path to Cassie's living quarters to bring in her luggage?"

"Reasonably," Jeremy said. "I suggest we carry as much as we can now. Noelle and I can come back down for the rest."

"I don't want all of us laden down with luggage," Levi said. "Makes it hard to draw a weapon."

"I have guards standing by at the entrance to the palace and at the corridor leading to the residence, but I'll understand if you want to keep a hand free." Jeremy motioned to the far side of the garage. "Let's clear the building, and we can unload."

"Sounds good." Levi verified that Noelle was staying with Cassie before he proceeded to start his sweep. A few minutes later, he and Jeremy met back at their vehicle.

"My side is clear," Levi said. "You?"

"We're good." Jeremy waved at his wife, who climbed out and opened the back door for Cassie.

Levi retrieved the cases that contained his guns and handed them to Jeremy. "Can you take these? I don't want any of my weapons left unsecure."

"No problem." Jeremy slid the straps over his shoulder.

Levi unloaded the other bags and pushed the ones with his personal belongings aside to retrieve Cassie's first. He turned two back-to-back so he could pull them one-handed.

"I can take something." Cassie reached for her carry-on bag.

"That's one way to blend in," Levi said. He wasn't sure what had happened to the woman who had waited for everyone to tend to her needs, but he rather liked this version of Cassie.

"If you take that one, I think we can get it all in one trip," Jeremy said. He took two cases with one hand and a third with the other, the gun cases hanging from his shoulder.

Noelle retrieved the remaining bags and closed the trunk. "Ready?"

"Lead the way."

* * *

Mixed emotions worked through Cassie when she entered the side door and started down the hallway toward her private quarters. The staff was noticeably absent, but tonight it was due to the security imposed for her arrival rather than the late hour.

Avoiding the main entrance where the shooting had taken place, Cassie took the path that ran along the back wall of the palace. They crossed through the grand ballroom, with its high ceilings and dripping chandeliers, past the music room, with the grand piano and full-sized harp, and through the main gallery, where many of her parents' favorite paintings were displayed.

"You have a beautiful home," Levi said, walking beside her.

"Thank you. The views from the ballroom windows are amazing when the garden lights are on."

"Are they usually on?"

"Yes." Cassie's steps slowed, a sense of unease coming over her.

"I had them turned off," Jeremy said. "I wanted to make sure we wouldn't be visible from the outside when we walked through."

Cassie noticed Jeremy adjust his grip on one of the suitcases and realized that half of them were Levi's. "Has a living space been assigned to Levi yet?"

"The captain of the guard said he could stay in the staff quarters."

"Where are the staff quarters?" Levi asked.

"In the wing opposite the residence," Cassie said. "If it's all the same to you, I thought you could stay in one of the guest suites. We have two in the residential wing."

"Aren't those typically saved for close friends and family?" Noelle asked.

"Levi qualifies," Cassie said. "Besides, I'd feel better if he isn't so far away."

"That makes two of us," Levi said.

"I'm not sure if the room will be made up for you, but we should be able to find linens and towels," Cassie said.

"I can rough it for one night," Levi assured her. "Which way?"

"The main residence is on the second level." They reached a stairwell, and Cassie pointed to an elevator to her left. "We can send the luggage up in the elevator."

Jeremy hit the up button. "The elevator isn't large enough for all of us with the luggage."

"Noelle, can you ride up with the bags? We'll meet you upstairs."

"No problem." The elevator doors slid open, and Noelle, Jeremy, and Levi loaded the bags inside. Noelle squeezed inside and hit the button for the second floor.

"I'll check out the stairwell." Jeremy jogged up the stairs at a quick enough pace that he would likely beat the elevator to the main residence hallway.

Levi took Cassie's arm, and they ascended the stairs together. When they reached the top, Noelle and Jeremy already had the bags stacked in the hall.

"My room is the second one on the left," Cassie said. "Levi, you can choose between the guest quarters next to my room or the one at the end of the hall."

"I'll take the one closest to you."

"Hallelujah." Jeremy hefted two large suitcases. "I don't want to carry these any farther than I have to."

"I don't blame you." Cassie opened the door to the guest quarters. "Levi, I hope this is okay."

Levi walked inside and set the gun case down on the narrow table beside the door. "I'm sure it will be fine."

With Jeremy's and Noelle's help, Cassie and Levi sorted their bags and deposited them in their respective sitting rooms.

"We'll leave you to settle in," Jeremy said. "The motion sensor alarms are active on the exterior of the palace. Tomorrow, I'll bring you up to speed on the other enhancements we have in place."

"I appreciate it," Levi said.

They all said their good nights, and Noelle and Jeremy disappeared down the stairwell.

"You have to be exhausted," Levi said.

"Yes, but I want to make sure you have everything you need before I turn in."

"I'll be fine." He leaned forward and pressed his lips to hers. "Sleep well."

"You too. I'll see you in the morning." Cassie went inside her room and closed the door. She took one look at the neatly stacked suitcases and promptly decided to ignore them. Unpacking could wait until tomorrow. Tonight, what was left of it, she wanted to spend in her own bed.

CHAPTER 31

LEVI WALKED INTO HIS NEW living quarters and locked the door behind him. The small sitting room was about the size of an average bedroom in the United States, not tiny but much more modest than what he would have expected in the residential guest quarters. A love seat occupied the space along the wall to his right, a chair angled beside it. A glass-topped table spanned the wall on the other side of the door, and a silk floral arrangement spilled out of a ceramic urn.

Levi sidestepped the pile of luggage that dominated the center of the room and crossed to the door that presumably led to the bedroom. He stepped through the opening and flipped the light switch to find he was most decidedly not in the bedroom. He quickly reassessed his impression of his new living space.

In the center of the open space before him, a long couch and three chairs created a seating area. Beyond the conversation area, eight chairs surrounded a dining table, a buffet pressed against the interior wall. French doors to his left led to a stone balcony.

Three evenly spaced archways along the interior wall provided access to the other living spaces in the guest quarters. Levi glanced through the first to find a door on one side that led to a half bath. Opposite the bathroom, double doors opened to reveal a well-supplied linen closet.

He moved to the next archway that led past a butler's pantry into a full kitchen that looked like it had come straight out of a design magazine.

Continuing to the last section, Levi entered a space that was a combination office/guest room. Levi passed through the office into another hallway. It made a bend, and he soon found himself in the master bedroom suite. Along the interior wall, he discovered an impressively large master bathroom and walk-in closet the size of his old bedroom when he was a kid. In the bedroom itself, the enormous four-poster bed in the center of the room should have dominated, but instead, it served as an accent piece the rest of the decor centered around. Blue throw pillows complemented the chairs clustered by another set of french doors.

Levi peeked through the glass at the balcony that stretched the length between the bedroom and main living area.

Realizing his stay in this suite would be short-lived, Levi retrieved his suitcases from the entryway and stacked them in the walk-in closet. He took the time to hang up his clothes for the next few days, and once that task was complete, he tucked his locked weapon cases inside his larger suitcases so they would be out of sight.

After he got ready for bed, he slipped his primary weapon into the second drawer of the bedside table, set an alarm, and plugged in his phone to charge. He dropped onto the bed, determined not to think about how few hours of sleep he would get before morning came.

He trusted Jeremy and Noelle did their best in securing the palace, but Levi wasn't going to sleep well until he knew for himself that Cassie was truly safe.

* * *

Despite the late hour of her arrival, Cassie rose with the sun. She needed to see her father, to speak with him in person.

Though she had been tempted to throw on her robe and go straight to her father's quarters, remembering Levi was currently residing next door, she took the time to shower and dress for the day first.

She opened the door leading to the hall to find Theo standing outside her father's room.

"Good morning, Theo," she said.

"Welcome home, Your Highness."

"Thank you." She continued forward. "Is my father awake?"

"He is."

Cassie knocked on her father's door, waited a brief moment, and opened it herself. "Papa?"

King Alejandro appeared at the entrance to the living room. "Cassie!"

Cassie rushed into his outstretched arms. "I missed you."

"I missed you too. Welcome home." He pulled back to look at her. "You lightened your hair."

"It helped me blend in for the first couple weeks I was in Meridia."

"Come in, and sit with me. I want to know how you have been. Did Prince Garrett treat you well?"

"Despite the reason for my visit, I had a lovely time in Meridia. Garrett and Janessa were very hospitable."

"As well they should be. We have been allies for generations."

"I'd like to think we're both allies and friends." Cassie followed him to the couch and sat beside him. "How are you feeling?"

"Better now that you're home."

Cassie gathered her courage and forced herself to speak what was on her mind. "When were you going to tell me about the cancer?"

Cassie sensed her father's surprise and saw him put his mask in place. She swallowed the tears that wanted to surface, determined to exhibit the strength she suspected her father needed from her right now. "Please don't hide the truth from me. I'm your daughter. I have a right to know that . . ." She trailed off and amended her words. "I have a right to know."

"I didn't want to worry you. You have so much on your plate already."

"You should have told me," Cassie insisted. "Like it or not, I am your heir."

"I know." He took her hands. "I should have realized you would figure it out eventually, but I hoped we both had more time to pretend things were normal."

"We can't pretend anymore."

"No, we can't."

Cassie pressed on. "It's time for you to let me share the burdens of leadership. I want to learn from you. I don't want to rely on what others tell me about you."

"I agree."

"You agree, yet you told relative strangers about your illness before you told your own daughter," Cassie said. "Why would you do that?"

"Who are you talking about? The only people who know about my illness are my doctors and your uncle."

"You must have told someone else because Levi told me." Cassie saw the confusion on her father's face.

"You're talking about Levi Marin? The man who was assigned to protect you in Meridia?"

"That's right," Cassie said. "I think King Eduard told him."

"King Eduard doesn't know." Alejandro's eyebrows drew together. "How did Levi know about my illness?"

"Obviously, he found out somehow. Regardless, I wasn't happy to hear my father has a terminal illness from someone I barely knew."

"I truly am sorry for that."

Though she wasn't sure she wanted to hear the answer, she forced herself to ask the question. "What have the doctors said? What is your prognosis?"

"A year, give or take, is what they're telling me." His hand squeezed hers, and he fell silent for a moment. "I wanted to wait until January to hand over the burden of leadership to you, but I'm afraid we may need to move up that time line."

Her father wasn't telling her anything new, but that didn't stop a fresh wave of regrets and fears from clawing to the surface. She struggled to focus on the practical rather than the emotional side of her father's announcement.

"Maybe you need to consider me your new apprentice," Cassie suggested. "Let me work beside you so I can learn as much as I can."

"I would like that, but first, we need to upgrade your security. The guard normally assigned to your personal safety is still in the hospital, and our royal guard is understaffed."

"I have someone in mind."

His eyebrows lifted. "You barely know the members of the royal guard. Who did you have in mind?"

"Someone new. Levi."

"I doubt the Meridian royal family will be happy if we poach one of their security people."

"He already agreed. In fact, he's probably still sleeping down the hall."

"What?"

"I put him in the west room."

"Here? In the residence?"

"Yes. He makes me feel safe, and I didn't want him staying on the other side of the palace."

"Cassandra, you know we can't set this kind of precedence. If we treat one servant in such a way, it will create an air of favoritism that will undermine the loyalty of our staff."

"Will it help if people think he's my boyfriend?"

"Yes, but I don't want to put you in the position of creating new fodder for the tabloids."

"I know, but Levi is special to me," Cassie said. "He was the head of security at the chateau and was preparing to transfer when he was asked to be my personal bodyguard."

"And you offered him a job here."

"Yes. I'd like for you to meet him. When you do, I think you'll approve of my choice."

"Your choice for a bodyguard or for a boyfriend?"

"Both."

Alejandro studied her for a moment. "What is your relationship with Mr. Marin?"

"We're still trying to figure that out, but I care for him, and he cares for me," Cassie said. "I think you'll like him."

"I look forward to meeting him." King Alejandro rose. "In fact, there's no time like the present. Invite him over. We'll have breakfast together."

"I'm not sure he's awake yet. We got in late."

"Then wake him." He looked at the grandfather clock that read six. "I'll give him time to properly prepare. We'll eat at seven thirty."

"Yes, Papa." Cassie took a step toward the door.

"Before you go, will you call the kitchen and order breakfast?"

"Of course." She noted her father's tie, which was slightly askew. "I'll also help you with your tie."

"It's good to have you home."

"It's good to be home."

CHAPTER 32

LEVI STARTLED WHEN HIS ALARM went off. He hadn't expected to sleep so soundly, but within minutes of his head hitting the pillow, he had drifted off and hadn't moved until the notes of "La Vida Loca" invaded his peaceful slumber.

Levi showered and dressed, choosing one of the suits he had purchased while living in Meridia. Having room and board paid for had allowed him to greatly improve his wardrobe, something he had needed while working for the royals.

He unplugged his phone and sent a text to Jeremy. *When can we meet? I want to walk through the security upgrades as soon as you're available.*

Jeremy's response came through within seconds. *I'm walking the perimeter in fifteen minutes. Want to join me?*

Where should I meet you?

The grand ballroom.

See you there.

He strapped his spare weapon to his calf and holstered his favored pistol at his waist. After checking to make sure neither was visible, he left his room and entered the main hall.

To his surprise, Cassie was approaching his door.

"Hey, there." Levi started to lean in for a kiss, but the presence of the guard standing down the hall caused him to rethink that decision. "I thought you would sleep longer."

"I needed to see my father."

Concern came into his voice. "How is he doing?"

"He confirmed what you told me." She glanced at the guard. "Let's talk in your room."

Levi opened the door and ushered her into the main living room. He waved a hand to encompass the generous space. "This suite is impressive. It's as big as a house in most places."

"I'm glad you like it."

Levi heard the strain in her voice and, acting on instinct, pulled her into his embrace. Her body trembled, and he could feel her tension as she fought against her emotions. Levi pulled back so he could see her face. "Tell me how you're doing. Really."

"It's hard. I look at him trying to pretend everything is normal, and part of me wants to go curl up in my room and cry myself to sleep so I don't have to think about it."

"And the other part of you?" Levi asked.

"Knows I need to spend as much time with him as I can, both as his daughter and as the heir to the throne."

"You may need to let both parts of you have their moment."

She blinked hard. "You're probably right, but my practical side has to dominate today." She rose to her toes and kissed him. "My father has requested we join him for breakfast."

Levi wasn't sure what to think about receiving a royal summons so soon after their arrival. "What time did he want us to meet him?"

"Seven thirty."

"That'll be tight, but I'll see what I can do."

Cassie pressed her lips together. "I don't think you understand. If my father gives a royal command, he expects it to be followed."

"I understand that, but my purpose for being here is to keep you safe," Levi said. "I'm heading out with Jeremy in a few minutes to get the lay of the land while he does his morning sweep."

"I appreciate your concern, but this is important," Cassie said. "I don't want your first meeting with my father to be one filled with disapproval."

Torn, Levi opted for a compromise. "Where are we meeting for breakfast?"

"His private quarters," Cassie said. "Across the hall from my room."

"I'll pick you up at your room when I get back."

"Thank you."

"You're welcome, but I'd better get going. I have a lot to do in the next hour." They walked back into the hall, and Levi asked, "What's the fastest way to the grand ballroom?"

"Do you want me to show you where it is?"

"No. I want you to stay out of sight for as long as possible."

"It's so strange to hear you say that in my own home."

"I know."

Cassie gave him directions, and he squeezed her hand. "I'll see you in an hour."

"Don't be late."

"I won't."

* * *

Cassie paced her sitting room and watched the grandmother clock as the minutes ticked by. Levi was going to be late.

Cassie had ridden with him plenty of times when he'd checked the perimeter of the chateau. He didn't rush when it came to security, and she suspected evaluating the coastline alone would take him the better part of an hour.

The clock chimed the quarter hour. Seven fifteen. Did Levi know that when her father demanded an audience with someone, he expected that person to be early? Levi had lived among royals long enough to understand that a king should never wait. Or a queen, for that matter.

Cassie swallowed hard. She had been born Her Royal Highness, Princess Cassandra of Sereno. She wasn't ready for her name to change, both because she didn't want to imagine a life without her father and because of her extensive inadequacies when it came to ruling a country. Ready or not, though, she would soon be Her Royal Majesty, Queen Cassandra.

Five more minutes passed. She retrieved her cell phone from her bedroom, struck by the oddity of having it in her hand again after three weeks without it. She set it back down. Even though she had memorized Levi's number, she doubted he would approve of her using her personal phone to call him. She hoped that changed soon.

Frustrated that she had no safe way to contact Levi, she walked back into the sitting room, her anxiety rising with each passing minute.

At seven twenty-four, Cassie decided she couldn't wait anymore. She would go to her father's suite and have Theo tell Levi where to meet them.

She opened the door to find Levi on the other side, his hand lifted to knock. "Ready?"

"I didn't think you were going to be back in time."

"Never keep a royal waiting," Levi said matter-of-factly. He offered his arm. "Shall we?"

"Yes." She tucked her hand into the crook of his elbow, and they crossed the hall to her father's door. She knocked, this time waiting for it to be answered.

The door swung open, and one of her father's butlers was standing inside.

"Your Highness." The butler bowed his head. "His Majesty is in the living room."

"Thank you." Cassie released Levi's arm and led the way inside.

Her father sat on the couch, a sheath of papers in his hand, an open file folder on the cushion beside him. He looked up and glanced at the clock before his gaze settled on her and Levi.

"Father, this is Levi Marin," Cassie said. "Levi, this is my father, His Royal Majesty, King Alejandro of Sereno."

"It is an honor to meet you in person, sir."

Worry flashed through Cassie that Levi would step forward and offer his hand, something that would be a breach of protocol. She needn't have doubted him. Levi remained where he was, a half step behind her.

The king pushed to a stand and stepped forward. Still, he didn't offer his hand, as though testing Levi. "I understand I owe you a debt of gratitude for keeping my daughter safe these last few weeks."

"Not at all. It has been a privilege to have the opportunity." Levi didn't expand on what opportunity had been his privilege, protecting Cassie or getting to know her. She considered the omission a wise one.

"I am grateful nonetheless." King Alejandro extended his hand.

Levi shook it, offering a bow of his head in acknowledgment of her father's position.

"Breakfast is ready." King Alejandro gestured toward where his butler stood in the archway that led to the dining room. "Shall we?"

"Of course."

Again, Levi's time serving royals shone through. He waited for Cassie and her father to lead the way into the dining room. Levi pulled out her chair and waited until everyone else was seated before he took his place beside her.

"I'm sorry I had Cassandra wake you so early this morning, especially knowing how late you got in last night, but my schedule is rather full today, and I wanted the chance to meet you."

"I didn't wake him, Papa," Cassie interjected. "He and one of his associates have been out walking the grounds."

"I see. And what do you think of our upgraded security?"

"I've only begun to assess what is currently in place," Levi said. "I suspect I will have a few more suggestions once I finish my analysis."

"I look forward to hearing about them," Alejandro said.

"If I may be so bold, I would appreciate it if you can schedule some time to meet with your daughter today. She has some information to discuss with you that could significantly reduce the threats against her."

"I have an hour until my first meeting." Her father's attention landed on Cassie. "What is this information of yours?"

Cassie gripped her hands together in her lap. She had envisioned sitting in her father's office and giving him a formal presentation on the contract she had signed and the reasons for her choice.

Levi's arm brushed against hers as though nudging her into action.

"During my time in Meridia, I did a significant amount of research into the top four oil companies we have considered to partner with for drilling in the Sereno gas fields."

"I expected no less from you."

Warmth spread through her at the subtle compliment. Her nerves eased. "In narrowing down the candidates, we discovered some frightening information."

"We?"

"Levi and I."

"You discussed classified proprietorial information with your bodyguard?"

"You said I could."

"No. I gave you permission to discuss our family's history with him, not the foundation of our country's economic future."

"It's all related to keeping our family safe," Cassie insisted. "Levi discovered that the assassins who tried to kill me were indirectly hired by Satori Oil."

"You can't be serious." Her father's face paled. "Someone tried to kill you for profit?"

"We believe so," Cassie said.

"How did you come to this conclusion?"

Cassie glanced at Levi, silently signaling him to answer.

"Your dislike of Americans is widely known. When your daughter narrowed the candidates down to three companies, two of which were based in the United States, a possible motivation for eliminating Princess Cassandra became clear," Levi explained. "If your experts came back with the same analysis and you were making the decision, it follows reason that you would have chosen the company that wasn't run by Americans."

"Your logic is sound, but how sure are you that Satori was involved?"

"I'm sure," Levi said. "My security team traced the payments to the assassins. The money was washed through a number of accounts, but it originated from a corporate account. The money was logged as a security payment, but it was four times the going rate."

"That does sound conclusive." He took a roll from the bread basket and set it on his plate. "I am impressed that you were able to gather so much information. I didn't realize Meridian intelligence had that depth of capabilities."

"I did call in a favor from Interpol," Levi said.

Before her father could comment on their involvement in the investigation, Cassie said, "Levi and I believe that announcing the winner of the drilling rights can eliminate the threat from Satori."

"You first have to iron out the contract details. That will take weeks."

"Actually, we did it in five days." Cassie took a deep breath. "I signed the contract yesterday."

"With?"

"Axion Oil. It is based out of Houston," Cassie said. "It's one of the companies Crispan suggested."

"Houston, Texas. In America."

"Yes, Papa. In America."

CHAPTER 33

LEVI ESCORTED CASSIE OUT OF her father's quarters and back to her room. The breakfast they had shared had been more meeting than eating, but after Cassie explained the contract points and the reasons for her selection, King Alejandro had calmed down.

Levi suspected Cassie's father recognized he wouldn't be here to see the fruits of his daughter's labors and, ultimately, had decided to trust her decision.

Cassie opened her door. "Can you come in for a minute?"

"Sure." He followed her inside. "What do you think? Did that go better or worse than you expected?"

"Honestly, I didn't expect to tell him so soon."

"I know."

"You know?" Cassie's eyebrows drew together. "Why did you do that? You had to know I wanted to prepare before meeting with my father."

"I know you were already prepared and that you would have wasted all day stressing over meeting with him," Levi said. "Now it's done."

Cassie folded her arms across her chest. "I should be mad at you right now."

Levi closed the distance between them and put both hands on her shoulders. He kneaded the muscles where her tension had settled. "You should be, but you aren't because you know I'm right."

"How did you get to know me so well in such a short time?"

"You let me." He leaned down for a kiss. He had meant to keep it brief, but the moment his lips touched hers, he couldn't resist pulling her closer. Her arms dropped to her side before lifting to rest at his waist. The gentle touch sent ripples of pleasure through him, his heartbeat quickening.

He deepened the kiss, drawing her closer still. His fingers tangled in her hair, the stress of the past few days falling away.

She was home, and he was startled by the thought that so was he. Wherever she was, that was where he wanted to be.

He pulled back and gave her one more quick kiss. "I don't suppose I'm allowed to do that in front of anyone, am I?"

"I'm afraid not," Cassie said. "I already miss being us."

"We're still us," Levi assured her. "We just aren't going to be us in public."

"Right. I'll try to remember that."

"I'd better go find Jeremy and get the latest updates. Will you be okay here by yourself?"

"Yes. I need to work on the press conference for tomorrow, and I thought I would drop a couple fake hints in the news about where I'm hiding out."

"Where are you today?"

"I was thinking Malta. I have a few photos I can leak that will keep the attention diverted away from here."

"That's a good idea. Can we meet for lunch?"

"I'd like that. Come by when you're ready, and we can order something up from the kitchen."

"I have a kitchen in my suite. Maybe Jeremy can help me get some groceries so we can avoid letting your staff know you're here for a little longer."

"Whatever works," Cassie said. "Come by whenever you're ready."

"Okay." Levi leaned down for a goodbye kiss. "See you later."

Levi exited Cassie's suite to find Theo standing across the hall.

"Sir, His Majesty has requested you come to his quarters."

"Are you sure? I was just there."

"Quite sure."

"Okay." Levi followed him to the door Levi and Cassie had exited only a few minutes earlier.

Theo knocked twice and opened the door. "He will meet you in the living room."

"Thank you." Levi found the king sitting in the same position he had been in when Levi and Cassie had arrived for breakfast.

"You wanted to see me, Your Majesty?" Levi asked. "I thought you had an eight-thirty meeting."

"You are my eight-thirty."

"I wasn't aware we had an appointment."

"Please, sit down." He waved to the seat opposite him. "We have a few matters to discuss."

Levi sat. "I'm listening."

"I understand you are the person who told Cassie about the change in my health."

"Yes, sir. I'm very sorry," Levi said. "And I'm sorry I denied you the opportunity to tell her in your own way, but we had to explore every potential motive against your daughter. The ascension to the throne was a logical possibility."

"And you have since discounted that possibility, favoring the idea that profit was behind the assassination attempt."

"One doesn't necessarily exclude the other."

"So you think my daughter may still be in danger even after the announcement of the drilling rights is made."

"I think it is my job to be diligent and explore every avenue to ensure your daughter's safety as well as the safety of you and the rest of your family."

"I appreciate that sentiment." King Alejandro set aside the papers he held. "Tell me, how did you come to uncover the information about my illness?"

"I'm sorry, but I can't reveal my sources, even to you."

"You're doing a lot of apologizing," King Alejandro said.

Levi didn't respond. For Cassie's sake, he wanted to be on good terms with her father, but regardless of Levi's loyalties, he couldn't abandon the fundamental truth that compromising sources was the fastest way to lose them.

King Alejandro tapped a finger on his knee. "Does my daughter know you are intelligence?"

Levi battled the instinct to deny it. The king might not know Levi was CIA, but the information they had discussed this morning had already revealed he had knowledge that went well beyond what a security guard would be able to access. "Not exactly."

"Which leads me to my next question. What are your intentions toward my daughter?"

"My intention is to do everything I can to keep her safe and happy."

"I find it interesting that you put her safety before her happiness."

"As do you," Levi said. "Otherwise, you wouldn't have sent her to Meridia."

"True," King Alejandro conceded. "I am more concerned about your personal relationship with my daughter. After speaking with her this morning, I suspect she has developed feelings for you."

Though his first reaction was to demand privacy in his relationship with Cassie, he had to remind himself that this wasn't only the king but her father too. "I have feelings for her as well. I don't have to tell you that your daughter is a bright, talented, and intriguing woman."

"And beautiful."

"She is that too," Levi agreed.

"You have worked with the royal family in Meridia for some time."

"That's correct."

"Then you know the pressure that comes when a royal develops a relationship with anyone, particularly a commoner."

"I am aware." Levi straightened. "I am also adept at staying out of the spotlight. Believe me, I have no interest in bringing unnecessary attention to your daughter or our feelings for each other."

"Are you prepared for the aftermath of what will happen if your efforts are unsuccessful?"

"Probably not, but I'm willing to deal with whatever comes. Your daughter is worth the effort."

"I couldn't agree more."

CHAPTER 34

CASSIE WALKED DOWN THE HALL, Theo on one side of her, Levi on the other. With each step, her sense of unease increased. For the past day and a half, she had remained in her private quarters, invisible to all except a few members of the royal guard, Levi, and her father. Now here she was, about to walk through the front hall, where lives had been lost, where her own life had almost ended.

She glanced at the artwork as she passed, her forward progress slowing.

"Are you okay?" Levi asked.

She nodded because it was expected, even though it wasn't true.

Levi took her by the elbow and came to a stop. Holding her in place, he spoke to Theo. "She needs a minute. Please make sure the main hall is clear."

"I'm okay," Cassie insisted.

"You're about to appear in front of the international press corps as the representative for your country." Levi turned her to face him. "You need a minute to deal with your anxiety before you step out in front of the crowd."

"Does it show that much?" Cassie asked.

"No, but I know you that well," Levi said. "We avoided the front entrance when we arrived, and you haven't talked about what happened in days." He gave her arm an encouraging squeeze. "You can do this. I'll be with you the whole way."

Cassie nodded again. This was a new day, but she couldn't quite shake the sense of déjà vu. Sure, Levi was beside her instead of her father, but that didn't change the truth. She was taking the same walk to the same place with someone she loved.

That thought startled her enough that her gaze lifted to Levi's and held. She loved him. How had this happened?

Concern reflected on Levi's face. "You're too pale. If you can't do this right now, we can do a televised conference from your private quarters or relocate the press to the ballroom."

"No." Cassie took a deep breath. "I can do this."

Theo returned to where they stood. "Everyone is in place, and the area is secure."

A new wave of anxiety tangled with the unfamiliar insecurity that came from knowing someone else held a piece of her heart. With a new resolve, she lifted her chin and started forward once more.

They reached the spot where she had taken cover during the shooting, the suit of armor that had been instrumental in protecting her from the assassins' bullets no longer present.

Cassie kept going. She entered the main hall; it looked like it always had before that awful night. The bullet holes in the walls were gone, and she couldn't see any trace of blood from the dead and wounded.

Her steps quickened only to slow again when they approached the reception hall, where the press conference would be held.

Levi put his hand on her back, a silent signal of support.

"The executives from Axion are already on stage," Theo said. "Are you ready, Your Highness?"

"Yes. Thank you, Theo."

Theo stepped through the door. A moment later, she heard his voice come through the microphone. "Ladies and gentlemen, may I present Her Royal Highness, Princess Cassandra of Sereno."

The rustle of fabric and the scraping of chairs sounded. Cassie waited a brief moment before entering, not surprised to find the entire audience standing.

She moved onto the stage and stepped behind the double podium that had been set up for today's address. "Members of the press and honored guests, thank you for coming."

The few whispers in the crowd ceased, and a hush came over the room. "I am here to announce a partnership between Sereno and Axion Oil to harvest the rich resources of natural gas and oil in our coastal waters. Mr. Keith Maloney has joined us today for the official signing of the agreement."

Cassie motioned to Keith. "Mr. Maloney, would you please join me at the podium?"

Keith stood and took his position beside her where a second microphone had been set up for his use.

Hands immediately shot up.

Though she was well versed in dealing with the media, rarely had she acted as the family spokesperson. She mentally went through the simple lessons she had learned from childhood. Shoulders back, speak slowly and clearly, look people in the eye.

She motioned to a man in his forties. "Your question, sir."

"I know several companies were being considered for the drilling rights. Who made the final decision?"

"The decision was mine." Cassie motioned to a woman in her late thirties.

"I am surprised the contract is being awarded to an American company. How does your father feel about that?"

"My father entrusted this decision to me because of my knowledge of resource management. He supports the agreement I have made."

Cassie and Keith entertained several more questions, many of them regarding the impact on Sereno when drilling began and the precautions that would be required to protect against potential spills.

When the question-and-answer portion of the press conference concluded, Cassie and Keith moved to the table where two copies of the agreement had been set out. Keith signed the copy on his side at the same time Cassie signed hers.

They straightened, and Cassie offered her hand to Keith. He shook it, holding on to her hand until the photographers' flashes faded.

"Your Highness, thank you again. I look forward to the future this agreement can create for both of us."

"As do I."

* * *

Julien watched the televised announcement. The princess was home.

His phone rang, the number for the chief executive officer of Satori Oil lighting his screen. Julien ignored the call. He already knew what the man was going to say. Julien had all but guaranteed Satori would get the drilling rights in Sereno.

No matter. Once Julien was in power, he could either cancel the contract with Axion and give the rights to Satori, or he could expose Satori's involvement in the assassination attempt. After all, no one could prove Julien had anything to do with the shooting.

His phone rang again, and again, he ignored it. He left the television on and crossed the room to sit at his desk. A few keystrokes on his laptop brought up the spreadsheet he used to track his finances. The money he had collected off the life insurance policies from the deaths of his parents had dwindled significantly over the past few months. Maybe he should have kept more than a 10-percent cut of the bank robbery money, but at the time he planned the heists, he had been faced with the simple fact that there was no honor among thieves.

Pratt had insisted the only way to enlist the help of so many top-end bank robbers was to guarantee them the majority of the take. Pratt had been right about that. The bank robbers had all taken their cuts and disappeared into the wind. Of course, Pratt had the added incentive of choosing people who would follow his directions since he had earned 5 percent of the proceeds as well. Julien supposed that was a small price to pay for the man doing all the legwork.

Until now, Julien had needed to ensure his anonymity. If things progressed as he hoped, he would step out of the shadows soon.

It was a shame that Sereno had awarded the drilling rights since Julien wouldn't be able to use Satori as a means to hire assassins again. He still had options, he assured himself. The princess was home, he thought again. Perhaps it was time he joined her.

CHAPTER 35

THE STAFF KNEW SHE WAS back. Levi had dreaded this moment, not only because of the increased security concerns but also because of the constant presence of household staff in the residential wing. How were he and Cassie supposed to have a personal conversation with maids and assistants constantly interrupting? It seemed to him Cassie's private quarters should remain exactly that: private.

Over the past three days, he had learned the routines and policies of the royal guard. It hadn't taken him long to understand how the assassins had managed to bypass the main gate and penetrate the second layer of guards. Security's strict protocols ensured everyone would be at their post, but those same protocols made guard movements predictable.

Jeremy and Noelle had done a good job of creating new security procedures and installing enhanced motion detectors along the perimeter of the palace grounds, but Levi wanted another layer of protection. He didn't want Cassie to ever experience the kind of trauma that had befallen her the night of the shooting again.

Levi approached the central portion of the palace, where Cassie's private office was located on the second floor, with the royal administrative offices. He stepped into the outer sanctum where a woman in her late twenties sat behind an antique desk, a slim laptop resting atop it, along with an office phone.

"You must be Anastasia," Levi said, naming Cassie's personal assistant. "I'm Levi Marin."

"May I help you?"

"Is she in?" Levi asked, waving at Cassie's closed office door.

"Do you have an appointment?"

"No, I don't."

"Can you tell me what this is regarding?"

Levi suppressed a sigh. Why couldn't he have fallen for someone living a normal life, someone who wasn't surrounded by red tape and danger?

"I'm part of the princess's new security team," Levi said. "Would you please inform Princess Cassandra that I wish to see her?"

"I'm sorry, sir, but without an appointment . . ." Anastasia trailed off when the door opened.

"Levi." Cassie's cheeks colored slightly. "Were you looking for me?"

"I am looking for you," Levi said. "Do you have a minute?"

"Yes, of course." Cassie gestured to her office before focusing on Anastasia. "Could you please set up a meeting with Keith Maloney for tomorrow?"

"Yes, Your Highness."

Levi followed Cassie into her office and closed the door behind her. He glanced around the large room, noting the stacks of papers on the worktable to his left and the open laptop on her desk.

"Are we really alone?" Levi asked.

She smiled. "Yes, we are alone."

His earlier objective forgotten, he closed the distance between them and slid his arms around her waist. "I've missed you."

"I've missed you too." Her hands lifted to rest on his shoulders, and she rose to her toes.

Their lips met, and Levi let himself fall. Every connection he had experienced with Cassie before strengthened, binding up his heart until it no longer belonged to him. Warmth started in his chest and spread outward, visions of forever hovering on the edge of his thoughts.

He pulled back, not sure he was ready to think about the challenges a future with Cassie could bring. He edged back a half step. "I'm starting to think I'm going to have to schedule an appointment to have alone time with you."

"My mom used to say the same thing to my dad."

"Occupational hazard, I guess."

"I'm afraid so." She dropped her hands. "What brings you by today? I thought you were working with Jeremy."

"I was, but I want to do a check of the extended grounds and hoped you might want to join me."

"On horseback?"

"That was my thought."

"I'd love to." She turned her laptop to face her and opened her schedule. "How long do you think we will be?"

"How much time can you spare?"

"None, but I need a break," Cassie said. "My father is having an infusion this afternoon, so I should be able to push my afternoon appointments to later in the week."

Cassie picked up her office phone. "Anastasia, I need you to clear my schedule this afternoon." She paused. "Thank you."

"All set?"

"Yes. Let me call the stables and have them saddle a couple horses for us."

"I'll take care of that," Levi said. "You go change. I'll meet you outside your suite in ten minutes."

"You really think I can get to my room and change in ten minutes?"

"I know you can." Levi leaned in for a quick kiss. "That's one of the many things I love about you."

Her cheeks flushed again.

Levi put his hand on the doorknob. "Come on. I'll escort you to your room to make sure no one tries to hijack you."

"You have your work cut out for you."

"Don't I know it."

* * *

Cassie hadn't realized how much she needed this. Fresh air, a horse beneath her, the man she loved riding beside her. Her cheeks warmed at the memory of Levi's earlier comment. If he loved her different traits, was that a precursor to him loving her?

And if so, what would their future look like?

To her surprise, her father had said little about Levi since meeting him. She had expected him to grill her for information about their relationship until he was satisfied Levi's feelings mirrored hers.

"What are you thinking about?" Levi asked as they walked their horses through a wide pasture.

"I'm surprised my father has been so well behaved regarding your presence."

"What do you mean?"

"You're staying in the royal residence, and he knows I think of you as more than a friend. I figured he'd be questioning me constantly about your intentions."

"He didn't need to. He asked me directly."

She reined in her horse and shifted in her saddle to face him. "He did what?"

Levi stopped beside her. "Right after breakfast that first morning."

"Why didn't you say anything?"

"It wasn't a big deal." Levi started forward. "I was impressed that he cares about you so much."

"What did he say?" Cassie asked as soon as she caught up to him.

"We chatted and got to know each other a bit."

"You had a private audience with the King of Sereno, and you didn't think it was a big deal?"

"I had a private conversation with my girlfriend's father," Levi corrected. "There was nothing royal about it."

A new appreciation for Levi rose within her. "I love that you can tell the difference between the man and the title."

"It isn't that hard."

"It is for a lot of people." She reined her horse in once more as she reached the top of a bluff overlooking the Mediterranean. From here, she could see the water without approaching the cliffs. "I love this spot."

"It's beautiful." He came to a stop beside her. "But, then, so are you."

Cassie saw him lean toward her for a kiss. "We're visible."

Levi instantly straightened and looked out at the horizon. A few motorboats dotted the blue water.

"I'm sorry," Cassie said. "I know I'm being paranoid, but the paparazzi have been known to sit out on those boats with their cameras aimed at the palace grounds."

Levi's jaw tightened, and Cassie could see him force his muscles to relax. "I'm not a fan of your title at the moment."

"Me neither." Cassie turned her horse. "Come on. There's another spot I think you'll like better."

They rode along the edge of the royal land that sloped to the beach. When they reached an outcropping of trees, Cassie led the way down a narrow trail to her secret spot, one only known to her immediate family.

They reached the small opening in the trees where a stone gazebo had been built when she was five.

She dismounted and looped her horse's reins around the branch of a nearby tree. "This is my favorite spot."

"I can see why." Levi dismounted and approached the structure. "It's like the rest of the world doesn't exist here."

"Which is why I love it." She walked beside him and climbed the three steps. Choosing her favorite bench, she sat and pointed at the break in the trees where the Mediterranean was visible. "I can see the water, but no one can see me." She paused and looked at him. "It's like your favorite place at the chateau."

"It is." Levi sat beside her and took her hand. "I guess we both like our privacy."

The oddity of his statement struck her. "If you like your privacy, why did you decide to get a job with the royals? That's a sure way to put yourself in the spotlight whether you want it or not."

"I guess you could say I sort of fell into it." His gaze met hers. "I have to say, I'm glad now that I did."

"Me too."

CHAPTER 36

ALEJANDRO SAT BEHIND HIS ANTIQUE desk, the mahogany surface clear except for a single file. The oddity of Cassie finding out about his illness from the Meridian royal family had raised his concerns, enough so that he had insisted on personally reviewing Darius's most recent report on the staff and his medical personnel. With the exception of the Canadian doctor his physician had brought in for a consult, everyone in the residence had worked for the royal family since before his wife had passed away.

The file in front of him included the information on everyone of concern, besides Dr. Lewis and Levi. Those analyses would be ready later today.

His desk phone rang. He hit the intercom button. "Yes?"

"Princess Cassandra is here to see you," his secretary said.

"Send her in."

A moment later, Cassie entered holding a file folder. "Can I get your opinion on something?"

"Of course." Alejandro motioned toward the chair across from him. "What is it?"

"Actually, it's two things." Cassie sat. "First, I would like to explore the possibility of building a resort outside Porto Blu."

"On our land?"

"Yes. We own more than twenty miles of that beachfront," Cassie said. "I'd like to use the section closest to town for a resort. With the increase in tourism we expect, I believe it would be a wise investment."

"Looking to diversify our holdings?"

"I am. Between the oil industry that will expand here and the possibility of the wind farm, I think it would be wise to diversify into something beyond energy and relying on our tax base."

"I agree." He noted the flush of pleasure in his daughter's cheeks. "Speak with your uncle Elliott about having designs developed."

"I will. Thank you."

"You said there were two things."

She offered him the file folder she held. "Levi asked me to give this to you."

He took it from her and opened the file. The evidence inside left no doubt as to who the inside source had been: a $10,000 deposit into Leon Cordova's Swiss bank account six months ago, followed by another $50,000 three days before the shooting.

As much as Alejandro wanted to trust his staff's loyalty, after seeing the evidence against Cordova, his confidence wavered.

"It appears your friend has found the culprit."

"He isn't convinced Cordova was the only person involved, but as he says, it's his job to keep looking." Cassie took a deep breath and straightened her shoulders, a sure sign she was preparing to ask for something. He missed the days when a pony was the golden prize.

"What is it?" Alejandro asked.

"Levi has been here for two weeks now. I would like to make his position official."

"What did you have in mind?" Alejandro closed the file and focused solely on his daughter. "I already have a captain of the guard, and Levi doesn't strike me as someone who is going to be happy working for someone else."

"That's true. He's been running the security at the chateau for the past two years," Cassie said. "I have something else in mind."

"Such as?"

"Well, dating someone who works for me would raise all sorts of issues, both personally and professionally."

"Not to mention the media when the story breaks."

"Precisely," Cassie said. "I propose he be hired as a security consultant."

"Whether you call him a consultant or an employee, he's still going to be working for you, and we'll still be paying him."

"That's true, but I believe the distinction is an important one, especially if our personal relationship continues as I hope it will."

Twenty-six years flashed through his memory. The moment Cassie was born, her first step, her debutante ball, the day she graduated from college, and so many other moments in between. His baby had grown up, and he'd barely had time to blink.

Alejandro forced himself to ask the dreaded question. "What are you hoping for?"

"The same thing I've always hoped for." Cassie's blush returned. "I want a happily ever after."

"You're in love with him."

"Yes."

"I see." And he did see. The confidence Cassie drew from Levi's presence, the adoration in Levi's eyes anytime he let his guard down, their afternoon rides together. "I will leave it to your discretion on how you want to handle his employment contract, but I must insist his living arrangements be adjusted."

"I realize having him in the residence can create an air of favoritism, but I truly don't feel safe when he isn't nearby."

"What about the tower apartment? It's close by but not officially part of the royal residence."

"That could work," Cassie said, clearly considering. "From the back staircase, he would be able to get here within a minute or two."

"He would be close enough but not too close to generate inappropriate rumors."

"Believe me, if there is one thing I know about Levi, it's that he prefers to be invisible if at all possible."

A knock sounded on his door. "Come."

Darius entered, a look of apology lighting his face when he saw Cassandra. "I'm sorry, Your Majesty. I can come back."

"It's okay, Darius," Alejandro said. "What is it?"

"I have that information for you."

That information, meaning the latest background check on the man her daughter was in love with. "Cassie, can you excuse us for a minute?"

"Of course." Cassie stood. "I need to get back to work anyway. I'll bring that contract over for you to review as soon as I finish it."

"Thank you." Alejandro waited for Cassie to leave the room before he took the file Darius held. "Anything new?"

"I'm afraid so." Darius clasped his hands in front of him. "I'm sorry, sire. This new information was not easy to find."

Alejandro flipped open the file and scanned the first page. "You think Dr. Lewis is the one who leaked my medical condition?"

"Inadvertently, yes. We believe the CIA intercepted an email between Dr. Lewis and Dr. Marois," Darius said. "Since Dr. Lewis's specialty is assisting high-profile patients with terminal cancer, we believe his presence raised a red flag with someone in the American intelligence community."

"So, the CIA knows I'm dying."

"It appears so." Darius clasped his hands together. "You will find more information in the file that I believe reveals another matter of which you need to be aware."

"Thank you, Darius."

Darius bowed his head and left the room.

Alejandro flipped the page to read through the report on Levi. He made it only to the second line before the pieces of the puzzle fell into place. He read through the information twice, hoping to find proof that the data could be faulty, but the facts remained. Levi was keeping secrets, and the man who Cassie hoped to build a future with was about to break his daughter's heart.

* * *

Levi crossed the flagstone that made up the patio outside the ballroom doors. He examined those doors now, checking the new motion detectors to ensure they were functioning properly and weren't noticeable. He could easily imagine a royal ball on the other side of the glass, the doors open and couples in formal attire spilling outside to enjoy the ocean breeze.

From where he stood, the Mediterranean spread out before him, the palace grounds high enough to provide protection against flooding but low enough to make the water appear in reach. In truth, the private beach was a fifteen-minute walk, which explained the paved path that connected the beach with the palace. Golf carts appeared to be the preferred mode of transportation to the beach, but during his first two weeks here, Levi had yet to see anyone make use of the sandy stretch of land.

The investigation into the shooting and the robberies had not yielded anything new during his time in Sereno. The lack of information concerned him. Someone had gone to a great deal of trouble and had employed a significant number of people to put something in play. Even though he couldn't identify the location of Raymond Escobar, Levi had to believe he was the man behind both crimes. A play for the throne was the only motive that made sense.

Levi took note of one surveillance camera that he needed to adjust to eliminate a blind spot on the terrace. He had to admit that overall, Jeremy and Noelle had done a good job with implementing the security enhancements. Another week or so and he would be ready to run some training exercises to make sure they had plugged all the gaps.

Levi rounded the corner of the palace and noticed a car parked by the main entrance, the trunk open.

Then Jeremy emerged from the palace, followed by Noelle.

Levi closed the distance between them. "What's going on?"

"I was about to call you." Jeremy loaded his suitcase into the trunk. "We have to leave for Bellamo."

"Is everything okay?"

"We received a tip that Dimitri Breuer arrived in Meridia this morning."

"Isn't he the guy who pulled off the theft in Paris last year?"

"Yeah. Over $3 million worth of diamonds disappeared from Lisbon."

The memory of the false alarm at the museum triggered in Levi's brain. He retrieved his phone and called Pierre. No answer.

He checked his watch. Four o'clock. The museum would still be open. Even if Pierre was unable to answer his phone, his assistant should have picked up. Levi checked his watch again, and this time, he noticed the date. Undoubtedly, Pierre was preparing for the exhibit.

Levi tried again but called Janessa. Again, no answer.

"Jeremy, try calling your sister." As Jeremy dialed, Levi made another call, punching in the number for the chateau security office. He let it ring seven times before he hung up.

"She didn't answer," Jeremy said. "That's not like her."

"Maybe the cell tower is down," Noelle suggested.

"No one is answering at the security office either," Jeremy said. "Someone must have interrupted the phone service."

"I'm sure Janessa or someone at the chateau is aware of it," Noelle said.

"Not necessarily," Levi countered. "There's a huge exhibit opening tonight. With everyone attending, they aren't going to be calling each other. Most of the royal family will be together in the same place."

"And since the royal guard uses a closed frequency, they won't realize anything is wrong," Noelle finished for him.

"Right."

"We'd better go." Jeremy shouldered his backpack.

Though Levi's sense of loyalty to the Meridian royal family demanded he accompany Jeremy and Noelle, his protective instincts wouldn't let him leave Cassie. "When you get there, ask Pierre about the display from Sereno. It may be the target."

"I'll call the police to see if they can get a message to him. I'll be in touch as soon as we get the phones figured out."

"Good luck."

"Thanks."

Levi headed back inside and spotted Darius. "Tell King Alejandro I need to speak to him. It's urgent."

"May I tell him what it's regarding?" Darius asked. "The king is not fond of people demanding an audience."

"It's a matter of your national security." Levi paused only long enough for Darius to dial his phone. Not waiting to listen to the conversation, Levi headed for the residence. It was time to have a conversation with King Alejandro about how to stop whoever wanted his daughter, or possibly daughters, dead.

CHAPTER 37

LEVI REACHED THE KING'S OFFICE, where Theo was standing in the hall. "King Alejandro is waiting for you."

"Thank you." Levi passed the king's personal assistant and knocked once. As soon as he heard the king grant permission for him to enter, Levi pushed open the door. "King Alejandro, I appreciate your making time to meet with me."

"Darius said it was urgent."

"It is. I need to know what you sent to Meridia for their art exhibit."

"Excuse me?"

Levi recognized the posturing as well as King Alejandro's surprise at being on the other end of someone's demands. "It's important."

"I don't see how a piece in an art exhibit relates to the safety and security of my family."

"Tell me this," Levi began, trying another tactic, "does it have anything to do with the agreement with the Escobar family?"

"When I told Cassie to share that information, I believed you were an employee of the Meridian royal guard." Alejandro's jaw tightened. "You didn't work for them exclusively though, did you?"

The accusation in the king's tone caused a ball of lead to form in his stomach. Levi told the truth, skillfully evading the underlying accusation. "I have not worked anywhere but at the chateau in Meridia for the past two years."

"I'm not speaking of where you worked but for whom."

Cassie rushed into the room. "What's going on? I heard Jeremy and Noelle are leaving."

"A well-known international thief was spotted in Meridia," Levi told her, hoping she could pry the information from her father. "You remember the false alarm at the museum in Bellamo?"

"Yes. What about it?"

"Pierre mentioned a display from Sereno that had never before been seen in public."

"I remember," Cassie said. "He said it was being stored somewhere else until the complete exhibit opened."

"I think that false alarm was someone testing the security system to prepare for the real theft," Levi said. "With the bank robberies, I have to wonder if the piece on loan from here is tied to the Escobar agreement."

"Why would my family choose to display anything to do with that?" Cassie asked. "The secrecy of the agreement has protected us from the interference of outside forces for years."

Levi saw the flash of awareness in the king's expression. "What does the agreement say that Cassie doesn't know about?"

"This is a private family matter, one I will not discuss with you," the king said.

"Papa," Cassie protested. "Levi is here to help us."

"To help us, or to spy on us?" Alejandro's eyes met Levi's. "Would you like to tell her who you really are, or shall I?"

Levi's tongue lodged in the back of his throat. Had Alejandro learned of his association with the CIA or simply of his extensive involvement with Meridia's intelligence service?

"Your friend here is an American."

"What?" Cassie shook her head. "He's from Meridia."

"No, my dear, he is not." Alejandro spoke the words as though they were poison on his tongue. "Levi Marin is an agent with the CIA. He is an American spy."

Levi's eyes darted to Cassie, and he silently pleaded for her to forgive him for the deceit.

Cassie's mouth opened and closed once before she managed to speak. "Is this true?"

"My assignment to protect you came from the Meridian royal family. I have answered primarily to them since arriving in Bellamo two years ago."

"But they aren't the only people you answer to," Alejandro said.

Levi fought against the lump in his throat and forced himself to speak the truth. "No."

"You have been playing me this whole time?"

"No, Cassie, I haven't."

"That's Princess Cassandra to you." Her chin tilted up, and her royal mask fell into place. "I can't believe I trusted you." Her hand lifted, and she motioned to the door. "I believe you know your way out."

"Don't do this," Levi pleaded. "My feelings for you are genuine. I'm not here to spy on you. I'm here to protect you."

"Then why did you plant a tracking device on my daughter's computer?" King Alejandro asked.

Levi hesitated a fraction of a second too long, and he knew it. "That was a tool I used to make sure I could find her again in case someone managed to get through our defenses."

"Or you wanted to keep tabs on my daughter's whereabouts for your agency."

"No. The CIA doesn't have access to the tracking code. They don't even know about it."

"I find that hard to believe."

"It's true. I love your daughter. I would never do anything to hurt her."

"I believe you already have." Alejandro nodded toward the door. "As Princess Cassandra said, you know your way out. Darius can make arrangements for your transportation back to Meridia. From there, where you go no longer concerns us."

Levi looked from Alejandro to Cassandra to find twin stares of animosity. As much as he wanted to convince Cassie of his affection, he knew she was beyond listening to him. Levi's jaw clenched, and he took a step back. Without another word, he turned and left the room.

* * *

The door to her father's apartment closed, and Cassie's heart shattered into a thousand pieces. From the day they had met, Levi had succeeded in chipping away at her royal facade to find the woman so few people really knew, and now she knew the truth about him. Levi had been deceiving her all this time.

For weeks, she had hoped he would someday come to love her. In her wildest imagination, she never could have anticipated hearing that declaration delivered quite like this. Not that she believed him for a minute. He had fooled her at a time when she needed to trust her judgment more than ever.

She blinked rapidly three times, the only outward sign of the tempest of emotions raging inside her.

"An American spy in my house and an American company in our business. I never thought I would live to see the day."

"Papa, I'm so sorry."

"He fooled us all," Alejandro said, compassion and frustration both evident on his face. "Tell me, though, how much influence did he have over who received the drilling rights here in Sereno?"

Suspicions bloomed, along with a searing pain that radiated through her entire body "He provided the information about Satori Oil. If he faked the reports . . ."

"He didn't," Alejandro assured her. "Darius did his own investigation and confirmed what Levi told you."

"At least he was honest about that," Cassie said. "How did you know Levi wasn't who he said he was?"

"He knew about my illness."

Cassie's eyebrows drew together in confusion.

"The information about my medical condition has been tightly held. When I had Darius look into how it could have been leaked, our security team discovered the CIA had intercepted some communication between my physician and a specialist he consulted with."

"That's it?" Cassie asked. "You figured out Levi was CIA because he knows you have cancer?"

"That and his birth record wasn't included in his background check. Darius found it today."

Cassie absorbed the facts and tried to reconcile them with the kindhearted man she had fallen in love with. His interactions with the chateau staff, the confidence of the Meridian royal family. Everything had indicated he was who he had appeared to be.

"How did King Eduard not know Levi was CIA?" Cassie asked.

"I suspect he did."

"But why wouldn't he tell you?"

"As Levi said, he's been working primarily for the Meridian royal family for two years. They have come to trust him. Obviously, they either didn't consider my aversion to Americans, or they deliberately chose not to tell me."

Cassie thought of the way Levi interacted with the royal guard. "No one ever acted like he was anything but a trusted employee of the royal family."

"Which is why we were so easily fooled." Alejandro reached out and took her hand. "I'm sorry, Cassie. I truly am, but we can't trust a man with your safety who reports to someone else."

"I know." Cassie squeezed his hand before she pulled hers free and stepped back. "I should get back to work."

"Before you do, I have something else we need to discuss."

Cassie's heart sank. All she wanted right now was privacy so she could let her emotions loose. "Can it wait?"

"I'm afraid not," Alejandro said. "Levi was correct about the exhibit in Meridia being tied to the succession agreement."

"What is being displayed?"

"Your future."

"My future?"

Alejandro hesitated a moment before he shared more details. "The exhibit in Meridia includes our portion of the succession agreement as well as six of the founding jewels."

"Why would you put those out in the public, and where are the rest of the founding jewels?" Cassie asked.

"Six of the gems were stolen the night of the shooting. The others have been lent out to various museums in Europe for safekeeping," Alejandro said. "The succession agreement will make its rounds to each of the museums to be displayed."

"Why?"

"Because someone in the Escobar family is trying to take over the throne."

"Do you know who?" Cassie asked.

"Yes. And I think I know where."

CHAPTER 38

THE TIGHTNESS IN LEVI'S CHEST increased until he could barely breathe. The guard who had escorted him from the king's apartment had thankfully allowed him privacy in his own quarters to pack.

Levi pulled his suitcases from his closet and tossed them on the bed. One bounced twice and tumbled to the floor. Levi left it where it lay and closed his eyes as he fought against the despair that threatened to drown him. He loved Cassie. He hadn't realized how much until the moment their possible future had been ripped away from him.

Levi looked around the bedroom he had come to think of as his own. He knew when he arrived, he wouldn't stay here indefinitely, but he had envisioned moving to another section of the palace once the security enhancements were complete. Now he knew the palace would never be his home.

Mentally, he went through the checklist of the remaining items to be completed for the security upgrades. The new fencing would arrive early next week, and the motion detectors on the beach would be installed tomorrow. Five more days were all he needed to complete the latest round of upgrades.

Darius had proven to be a good man, quick to incorporate the improvements, but that didn't change the fact that Levi was being forced to entrust Cassie's safety to another. If only the king hadn't discovered his true identity.

Levi opened the suitcase on the bed and removed his weapon cases. Systematically, he collected his belongings and packed them. He completed his task and stacked his luggage by the door before the question surfaced: How did King Alejandro know Levi was CIA?

Levi's cover story had been in place so long, no one should have been able to penetrate it, at least not without the Agency seeing some significant red flags. Had King Eduard told King Alejandro, or had Cassandra's father learned some other way?

His phone rang, and Director Palmer's number lit up the screen. Maybe those red flags had been flying and no one had managed to tell Levi in time.

Levi answered the phone. "Did you already hear the news?"

"If you're talking about an Escobar living in Sereno, yes."

"A member of the Escobar family is here?" Levi asked. "Who? Where is he?"

"Raymond Escobar is going by Theo Nalar. From what I can tell, he appears to be working inside the palace."

"He is." Panic streaked through him. For the past two weeks, Levi had focused on protecting Cassie and her family from outside threats. How had he, Interpol, and the royal guard all missed that the danger lurking within the palace walls was the king's personal assistant?

"Apparently, he disappeared after his father passed away. One of our analysts managed to track him to a fishing village in Italy. A few days later, Theo Nalar surfaced at the port in Sereno. A day after that, he was inside the palace."

"Why would he have waited so long to make his move against the royal family?" Levi said, talking more to himself than to the director.

"Make his move for what? Why did you have us looking into the Escobar family?"

Levi realized he had said more than he should have. Even though Cassie and her father wanted nothing more to do with him, Levi couldn't bring himself to break the confidence. "Director, I'm going to have to call you back."

"There's something—"

Levi hung up and pocketed his phone. Whatever the director had to say would have to wait. For now, he had to find Theo.

He opened the door, and Darius was waiting in the hall.

"I've been instructed to escort you off the grounds," Darius said.

"Where's Theo?"

"That's none of your concern."

"The princess is in danger." Levi's frustration level hiked up another notch. "At least post a guard at her door until Theo is questioned."

Though Darius didn't respond, the flash of concern on the man's face sent alarm bells off in Levi's head. "Where is Princess Cassandra?"

"A car is waiting outside the front gate to take you to the airport." Darius reached past him and picked up the two weapons cases. "Please collect the rest of your belongings."

Levi looked down at the two suitcases. As soon as he left the guest suite, he would be escorted until he was off the grounds. He couldn't leave now, not until Cassie knew of the danger.

His grip tightened on his cell phone. "I forgot my phone charger in the bedroom. I'll be right back."

Levi left the front door to the apartment open and retreated through the living area. As soon as he reached the bedroom, he closed and locked the door. He crossed the room, passed the phone charger that was indeed still plugged in beside the bed, and opened the door leading to the balcony.

He looked out and analyzed the guards' movements below. Even if he could find a break in the coverage on this side of the palace, he had made sure no one could use Cassie's balcony as a point of entry. Since his room was beside hers, he had inadvertently left himself without a means of escape.

"Levi, time to go." Darius's voice carried through his apartment.

If Darius was inside Levi's quarters . . .

Levi's thoughts raced, and his action followed. He grabbed his phone cord, hurried outside onto the balcony, and pulled the french doors closed behind him. He then used the cord to tie the two handles together to create another barrier between himself and Darius.

A knock sounded on Levi's bedroom door.

Levi checked out the only guard visible below. The man's back was turned, his focus on the wide expanse of lawn that separated this side of the palace and the ocean that lay beyond.

Levi put his hand on the stone railing that separated his balcony from Cassie's. With another glance at the guard below, Levi climbed the four-foot-tall barrier and ducked down outside Cassie's balcony door.

He curtailed the instinct to knock before entering Cassie's apartment, afraid that the guard or Darius would hear him.

He pulled on the door handle, but it was locked. He retrieved his lockpick kit from his pocket and, ten seconds later, opened the door.

"Cassie?" Levi called out softly. No answer. He pushed the gauzy white curtains aside and closed the door behind him. "Cassie?"

His gaze swept over her bedroom. Walls the color of toasted almonds, a mahogany bed offset by an off-white bedspread, and a love seat in pale blue. The laptop on the bedside table told him what he already suspected; Cassie wasn't in the residence.

Ever thorough, Levi passed through her bedroom and checked the main living areas, but they were empty as well.

A shout sounded from the room next door, followed by a loud thud.

A sense of urgency enveloped him. He had to find Cassie before anyone stopped him. Or he had to at least find Theo.

An alert sounded on his phone. Levi glanced down. A proximity alarm had triggered along the east perimeter, the same place the new fencing was being installed. Had a construction worker strayed a little too far from the construction zone, or did Theo have friends here to help eliminate Cassie? Unwilling to take any chances, Levi headed for the door. With any luck, Darius was still in his quarters, which meant he wasn't in the hall.

* * *

Shouts sounded from the hall. A heavy fist pounded on the door.

Alejandro set aside the report he held. "Come."

Darius rushed into the room. "Levi is gone."

"Define 'gone.'"

"I escorted him to his quarters to pack. When I went inside a couple minutes later, he was gone. It looks like he escaped through the balcony doors."

"Find him. He can't have gone far."

"There's something else," Darius said. "Levi asked about Theo and wanted me to put a guard on Princess Cassandra. Levi insisted your daughter is in danger."

Alejandro's heart picked up speed. Had Levi misinterpreted information he had uncovered, or was a new threat present?

"Sire, the last time I saw Theo, he was with the princess."

Alejandro's hand fisted. Had he made a mistake in giving Theo a place in his home? Or was Levi jumping to conclusions? Alejandro couldn't take a chance with his daughter's safety. "Find Cassandra. I want her back inside her apartment with two guards posted until we sort this out."

"Yes, Your Majesty." Darius took a step back as his cell phone rang.

Alejandro waved his hand to give permission for Darius to answer.

"Yes?" Darius paused, a new level of concern entering his voice when he asked, "Where?"

Another pause. "Find Princess Cassandra. Tell her she is needed in the residence immediately."

Darius hung up the phone. "A sensor alarm triggered along the east wall."

"Near the stables?" Alejandro asked.

"Yes, sire." Darius took a step back. "I will inform you as soon as your daughter returns."

Alejandro swallowed the lump in his throat but couldn't form words. Instead, he nodded his approval and watched Darius leave. Was Levi the cause of the alarm, or had he bypassed the security he had helped create in order to protect his daughter?

The alarm on his phone went off to signal it was time for his next pain pill. Somehow, he doubted the medicine was going to have the desired effect until his daughter was once again safely at his side.

CHAPTER 39

JULIEN STOOD AT THE BASE of the mountain, the trees shielding him from view. From his position above the palace, the royal grounds spread out before him. The white towers of the palace contrasted against the cloudless sky, the grassy expanse creating a natural defense to allow the guards to see anyone who dared approach. Waves rolled up on the beach, the royal yacht docked at the edge of his view. It was a fairy tale in the making, a fairy tale Julien was determined to claim as his own.

Pratt crouched beside him and studied the lay of the land. "Are you sure about this? If you get caught—"

"I'm not taking the chance that this doesn't get done right. If my brother really is here, he could ruin everything we've worked for."

"Yes, but if anyone learns you're involved, you could lose your claim to the throne."

Julien rubbed a gloved hand over his shaved head. "No one will ever know I was here. Besides, you're going to kill the princess. I'm here to tie up my own loose ends."

"You're the boss." Pratt slipped a set of earphones over his head that would allow him to hear the communication among the royal guards.

"Anything?" Julien asked.

"Not yet. If the princess follows her normal routine, she should head to the stables within the next hour."

Julien picked up his binoculars and trained them on the work crew along the east gate. That was their entry point, the one vulnerability that still existed on the palace grounds. It wouldn't be long now. The workers would take their lunch soon, and when they did, Julien would be able to walk right through the gap in their defenses. If he and Pratt had to eliminate a guard or two on their way onto the palace grounds, so much the better.

Julien twisted a silencer onto his pistol. He was ready, and this time, he would succeed.

* * *

Levi slipped down the back staircase, disabled the alarm on one of the ball-room windows, and navigated his way through the blind spot he had discovered only a short time ago.

If he had read Darius's expression correctly, Cassie was no longer with her father. Levi guessed she had left the residence shortly after he'd been escorted out the king's chambers.

Though there were dozens of places she could go on the palace grounds, only one made sense to him: the gazebo.

Assuming his status with the royal guard had changed from guest to enemy, Levi tucked his earpiece into place and used his phone to find the new frequency for the guards' communication. It took him only two tries to find it. That was something else security needed to change. Of course, if they had approved the scrambler he had recommended, he wouldn't be able to track their activity now.

He listened for a moment as the guards orchestrated their movements to compensate for the motion sensor that had sounded. Levi played the guard formations through his mind and chose his course. He pressed his body along-side the palace wall to keep himself out of view of the cameras and made his way to the northeast corner.

Should he hike straight to the gazebo or retrieve a horse? Going on horse-back would certainly be faster, and depending on how long ago Cassie had left the residence, she might still be at the stables.

With a destination in mind, he continued forward. He scanned the area, searching for any movement out of place or any guards who might intercept him. From the voices coming through his headset, security had yet to locate the source of the sensor alarm. He itched to have access to the control room and the video images feeding onto the screens there.

One voice cut through the rest of the chatter on his headset with a sense of urgency. "Intruder on the east side. Looks like he's heading for the stables."

Levi's heart squeezed in his chest. If he was right, whoever was on the grounds was headed straight for Cassie.

* * *

"Well, well, well. If it isn't my big brother." Julien lifted his weapon and took aim. "I have to say that was very clever coming to work for the Rossi family. I never thought to look for you here."

"Put the gun down. I'm not a threat to you."

"Oh, but you are. You and those three princesses are all that stand between me and the throne."

"I abdicated my claim when I came to work here. It was the only way King Eduard would agree to protect me."

"Then he knows."

"He only knows you exist. He doesn't know your name or anything else about you."

"Someone does. Otherwise, I wouldn't have found a surveillance team outside our old apartment in Malmo."

"I don't know what you're talking about. King Alejandro didn't have anything to do with that," Theo insisted. "If he had ordered a surveillance team, I would have known about it."

"Maybe. Or maybe he didn't trust you as much as you believed."

"What do you want?" Theo asked. "You know as well as I do that if you kill any of the heirs, you will lose your claim."

"That's not what the agreement says," Julien said. "It says if a member of the Escobar family kills any of the sons in line for the throne, the agreement will be invalid."

"The law was changed to allow female succession in the royal house thirty years ago."

"The law in Sereno was changed, but the agreement never was." Julien sneered. "As long as I don't kill King Alejandro, I don't have anyone standing in my way. Except you, that is."

"I told you I abdicated my claim to the throne."

"So you say, but I'm not taking any chances." Julien took aim. "It was good seeing you again, Raymond."

Julien squeezed the trigger at the same time his half brother dove for cover.

Raymond cried out as he dropped to the ground behind a stable door. Not taking any chances, Julien rushed forward. He was within a meter of Raymond when his brother kicked the stable door open into Julien. Julien stumbled backward, and his weapon fell from his hand.

Footsteps approached, along with a shout. "Theo!"

His heartbeat quickening, Julien searched the ground for his pistol as the shout repeated and the footsteps grew closer. He found the gun beneath a wheelbarrow and scooped it up.

The stable doors behind him burst open, and sunlight spilled in. Julien took off, sprinting for the far doors.

"Freeze!" a man called out.

Julien ignored him. No one was going to stop him.

* * *

The last thing Levi expected when he rushed into the stables was to find Theo on the ground and a man running out the other door. Levi hurried to Theo's side; the man was holding his shoulder, blood seeping between his fingers.

"What happened?" Levi asked. "Who was that?"

"He's after Princess Cassandra. You have to stop him."

"I thought you were after her."

"No."

"But after the Rossi family, you're next in line for the throne," Levi said, his confusion rising.

"I never wanted the throne. My brother did." Theo moaned in pain as he tried to sit up.

"Brother?"

"There's no time to explain. The princess rode off a few minutes ago. If Julien finds her, he'll kill her." Theo motioned to the saddled horse tethered outside. "You need to find her."

"I will." Levi pulled out his phone and called the guard office. "This is Levi Marin. You have a man down in the stables, and we have a perimeter breach. At least one man is on the grounds."

"We'll take care of it, but you need to come back to the palace," the man on the other end said.

"Not until I'm sure Cassandra is safe." Levi hung up and pocketed his phone. He untied the horse and swung himself into the saddle. He circled the barn and immediately spotted a horse and rider on the slope of ground leading to the wooded area where the gazebo was. The brown ponytail left no doubt as to who it was.

Levi urged his horse into a gallop. The man he had chased out of the barn was out there somewhere, and Levi had to get Cassie to safety before she became his next victim.

* * *

Cassie urged her horse up the rise and headed for the gazebo. She needed time to think, time to feel, and time to consider her future now that Levi wasn't a part of it.

A new wave of loss crested over her, overshadowing the hurt and embarrass-ment that came from learning Levi had fooled her during their weeks together. She thought about it now, the way Levi never talked about his family or his home, his comment about not having a choice in his reassignment, even his friendship with Janessa. Pierre had mentioned Levi's arrival in Meridia had coincided with hers. Could he have come to protect his fellow American citizen originally? Obviously, the Meridian royal family appreciated his skills enough to want him to stay. What would have happened had Levi been honest with her from the beginning about who he was?

She knew the answer the moment the thought formed. If her father hadn't rejected his help, she would have. The walls would have been erected between them, and she never would have fallen for him.

Her first thought was she wished she had never met Levi. The memories of her time with him overshadowed the pain. Despite the deceit, she couldn't deny that he had opened her heart in a way she had never before experienced. If only he could have been the man she believed him to be.

The information her father had shared with her clarified so many things, details that explained many questions Levi had been asking for weeks. Had they been working together, perhaps Levi could have helped her family neutralize the true threats against them. Of course, she could hardly fault her father for holding back. After all, he was right not to trust Levi fully.

Cassie noted the work crew along the east fence. Another few days and the security improvements would be complete. But now they would have to be revamped again to make sure the CIA didn't have too much insight into their internal affairs.

She rolled the information her father had shared over and over in her mind, the pieces of the puzzle finally falling into place. King Eduard hadn't told Levi of her father's illness, which meant the CIA knew her king was dying.

A new wave of uncertainty bloomed within her. Could she rule her country effectively when her father turned the reins over to her? Or was she destined to let outsiders take over the empire her family had fought so hard to build?

Something rustled in the trees, and Cassie turned toward the sound. She saw a flash of movement to her left even as she heard a horse quickly approaching from the right. She reined in her own mount and looked behind her at a horse approaching at a full gallop, Levi on his back.

"Take cover!"

The urgency of his words jarred her into action. Cassie wheeled her mount to the right, intent on moving into the trees.

A shot sounded, and her horse reared. Her heart jumped into her throat, and her fingers tightened on the reins. She managed to stay seated, but when the stallion reared a second time, she lost her balance and tumbled to the ground.

CHAPTER 40

LEVI SAW CASSIE FALL, AND his heart stopped. He forced in a breath, his pulse kicking into high gear when Cassie's mount raced down the hill toward the stables.

Levi drew his weapon and evaluated the area. He couldn't think about what he would do if the shooter had been successful in killing Cassie. He had to believe she was still alive, if only to give him a reason to keep moving.

Cassie moaned and started to sit up.

Levi's relief rose only to be overshadowed by his training.

"Stay down!" Levi shouted. He drew his weapon and urged his mount forward. He fired off a shot toward the woods, hoping to keep the shooter at bay.

His horse broke stride and jerked to the left. "Easy." Levi urged the animal into motion again, racing forward until he reached where Cassie lay.

He swung down from the saddle and kept the horse between Cassie and the trees where the shot had originated. "Are you hurt?"

"I don't think so." She rolled onto her side. "Can I sit up now?"

"Yeah." Levi put his hand on her arm. "Come on. We need to take cover."

"Was that someone . . . ?"

"Someone was shooting at you," Levi said. He evaluated the surrounding area. The only place the person could shoot from while hidden was the woods along the nearby ridge. That was also the only place they wouldn't be exposed unless . . . Levi's thought trailed off, his gaze now trained on the cliffs to their left. "I know you aren't going to want to hear this, but I need you to hide on the cliffs."

Panic immediately flared on her face. "Levi, I can't."

"You have to. The shooter is in the woods, and we can't hide behind the horse forever."

Another shot sounded, and Cassie squeaked in alarm. Levi's mount jerked his head back, the reins cutting into Levi's fingers.

Another gunshot, and the horse jerked again, this time rearing back enough to break free.

Out of options, Levi fired off two shots, grabbed Cassie's arm, and pulled. "Come on!"

Cassie barely had her feet under her before Levi started running toward the cliffs. He squeezed off another shot to provide them cover. Levi thought Cassie's fear of bullets had succeeded in helping her overcome her fear of heights because she kept pace with him right until the drop to the water came into view.

Immediately, her gait changed, and she stutter stepped to a stop. "I can't."

Levi couldn't understand how Cassie could let her fear of heights overshadow the fact that someone was shooting at them. "It's only a few more feet."

"I can't," Cassie repeated.

Levi pulled her to the right as another shot fired. He whirled and squeezed off a shot of his own, relieved to see guards heading toward the trees.

Trusting the royal guard to deal with the threat, Levi holstered his primary weapon. He wrapped his arm around Cassie's waist, leaned down, and scooped her into his arms.

She let out a gasp of surprise, and her body stiffened the minute he moved toward the cliffs.

"Close your eyes," Levi said.

Instead of obeying the command, she locked her gaze on his.

"You can trust me." Levi took another step toward the nearest bluff. "Close your eyes."

More gunfire erupted behind them. Cassie squeezed her eyes shut, but Levi couldn't tell if she was complying with his request or trying to block out reality.

He hurried forward and ducked behind a huge boulder to his left, then let himself fall to the ground, his body cushioning Cassie so his backside absorbed the weight of both of them.

When he saw that he and Cassie were only a few meters from the spot where the land dropped off into nothingness, he used his feet to push himself back, Cassie still cradled in his arms.

Another volley of gunfire sounded, but Levi didn't dare look to see if the guards had been successful. For now, his only purpose was protecting the woman he held, the woman he loved.

Levi leaned back against the rock. Cassie must have taken the subtle movement as a signal that all was well because her eyes flew open. Her gaze locked on the cliff and the contrast of land against the water below, and she screamed.

Levi's hold tightened. "It's okay."

Cassie twisted in his arms, her feet connecting with the ground. Levi tightened his grip, but she turned and clawed at the ground to pull herself away from the edge and toward the pasture and danger.

"Cassie, stop," Levi pleaded and demanded at the same time. "Close your eyes. I've got you."

Like a caged animal, she didn't hear anything he said. She grabbed the edge of the boulder and pushed with her legs again, finally pulling free of his grip.

Levi grabbed for her ankle to keep her from diving back into the danger zone. As he did, he pushed off on his left foot, but the ground gave way. When he started sliding down the incline toward the cliff, Levi decided Cassie's fear of heights wasn't so irrational after all.

* * *

Cassie gripped the side of the rock, each breath a struggle. She looked out at the field in front of her. One guard lay motionless on the ground. Another crouched over him and fired a weapon into the trees.

It was happening again. People were fighting because of her, possibly dying because of her.

Levi cried out behind her.

The sound was so unlike him that she turned toward it despite the presence of the cliffs. Her heart nearly stopped beating when she saw Levi's legs stretched beyond the land and all but his thighs were suspended in open air. Only his grip on a half-buried rock the size of a bowling ball kept him from sliding off the edge and into the forty feet of open space below.

"Levi!"

"Cassie, take cover!"

She ducked a fraction of a second before a bullet whizzed over her head.

Logic broke through her fear long enough for her to recognize the simple fact that while falling from a cliff could kill her, staying exposed to a shooter practically guaranteed she wouldn't survive the day.

She pressed against the boulder and circled it until she was shielded from the would-be assassin's gunfire. Another bullet hit the rock a few inches from her, debris exploding into the air.

She closed her eyes, both to protect them and to will this to all be a dream. When she heard guards shouting, she forced her eyes open again and stared at reality. Levi was in as much danger as she was.

The ground surrounding the rock Levi held loosened as dirt gave way.

Cassie swallowed hard and looked around for anything she could use to help him climb back to safety. Tufts of grass fought through the soft ground between huge boulders, but nothing lay on the windswept land besides the rocks that had long ago become part of the landscape.

Levi managed to bring his second hand up beside the rock he clung to. He fisted a handful of grass, but it ripped free of the ground. He grunted, but Cassie couldn't tell if the sound was born from frustration or fear. His hand clawed at the ground, his fingers digging into the mud but not able to keep from slipping.

The rock loosened further. Cassie gasped. It wasn't going to support Levi's weight much longer.

She gauged the distance between them. A meter. Maybe a meter and a half.

Her fears welled up inside her, combating the truth. No matter who Levi was or wasn't, she loved him. She couldn't watch him die right in front of her, not when she could do something to prevent it.

One hand still clinging to the boulder, she slid her body toward Levi and stretched her leg toward him. "Here. Grab on to me."

"No. I don't want to take you with me."

"The rock is pulling loose. You don't have a choice," Cassie said.

Levi tried to find a handhold again without success.

"Levi, let me help you." Cassie rolled onto her side so she could extend her reach farther while still keeping her hand on the boulder that had become her lifeline.

This time, Levi took hold of her ankle. The mere thought of his weight pulling her down with him was enough to send a new wave of panic over her. She bent her knee, trying to pull her leg back, and the movement brought Levi sliding upward.

He bent his left knee as though trying to clamor back onto solid ground, but he was still too far over the edge to find success. Using every ounce of strength, she leaned back and tried to bend her leg further.

Her muscles burned as Levi tried again to get his legs under him. This time his knee made contact with the spot where the ground gave way to air. He inched forward, using the rock to pull himself up as he kept one hand on Cassie's ankle.

Levi was going to make it. He was going to be okay. Those thoughts rattled around her mind as hope overshadowed her fear for a brief moment. Then the rock he clung to pulled loose.

"Watch out!" Cassie cried.

Levi's grip on her ankle tightened when he let go of the falling rock. He rolled to his side, and the rock tumbled past him and over the edge.

The sudden loss of his handhold doubled the weight pulling against Cassie. The boulder cut into her hand, and she gasped, her heart pounding.

She pulled herself upward with every ounce of strength she possessed. Inch by inch, Levi drew closer, finally reaching the spot beside her.

He sat up and pressed his back against the rock. His breathing came out in ragged breaths. "You could have been killed."

"I couldn't . . ." Cassie began. "I couldn't . . ."

Levi put his hand on her knee. "Thank you."

She nodded, unable to form words.

A new round of gunfire sparked the air.

Cassie cringed. "I hate to complain, but I'd really like for the shooting to stop."

"I'll see what I can do." Levi seemed to gather his strength before he pulled his legs underneath him and prepared to stand. "Can you stay here?"

"I'm not going anywhere."

CHAPTER 41

JULIEN GASPED WITH EACH SHOT fired. Pratt had taken position in a mature olive tree. He had chosen his spot perfectly, sitting low enough that the guards would assume he was at ground level but high enough for their bullets to pass beneath him.

Pratt picked off a second guard and sent a spray of gunfire in a wide semi-circle to keep reinforcements at bay, and Julien cringed when a guard at the edge of the trees sent more bullets flying only to be forced to take cover when Pratt's bullet came within an inch of the man's arm.

Julien looked down at the gun in his hand, his palm sweating, his arm trembling from the weight of his weapon. How did people stand this? When he was king, he was going to make sure no one could make it onto the royal grounds. He had certainly spent enough time analyzing the property for weaknesses to know where they were.

From where he crouched twenty meters behind Pratt, he saw two more guards skirting through the edge of the woods toward him. Julien ducked out of sight behind a thick tree trunk. Footsteps grew closer, one cautious step after another. Julien pressed his lips together in an effort to contain his sudden fear of discovery. He didn't like this lack of control. Why didn't Pratt see them? Why didn't he take care of their newest threat?

"Do you seem him?" one man whispered to the other.

"Negative."

Him?

The footsteps slowed, then stopped mere feet from where Julien hid.

Julien's heart pounded, his pulse echoing so loudly in his ears he was certain the men standing a few feet away must be able to hear it.

"The shots came from this direction," one man said. "He has to be around here somewhere."

"You go that way," the other responded. "Stay alert."

He. Julien processed the single word. The guards didn't know there were two of them. Did that mean if one of them was discovered, they would think they had accomplished their objective?

The two guards moved on, only an occasional footstep audible in the ensuing silence. Did Pratt know if he shot again, he would give away his location? Were there more guards heading their way?

The answer to his second question was answered when someone shouted, "Up here!"

The stampede of footsteps was enough for Julien to reach an unexpected decision. If he didn't act now, he would be found, and everything would be ruined. He peeked out from behind the tree and spotted Pratt sitting motionless on his perch.

"Sorry, Pratt," Julien whispered under his breath. He lifted his gun and fired off a single shot. The silencer masked the sound, but when the bullet impacted the tree a few inches from where Pratt sat, bark went flying, and Pratt jerked in surprise.

That was all the movement needed for the half dozen guards to finally spot him.

"Up there!"

Gunfire sparked in the air again, from Pratt and the guards. Ten seconds was all it took for a bullet to find its home and for Pratt to tumble to the ground.

* * *

Levi kept his body pressed against the boulder as he worked his way to the far side of it. He gripped his pistol tighter, willing his hand to stop shaking. The mere thought that Cassie could have died trying to save him unnerved him.

He glanced behind him where she sat a few feet away, her eyes closed, her breathing coming in deep, even breaths. She couldn't bear to look at the cliffs, yet she had risked everything when he'd been in danger.

She had saved him. Now it was time to return the favor.

Levi looked around the edge of the boulder. The shooting had ceased, a new flurry of activity surrounding the wounded guards and the edge of the woods. A man was pulled out of the underbrush but didn't move, and from the awkward angle of the man's head, Levi doubted he was still breathing.

Darius appeared in the clearing and motioned his men into action. Four headed into the woods, and two more tended to the wounded guards. Two golf carts came into view, heading for Darius.

"What's happening?" Cassie asked from where she sat with her eyes closed.

"It looks like they neutralized the suspect," Levi said. "I know it's uncomfortable, but I want to stay here until we're sure he didn't have any friends."

"How . . . ?" Cassie began. She swallowed and tried again. "How did you know someone was here?"

"A motion sensor went off. I think the guy came in where the new fence is being built." Levi sat and scooted over until he was beside Cassie. "The royal guard hasn't upgraded their communication system yet, which would have made it easy to monitor their response."

Cassie turned her head toward his voice and opened her eyes. "I thought you already left."

"I couldn't go when you might be in danger." The realization that this could be the last time he would ever see her hit him hard. A hollow sensation started in his center and spread outward. "I never meant to mislead you."

"But you did."

"I've spent the past seven years living parallel lives. Every time I was with you, I was Levi Marin, head of security at the chateau. I wasn't a CIA agent."

"Ever?" Cassie asked. "What about the tracking device on my computer?"

Once again, Levi found himself perched on the edge of a cliff, only this one had him wavering on whether to protect his agency or trust the woman he loved. The debate lasted only a second. "I admit I was asked to plant a snooper program on your computer, but I didn't. Instead, I ignored my orders and did what I thought would protect you instead."

"It didn't work out very well for you."

"No, it didn't, but if someone at Satori Oil had been after you, your laptop could have been a target," Levi said. "I had to prepare for any threats that might arise."

Cassie's gaze strayed from his. She tensed when she took in the cliffs. "Can we go somewhere else?"

"Let me see if the guards have completed their search." Levi pulled his phone from his pocket and called Darius.

Darius answered on the first ring. "We can't find Princess Cassandra. Is she with you?"

"Yes. I have her," Levi said. "What's the situation? Have your men cleared the woods?"

"They're doing that now," Darius said.

"Call me when they're done, and I'll bring her back to the palace."

"I'll come to you."

"After you clear the woods," Levi insisted. "If someone else is on the grounds, they'll be watching for you or your men to lead them to the princess."

"I want her inside, away from danger."

"That makes two of us, but we have to identify the danger before we can accomplish that," Levi said. "Call me when you're done."

Cassie closed her eyes again and blew out a breath. "I can't go out there yet, can I?"

"Not quite yet." Levi put his hand on hers. "Close your eyes. It will only be a little longer."

"A little longer," she repeated. Her hand turned over and gripped his, a remnant of the trust they had once shared.

Levi stared at her profile: the dark eyelashes against flawless skin, the line of concentration on her brow, the strand of hair that caught in the breeze.

Cassie's father was right. She was beautiful. Levi had no doubt that her face would haunt him when he left here, because he couldn't imagine ever finding anyone who touched his heart the way she had for as long as he lived.

* * *

Julien never liked hide-and-seek. He especially didn't like it now when the people looking for him were armed.

He had abandoned his hiding place during the commotion after Pratt had fallen from the tree. Working his way deeper into the woods, he had stumbled onto a worn path, the ground packed hard enough to hide his footprints. He took advantage of the level ground to quicken his pace. The sound of voices and rustling branches filtered toward him.

He passed several small trees, a fallen log his newest objective. He reached his intended hiding place and looked behind him. The path remained empty, but the voices grew louder. He stepped over the log and crouched down. A quick glance in the other direction revealed a small clearing, a stone gazebo in the center of it.

A guard passed into view on the far side of the clearing, and Julien ducked down. Movement on the other side of him sent his heart racing. He was surrounded with no place to go.

As soon as the guard on the other side of the clearing disappeared into the woods, Julien hurried back onto the trail and rushed to the side of the gazebo. Squatting down, he listened once again for his pursuers.

One approached, following nearly the same path Julien had taken a moment ago. He climbed the steps of the gazebo, and Julien pressed himself against the side so he would be invisible beneath the small stone ledge above him.

Shoes against stone gave away the guard's position. Julien trod softly, timing his steps to match the other man's. When the guard descended the stairs, it took Julien a moment to determine which direction he had gone. The guard was nearly upon him when Julien realized the man was circling the gazebo.

His pulse hammering, Julien once again timed his footsteps to match the guard's and made his way around the gazebo, the guard close enough behind him for Julien to hear but far enough for Julien to remain unseen.

Julien reached the steps of the gazebo and climbed up them, keeping his body bent over to stay out of sight.

Someone called out. "Do you see anything?"

"Nothing," the guard nearest him said.

Julien scooted onto the floor of the gazebo, rolling against the side so he wouldn't be seen in case anyone walked by the entrance.

"Where else do we need to look?" the first guard asked.

"Circle down the path again. I'll have Paciano and Arturo take the trail by the cliffs. Anything beyond the stables will be picked up by the motion detectors."

"I'll meet you back at the guard house. Don't forget to check in with Darius as soon as you're done."

"Yes, sir."

Julien lay motionless for several more minutes, his breathing shallow and quiet. Motion detectors by the stables. That explained why he'd been found so quickly. The question now was, How would he find the princess again and get off the grounds without being seen?

He lay his head back against the stone floor. He'd take another few minutes to ensure he remained unnoticed. Before long, the search would end, and he could plan his next move.

CHAPTER 42

CASSIE DIDN'T KNOW HOW LONG she sat with her eyes closed, her only comfort coming from Levi's hand in hers. Whatever courage she had found when she'd helped Levi had faded, a new, deeper fear replacing it. Her body trembled.

"It's okay." Levi rubbed his thumb over the back of her hand. "It shouldn't be much longer." His phone rang. "Marin."

Cassie could hear the murmur of another male voice but couldn't distinguish the words.

"You're sure?" Levi asked. He paused and listened to the response. "Okay. We're on the cliffs." Another pause. "I'll bring her to you."

Levi squeezed her hand. "That was Darius. He's going to meet us by the woods."

As much as Cassie wanted to get away from the cliffs, she couldn't move.

"Cassie?" Levi used her nickname, apparently ignoring her earlier demand to be called by her title. At the moment, she couldn't bring herself to care.

"Cassie," Levi repeated. "Can you stand?"

She squeezed her eyes tighter.

Beside her, Levi moved. She tightened her grip on his hand for fear Levi would once again tumble toward the edge of the cliffs.

"It's okay." He tugged on her hand to prompt her to stand. "Stand up. I've got you."

"Last time you had me, you nearly went off a cliff."

"We're going to take this one step at a time," Levi said, ignoring her comment. "I need you to stand up. Then we're going to circle to your right until we're on the other side of the boulder."

Cassie tried to visualize what he described but still couldn't get her body to move.

"Come on, Cassie." Another tug of her hand. "You want to be on the other side of this rock. Help me get you there."

She took a deep breath, blew it out, and repeated the process.

"You can do this." Levi's lips pressed against the back of her hand. "Trust me."

I can do this. She played the words over in her mind, finally managing to put her body in motion.

With her hand still in Levi's, she turned toward the rock, pushing up onto her knees while her free hand gripped the boulder.

"That's good. Now one foot at a time, I want you to stand up."

She placed her right foot on solid ground. Her heart jumped into her throat, blocking her air as she struggled to take that next step.

"One more." Levi put his hand on her back, giving her the sense that he could hold her in place.

She gave in to the illusion and managed to stand.

"Now, take a step with your left foot," Levi said. "Five or six steps. That's all it's going to take."

Again, she froze.

"It's just like on the boat," Levi said. "I'm here, and I won't let you fall."

Cassie bobbed her head up and down in an effort to convince herself. She slid her foot to the side. Pain surfaced with the movement but was overshadowed by her fear.

"That's good. Now another step."

Little by little, Cassie shuffled her feet, her back pressed against the rock. When she reached the edge of the boulder, she opened her eyes and looked behind her at the grassy field. The view of solid ground was all it took for her to scramble the rest of the way to safety.

Levi followed.

In the distance, she saw Darius approaching. In a matter of minutes, the royal guard would take her away, and Levi would disappear forever.

As though he didn't understand the implications, Levi took Cassie by the arm and started forward.

Cassie took one step and stumbled, pain shooting through her ankle. "Ow."

"What's wrong?" He turned to look at her, his hand still holding on to her.

"My ankle. I think I twisted it."

Levi squatted and put his hand on her left ankle. "This one?"

He pressed on a particularly tender spot, and Cassie sucked in a breath. "Yeah."

"I'm so sorry. I think you hyperextended it when you helped me."

"A minor injury is insignificant considering the alternative of watching you tumble over a cliff," Cassie said. "That wouldn't have helped my fear of heights in the least."

"I suppose you're right." Levi's body stiffened when Darius reached them. "Princess Cassandra is injured. We'll need a cart or a horse to take her back to the palace."

"I'll take care of it," Darius said. "As for you, there's a car at the main entrance waiting to take you to the airport."

"I'm not leaving until she's safely inside," Levi said.

"That wasn't a request. The king was very adamant in his instructions."

Cassie sized up the two men who had squared off on either side of her. With her own emotions in a turmoil, she struggled to regain her composure. When she thought of Levi leaving her side while she was out in the open, a wave of panic flooded through her.

"Darius, I'm sure my father will understand if his orders are delayed," Cassie said. "He certainly didn't expect another shooting today."

"Yes, Your Highness, but—"

"Levi will remain with me until I return to the palace." She looked at Levi, love and betrayal battling for dominance. "Besides, Mr. Marin and I have some things to discuss before he departs."

"Yes, Your Highness." Darius retrieved his phone. After he called one of his men and explained the situation, he hung up and said, "If it's all the same to you, I'll wait here with you."

"Of course." Cassie looked down at the palace grounds below where emergency vehicles had gathered at the edge of the gardens. "How are your men?"

"Two wounded. I think they'll make it."

"I was afraid—" Cassie broke off. "What about the man who was shooting at us?"

"He was killed. His body is being taken to where Theo is being treated so he can identify the shooter."

"Theo? Why would he know the shooter?"

"Because we believe it was his brother." Darius glanced at Levi, apparently debating whether he should say anything further.

"Levi has already been given access to everything. I don't think there's anything you can say that will surprise him at this point."

"Theo's real last name is Escobar."

Cassie's jaw dropped. "What?"

"He came to King Alejandro three years ago after his father died, looking for protection."

"Protection from what?" Cassie asked.

"Not from what. From whom," Darius said. "After your family, Theo was the next in line for the throne here in Sereno. He abdicated his claim in order to work for the royal family. In exchange, the king helped him hide his location," Darius explained. "The man who shot Theo in the stables was his younger brother."

* * *

Alejandro paced across his living room, his cell phone in his hand. Darius continued to give him updates on the situation outside, Alejandro's blood pressure steadily rising.

"Alejandro, you need to sit," Elliott said, addressing him as he only did when they were in private.

"You can't sit still either," Alejandro pointed out as Elliott paced the room.

"I'll sit if you will."

Alejandro's phone rang, and he answered on the first ring. "Yes?"

"Your daughter is safe," Darius told him. "She injured her ankle, but one of my men will bring a cart up to the cliffs to retrieve her as soon as the injured are delivered to the ambulances."

"Thank you." Alejandro hung up the phone and turned to Elliott. "Cassie's okay."

"Thank goodness. Where is she?"

"Darius is bringing her down in a few minutes." Alejandro headed for the door.

"Don't you think you should wait here?" Elliott asked. "You had people shooting at your daughter a few minutes ago. I think it would be wise to stay out of sight until security has time to recover from the incident."

"I need to see my daughter." Alejandro continued into the hall. As much as he wanted to rush down the stairs, he recognized his fatigue and stopped at the elevator.

"I really think you should wait in the residence," Elliott said.

"You can wait here. I'm going downstairs." The elevator doors slid open. Alejandro wasn't surprised when Elliott followed him inside.

They made their way outside to where three ambulances occupied the driveway by the main entrance. A guard lay on a stretcher as paramedics tended to him. A second guard sat in the back of a golf cart while another paramedic applied a bandage to his leg.

Theo sat on yet another stretcher.

Alejandro headed his way. "Theo, what happened?"

"I'm sorry, Your Majesty. I don't know how he got here."

"Julien?"

"Yes." In a complete breach of etiquette, Theo grabbed Alejandro's hand. "He's after Princess Cassandra. He'll kill her, and when he's done, he will go after your other daughters. Someone has to stop him."

"Someone already did." Alejandro looked up at a guard driving a golf cart toward them, a prone figure visible on the backseat, a sheet draped over it.

The guard parked a few meters away. Another guard joined the first, and together they lifted the body, sheet and all, from the golf cart and lowered it onto the ground.

"That's Julien?" Theo asked, now addressing one of the guards.

"This is the shooter."

"I need to see him." Theo struggled to stand. "I need to know he can't hurt anyone else."

The guard looked at Alejandro for approval. Alejandro nodded.

As soon as Theo stood beside the body, the guard pulled the sheet back far enough to reveal the man's face.

Theo took a hasty step backward. "That isn't him."

"What?"

"I saw my brother. He's the one who shot me," Theo said, his voice panicked. "That isn't him. Julien is still out there."

CHAPTER 43

LEVI TOOK IN THE NEWS Darius had dropped on them, his protective instincts surging. He and Cassie had been right. The person after her, Julien Bartolli, was after the throne.

"I don't feel comfortable sitting out here in the open. We need to take cover," Levi said. "You take point. I'll carry Cassie." Darius opened his mouth to respond, but Levi cut him off before he could argue. "Unless you'd rather have me pointing a weapon."

"I'll take point."

"Can't we just wait here?"

"I don't want to stay exposed," Levi said. "Hopefully, Julien was working alone, but I don't want to take the chance." He squatted down in front of her. "Come on. Time for a piggyback ride."

Cassie hesitated a brief moment before she linked her hands around his neck. Levi boosted her onto his back as he stood.

"Head for the trees," Levi said.

His gun in hand, Darius angled toward the nearest section of woods. They cut the distance in half, with another twenty meters to go when Darius's phone rang.

He answered it with his free hand. "Yes?"

Levi didn't know who was on the line, but Darius listened for only a second before he dropped the phone and yelled, "Run!"

* * *

Julien squeezed the trigger a moment after the guard shouted. He missed.

He couldn't fail. Not this time.

Again, he aimed at the princess clinging to the other man's back. Julien shot a second time, but the guard cut into his line of fire and fell to the ground. The man carrying the princess kept going.

Another few seconds and they would reach the woods. A third shot. Another miss. Julien cursed under his breath. Would the woman not die?

His mind raced. He couldn't go through this again. He aimed for the space right in front of where the man was headed. The man dove for the brush as Julien shot again.

From where Julien stood, he could see the princess fly off the man's back and roll onto the ground, but Julien couldn't tell if he had hit his target.

Not willing to take any chances, he abandoned his position and angled toward where the princess had fallen. If he was lucky, Cassandra was already dead. The man with her was next.

No witnesses, Julien promised himself. He needed the loyalty of the palace employees when he took over here. Besides, the longer it took for the royal guard to figure out what had happened, the better.

* * *

Levi fought back a moan when he pushed up on his elbow. His shoulder throbbed from where he had landed, and he could only imagine Cassie had her own share of aches and pains from when she had hit the ground.

She rolled over so she was facing him and opened her mouth to speak.

Levi lifted his finger to his lips. "Shhh."

She nodded.

He scooted closer to her and whispered, "Are you okay?"

"I am, but Darius . . ."

"We can't do anything for him until we're sure we won't get shot." Levi hated that, but he knew the fastest way to help Darius was to neutralize whoever had shot him.

Levi listened for a moment, unable to discern any movement nearby. He pushed himself up with his good arm. "Come on. We need to get out of here. The shooter knows where we are."

Cassie followed his lead and stood.

Levi ignored the throbbing in his shoulder and drew his weapon. With his free hand, he motioned Cassie forward. Cautiously, he sidestepped the bushes to his right, keeping his body between Cassie and the direction the shots had come from. A twig snapped to his left, and Levi pulled Cassie behind two trees that had grown together at the base.

A gunshot rang out, and Levi acted on instinct. He grabbed Cassie's arm and pulled her to the ground. "Stay down."

Another bullet splintered into the wood a few inches above him. So much for hiding. His hand gripped his weapon, and he listened for any sound.

The click of an empty cartridge being expelled from a gun sounded, followed by a new one snapping into place. Their pursuer had come prepared, and Levi didn't doubt the man wanted both of them dead.

Levi straightened, aimed in the direction of the sound, and fired. A blur of movement flashed in the bushes. Levi shot again, and his opponent returned fire.

Levi ducked, retrieved a clip from his holster, and reloaded. He leaned back against the tree currently protecting him.

Cassie scooted closer. "What now?"

Levi looked at her and stared. Someone was shooting at them, and her voice was relatively calm. Yet, when they had been safely hidden behind the rocks by the cliffs, she had fallen apart.

Another shot sent bark flying. Cassie flinched but didn't scream.

"Since when are you this calm under pressure?"

"I'm learning," she said before repeating her question. "What do we do now?"

"We call for reinforcements." Levi pulled his phone from his pocket to send a text message, then realized everyone he had worked with directly had either left the country or was wounded.

He handed Cassie his phone. "Text your father. Tell him Darius is wounded and there's another shooter."

Cassie took the phone as another shot fired. His cell slipped through her fingers and fell into the underbrush. She leaned down to retrieve it, patting the ground as she searched the knee-high grass.

"Where did it go?" Cassie asked. A hint of panic entered her voice when she added, "Levi, I don't see it."

Levi scanned the ground but to no avail. "Do you have your phone with you?"

"It's in my saddle bag."

Levi analyzed the surrounding terrain. If he was right, the shooter was still in the thick brush thirty meters to their left. The open trail that led to the gazebo spanned the space between them, and a handful of young trees dotted the landscape but didn't provide sufficient cover to mount an attack.

Conversely, their would-be assailant had chosen his spot well. Thick bushes filled in the space between a couple mature trees. The man was exposed on his right, but Levi didn't have a chance of getting into position without someone to lay down cover fire.

Another bullet impacted the tree behind them mere inches from Cassie's head. Their assailant was on the move, angling to get a clean shot.

Levi pulled Cassie to the ground, using the grass for cover. It didn't matter if help was coming. They were running out of time. Another few seconds and one of the bullets was going to find a target.

Levi reached for his spare weapon and pulled it free of his ankle holster. "Take this."

Cassie stared at the weapon for a second before she accepted the offering.

"Do you know how to use it?" Levi asked.

She swallowed hard and nodded.

"When I tell you, I want you to fire off two shots, roll to your left, and shoot one more time."

"Where am I aiming?"

"That way." Levi lifted his chin in the direction of the shooter. "I'm going to circle around this guy and see if I can get the jump on him."

Cassie's eyes widened. "You'll be out in the open."

"Which is why I'm having you lay down cover fire for me," Levi said with more confidence than he felt. "He can't shoot me if he's hiding from your bullets."

"Be careful."

"I will, but if I do go down, fire off another shot, and take off that way," Levi said. "Zigzag through the trees so he can't get a clear shot."

"Levi—"

"Please. Do what I ask," Levi pleaded. He saw the change come over Cassie, the acceptance of what they needed to do. "Are you ready?"

Cassie drew a deep breath and nodded. "I'm ready when you are."

* * *

Cassie watched Levi push into a low crouch, like a sprinter ready for the starting gun to go off. She wished the bullets flying today were because of a sporting event.

Cassie took aim in the direction Levi had indicated, the weapon heavy in her hands. The thought that her bullet might hit a target gave her a moment of unease, but she reminded herself that whoever was out there wanted her dead. It was him or her.

"Now!" Levi whispered.

Cassie squeezed the trigger, her shoulders absorbing the impact of the shot. Levi sprang into action, and she squeezed off another shot.

Levi's footsteps pounded. Cassie rolled over. Another shot rang out before she once again took aim. She fired and rolled again, then peered through the grass as Levi raised his weapon and took a shot of his own.

The faint puff of displaced air sounded. An instant later, Levi stumbled a step and dropped to the ground.

"No!" The single word escaped her in a whisper.

Cassie started to rush forward but stopped herself. Levi told her what to do. She raised her gun to fire off another shot, then lowered her weapon again. She couldn't leave Levi. There had to be another way.

Another puff of air, this time followed by a cloud of dust rising a few feet from where she now lay. It took only a moment for her to realize the shooter had aimed for where she had been when she'd fired off her first two shots.

Cassie held her breath for several seconds, afraid the mere sound of inhaling and exhaling might give away her position. The instinct to roll again surfaced, but she fought against it. If the shooter thought he'd succeeded, would he leave her alone? Or would he come out to see if she was really dead?

Her grip tightened on the gun handle. If he came out in the open, could she bring herself to shoot another human being? Would she hit her target if she tried?

Her gaze landed on Levi, who lay motionless on the ground. She pressed her lips together as myriad emotions crashed over her, though fear, regret, and panic dominated, dousing the tiny flicker of hope that Levi was still alive.

She blinked against the tears that sprang to her eyes. Levi lay ten meters away. Darius lay in the field forty meters behind her. She owed it to both of them to stay alive, if for no other reason than to see if her prayers for their survival were fulfilled the way she hoped.

Her hand loosened and tightened on the gun grip again. She didn't know if she was ready for what would come, but she was most certainly waiting.

CHAPTER 44

LEVI MUSTERED EVERY OUNCE OF willpower to keep himself from moving. A trickle of blood seeped into the fabric of his pants. Apparently, the sensation of getting slapped had actually been a bullet to the fleshy part of his thigh.

His shoulder throbbed with each heartbeat, but he ignored the pain and focused instead on the sounds around him.

His hand still gripped his gun, and he hoped the shooter would expose himself when Cassie ran away.

No footsteps. Why wasn't Cassie running? Had their assailant managed to shoot her? He couldn't entertain such a thought. She had to be okay. He had to make sure she stayed that way.

For several seconds, the only sound was the rustle of the leaves in the breeze. Cassie didn't move. She didn't shoot.

A hollowness started in his stomach and spread outward until it encompassed his entire body. Cassie couldn't be dead.

The thought of living without seeing her every day had devastated him when she'd kicked him out, but that was nothing compared to what the world would be like if she was no longer part of it.

His mind raced, searching for options. Did he wait for the shooter, knowing Cassie could be bleeding to death in the grass a few meters away? Should he spray the last of his bullets into the bushes in the hope he hit the assassin even knowing that if he failed, he and Cassie would both die?

The possibilities swirled through his mind. In the distance, the hum of a golf cart broke through the silence. Help was coming. Would it arrive in time? Or was it already too late?

A footstep against the dirt was followed by another.

Levi's heartbeat quickened, his anticipation overshadowing the throbbing in his shoulder and the tightness centered in his thigh. He didn't move, willing the shooter to continue toward him, praying the intruder wouldn't shoot him again.

In his mind, he visualized how many steps it would take for the shooter to expose himself. Four? Maybe five?

A countdown started in his head. Another step. One. Then another. Two.

The muscles in Levi's arms tightened in anticipation of springing into action.

A gunshot rang out. It took a split second for Levi to realize that it had come from Cassie's direction. Hope leapt within him.

He pushed to a stand, but his right leg buckled as he squeezed the trigger.

The shooter took aim and shot. Levi fell back to the ground, a bullet impacting the dirt inches from him.

He rolled and aimed, but this time, he took the split second necessary to anticipate his adversary. He squeezed off another shot, a second gun firing almost in unison with his.

Levi didn't know whose bullet hit the mark, but the shooter's arm jerked back when he took a hit in the shoulder. Despite the injury, the man raised his gun again.

Before he could take aim, Levi fired two more shots, and the man in front of him dropped to the ground.

* * *

"Levi!" Cassie pushed herself up just as a hand grabbed her from behind.

"Your Highness, we have to get you to safety."

Cassie looked at the guard who held her arm. "I need to make sure Levi is okay."

A second guard moved past her, shielding her from Levi and the attacker who lay on the ground. "I'll check on them. You get her to the palace."

The man holding her arm tugged on Cassie, leaving her no choice but to follow or fall down.

Cassie took a few backward steps, her concern for Levi giving her a new resolve. "Let go of me. I can walk on my own."

"Your Highness, the king insisted we bring you to safety."

Cassie stepped behind a tree. "I'll wait here, but I'm not leaving until I know if Levi is okay." She motioned to the shooter. "And I want your assurance that the man over there isn't going to harm anyone else."

"Yes, Your Highness." The guard didn't leave her side, but he called out to his partner. "What's the status on those two?"

Cassie watched the other guard collect the shooter's weapon and check for a pulse. "This one is dead."

He moved to where Levi now lay.

"Call another ambulance. He's got a leg wound."

The guard beside her made the call.

"What about Darius?" Cassie asked.

"A medic is with him now." The guard motioned toward the pasture. "Please, Your Highness. I insist you let me take you back to the palace."

Levi rolled his head toward her. "Go with him, Cassie."

"But . . ."

"Go with him. I want you safe."

Cassie pressed her lips together and nodded. Her body trembling, she turned away from Levi and followed the guard toward the transportation that would take her home.

* * *

Levi watched Cassie disappear through the trees, a tangle of worry knotting in his stomach. Would he ever see her again?

He turned to the guard beside him. Levi flipped through his memory for the man's name. "Arturo, how is Darius?"

"Alive. He took a bullet to the back, but he was conscious when we got to him." Arturo motioned to Levi's leg. "Is that the only place you were hit?"

"Yeah." Levi struggled to sit up. He looked down at the small hole in his pant leg, the bloodstain barely noticeable.

A cell phone rang. It took Levi a moment to remember he had lost his in the grass. "My phone fell over there. Can you see if you can find it for me?"

"Sure."

The phone stopped ringing, then started a moment later. Arturo followed the sound, locating Levi's cell within seconds. He looked at the screen. "It's someone named Janessa."

Levi took the phone from Arturo as it stopped ringing a second time and pressed the screen to call Janessa back.

"Hey, Levi. Sorry I missed your call earlier. Our phones were out."

"I think someone was scrambling the cell signals," Levi said. "Are you at the museum?"

"I'm heading there in a few minutes."

"I need you to get ahold of Pierre. I think there's a robbery happening tonight."

"Do you know what the target is?"

"I'm pretty sure it's the exhibit on loan from the royal family here in Sereno," Levi said. "Jeremy and Noelle are heading your way. They found out Dimitri Breuer arrived in Meridia today."

"The art thief?"

"That's the one."

"I'll get the word out and talk to Pierre."

"Thanks." Levi glanced at the bloodstain on his pants. "I'm a little tied up here, but keep me informed."

"I will."

Levi hung up. He hated feeling helpless, and at the moment, he wasn't capable of doing anyone any good. As much as he despised it, for now, he had to trust Sereno's royal guard to keep Cassie safe, and he had to trust Janessa, Jeremy, and Noelle to protect Sereno's national treasures.

He looked down at his leg again. Getting shot was extremely inconvenient.

* * *

Alejandro sat on a ridiculously uncomfortable bench beside the window in the front hall. When the gunshots had started again, the guards had ushered him inside to safety, and his anxiety had been rising with each passing minute.

He had paced for ten minutes but had expended what little energy he had. Exhausted both physically and mentally, he had ultimately collapsed onto the seventeenth-century example of woodworking. No wonder cushions had been invented.

On the other side of the room, Elliott paced enough for both of them.

One of the guards walked inside.

"What's the latest?" Alejandro demanded.

"Your daughter is safe."

"Theo's brother?"

"Dead," the guard said. "I don't know many details beyond that."

"Where is Cassandra now?" Alejandro asked.

"The stablemaster is taking a couple horses up to the ridge to bring her down now."

"What about the golf carts?" Elliott interjected. "Those are closer."

"They're still being used to transport the wounded," he said. "Darius was shot. So was Levi."

Alejandro had to swallow before he could voice his next question. "How bad?"

"Darius needs surgery. The medics are hopeful he'll pull through."

"And Levi?"

"The Meridian took a bullet in the leg. He'll be okay."

The guard's reference to Levi as a Meridian rather than an American demonstrated Darius's discretion. Apparently, his captain of the guard had kept Levi's true identity private, allowing Alejandro to decide who to share the information with.

One of the golf carts that had been sent up to the woods returned. Alejandro recognized the uniform of his captain of the guard and turned to his brother-in-law. "Elliott, I want you to call Dr. Marois. Let him know Darius is on his way in," Alejandro said, not taking his gaze away from the window. "I want Dr. Marois to oversee his care personally."

"Of course."

Alejandro watched a medic rush toward the golf cart with a stretcher.

"If you'll excuse me, Your Majesty," the guard said. "I'll see to it your daughter is brought to you as soon as she returns."

As much as he hated doing it, Alejandro forced himself to put caution first. "Make sure there aren't any more shooters out there before my daughter is brought back to the palace."

"It will take at least twenty to thirty minutes to conduct a thorough search."

"I want my daughter back by my side, but we can't afford to take any chances," Alejandro said. "The open space between the woods and the palace is too vulnerable if someone is out there waiting to take another shot."

"I understand." The guard nodded. "I'll take care of it, Your Majesty."

"Thank you."

CHAPTER 45

CASSIE RODE ALONG THE EDGE of the woods, the stablemaster on one side of her and a guard on the other. Though her first thought had been to urge her horse into a full gallop to bridge the open space between the woods and the palace, her guard had dictated their pace as well as their route. It appeared as though no one wanted to take the chance that there might be another shooter waiting in the shadows somewhere.

She could see three guards on foot working their way through the trees. They moved methodically, checking behind every bush, searching every high branch, tromping through every patch of high grass. Cassie didn't know why the guards had bothered to have a horse brought to her when they could walk faster than their current progress.

Paciano motioned for her to stop as the three guards in the woods moved to the next section. Another two hundred meters and they would reach the edge of the trees.

An ambulance pulled away from the palace as another one arrived. A golf cart started up the hill, presumably to transport Levi from where she had left him to the waiting ambulance.

Cassie's stomach clenched as images of the latest shooting played through her mind. Had she shot the man trying to kill her, or had Levi? She couldn't be sure. In truth, she wasn't sure she wanted to know. Just the memory of aiming the gun at another person made her shudder.

"Your Highness, we're clear," the guard said.

That was all Cassie needed to hear. She urged her horse into a canter, and the two men once again took position on either side of her. Cassie bypassed the path leading to the stables and instead headed straight for the entrance to the residence.

The guard stationed by the door opened it for her. Cassie swung down from the saddle, let the reins drop, and limped inside.

"Where is my father?" Cassie asked the guard.

"In the front hall."

"Thank you." Cassie ignored the pain that shot through her ankle with each step as she continued forward. She made it only halfway to her intended destination before she was intercepted by her father and uncle heading toward her.

"Cassie!" Her father rushed forward and scooped her into his arms. "Thank the heavens you're safe."

Cassie buried her face in his chest, her emotions spiraling as her father's arms pulled her close.

Her uncle's hand came down on her shoulder as though he too needed to make sure she was still breathing. "Cassie, I'm so glad you're okay."

She nodded but couldn't speak. Tears threatened, and she squeezed her eyes closed to fight against them. Then she took a ragged breath and struggled to control her breathing.

"Let's go into my apartment," Alejandro said. "I want to know what happened."

Cassie took a step toward the elevator and stumbled.

Her father caught her by one arm, and her uncle grabbed the other.

"Are you okay?" Elliott asked.

"It's nothing serious. Just my ankle."

"Lean on me. I'll help you upstairs." Her uncle slipped his arm around her waist. Cassie let him support her weight with each step on her left foot. When they finally reached her father's living room, she sat on the couch.

The sense of security she expected to feel once she was home didn't come, and she couldn't help looking around to make sure they were really alone.

"It's okay. You're safe now," her father assured her. He sat beside her.

"Can I get you something?" Elliott asked. "Some water or lemonade?"

"A glass of water would be wonderful, thank you," Cassie said. "Did the guards tell you that both the shooters were killed?"

"Yes." Alejandro laid his hand on hers. "I'm so sorry, Cassie. I should have enlisted the help of Interpol when Theo first came to me."

"Why did you let Theo come to work here if you knew he was an Escobar?"

"I did it to protect you."

"Protect me how?"

"He came to me shortly after his father died. His younger half brother learned of his heritage and tried to kill Theo to get one spot closer to the throne. Theo rightly assumed Julien intended to kill you and your sisters."

"Which is why you upgraded security."

"Yes." Alejandro put his hand on hers. "I'm so sorry I let him get too close."

"It's not your fault," Cassie insisted. "And you made sure Annabelle and Victoria stayed safe."

"I should have let you go with them to the hideaway."

"My place is here," Cassie said. "Now that Julien is dead, we can make our home safe again so my sisters can return."

"I'd like that."

Elliott returned holding two glasses of water. He offered one to Cassie and the other to Alejandro.

"Thank you." Cassie took a sip and set the glass aside. She motioned to her ankle. "Uncle Elliott, can you please arrange for someone to take me to the hospital?"

"There's no need for that," Alejandro said before Elliott could respond. "I'll send for Dr. Marois. He can treat your ankle here."

"I know, but I want to see Levi and check on our wounded guards."

"The hospital will give us updates. I don't want you out in public right now," Alejandro said. "Besides, I already told you who Levi really is."

"I know who he is," Cassie said.

"Then you understand why it's best to keep your distance."

The experiences of the past two hours culminated in her mind and gave her a new sense of clarity. She couldn't deny the sense of betrayal she had experienced when she'd learned of Levi's deceit, but when faced with danger, Levi had put her first every time. "Papa, Levi saved my life. I want to be there for him."

"Absolutely not. I forbid it."

Cassie pushed to a stand and turned to face her father. "You have two choices: you can either accept that I'm going to the hospital or you can arrange for him to recover here. The decision is yours."

"Have you forgotten that I am your father?"

"I haven't forgotten, nor have I forgotten that you are my king," Cassie said. "But whether you want to admit it or not, Levi is the reason I'm still standing here. I owe him my life."

"Don't let your gratitude confuse the truth."

"Like I said, I know who Levi is. It's not a fact I'm likely to forget anytime soon."

Alejandro motioned to Elliott. "Can you please help Cassie to her room? I'll make the call to the hospital."

"Yes, sire."

* * *

Levi lay back on the stretcher as the paramedics rolled him through the hospital entrance. He lifted the cell phone he gripped in his hand to check the time. Over an hour had passed since Janessa's call, an hour with no news.

He wasn't sure what the king's motivations were to put his family's section of the royal agreement on display, but whatever it was, he hoped it didn't backfire.

Unwilling to wait any longer, Levi hit the button to call Janessa again.

Janessa answered on the second ring. "Levi. I was about to call you."

"What's the latest?"

"You were right. Dimitri Breuer was going for the display from Sereno," Janessa said. "He tried to sneak into the museum with the caterers."

"Then he was apprehended?"

"Yes. He isn't talking, but Jeremy and Noelle will work on tracing his funding. I'm sure someone of his reputation insisted on being paid something up front."

Relieved that the theft had been averted, Levi lay back and watched the tiles on the hospital ceiling pass by. "I think King Alejandro can give them an idea of where to start looking."

"King Eduard is speaking to him now." Janessa paused, and then continued with a new sense of urgency. "I just heard there was a shooting in Sereno. Are you okay?"

A nurse approached. "Sir, you need to put your phone away. We need to take some X-rays."

"Levi?" Janessa asked.

"Cassandra is fine. We're waiting to find out about the guards who were injured."

"And you?"

The nurse reached for the phone. "Sir, I must insist."

"Sorry, Janessa. I've got to go."

"Levi—"

Knowing Janessa could be every bit as forceful as the nurse currently standing by his side, Levi said, "Bullet to the leg. I'll be fine." Before he could say anything further, the nurse snatched his phone from his hand and hung up on Janessa. "Do you realize you just hung up on a princess?"

The nurse glanced at the phone for a brief moment as though second-guessing herself. Then she seemed to shake off any uncertainty. "If she were here, I'm sure the princess would want you to get treated as soon as possible."

Levi's mind immediately jumped from his friend the princess to the princess he loved. "I'm sure you're right."

CHAPTER 46

LEVI HADN'T FOUND A DUNGEON in the palace during his security analysis, but when his nurse, Ivan, pushed his wheelchair into the palace, Levi wondered if that was where he was headed. Why else would the royal family invite a known spy into their home?

His suspicions had risen steadily since learning he was being released from the hospital only hours after being treated for a bullet wound.

He had been fortunate the bullet had missed bone. The exit wound would leave a nasty scar, but from everything the doctor had said, Levi could expect a full recovery. Thankfully, the pain in his shoulder had subsided despite the nasty bruise his impact with the ground had left behind.

A butler greeted them in the main hall and escorted them to the apartment that had been his home for the past few weeks.

"Mr. Marin, your luggage has been stored in your closet. If you wish assistance in unpacking, I'm happy to take care of it."

"I'll be okay, but thank you." As soon as he was left alone with his nurse, he said, "I've never had a private nurse before. How does this work?"

"Accommodations have been made for me in the staff quarters," Ivan said. "Another nurse will relieve me for the night shift."

"And who arranged for me to have such personalized care?"

"That would be me." Dr. Marois emerged from the kitchen. "Let me take a look at your leg."

"I think I've been poked and prodded enough for one day."

"I'm sure you're right, but indulge me anyway."

Levi remained in the wheelchair while the doctor examined his leg.

"I understand you also injured your shoulder," Dr. Marois said.

"It's just bruised. Nothing some rest can't fix."

Again, the doctor poked and prodded. Once he completed his examination, the nurse rebandaged Levi's leg.

"Ivan, I think our patient will be okay for a few minutes without us," Dr. Marois said. "Come with me, and we can discuss his treatment plan."

The two men left, and the door closed behind them. Movement sounded in the kitchen, and Levi turned toward it.

Cassie appeared in the opening between the living and dining areas, a pair of crutches assisting her forward progress. Levi's heart squeezed in his chest at the mere sight of her. She was the future he could never have and would always regret.

The bandage on her ankle reminded him how close they had both come to dying today. He shuddered at the thought.

Cassie held her position beneath the archway. "Thank you."

Levi wasn't sure what he'd expected her to say, but that wasn't it. "If you're thanking me for saving your life, I think we're even. I wouldn't still be here if it weren't for you."

"You never would have been on that cliff had you not come after me," Cassie countered. "Truly, I owe you my life. I don't know how I can ever repay you."

"You can forgive me."

Cassie used her crutches and closed the distance between them. She lowered herself onto the couch, facing where Levi still sat in his wheelchair. "I hope you don't mind staying here instead of the hospital."

"As long as you and your father aren't planning on throwing me in the dungeon, there's no place I'd rather be."

"We don't have a dungeon."

"Good." Levi glanced around the empty room. "I assume you know one of the shooters was the man after the throne."

"Yes. Julien Escobar, although he was going by a different last name," Cassie said. "Interpol already traced him back to where he had rented an apartment in Copenhagen. An agent recovered the missing founding jewels and the twenty-two missing pieces of the succession agreement."

"That's quite a find."

"Yes. Jeremy and Noelle are going to work with my father to get the pieces returned to where they belong."

"I'm glad."

"Me too," Cassie said. "I think I've had enough trauma in the past few months to last a lifetime."

"Yes, you have." Levi reached for her hand and spoke from the heart. "I know you may not believe this, but I meant what I said in your father's apartment. I do love you."

"I love you too."

Levi's eyes widened. "You do?"

"Finding out you hadn't been completely honest with me hurt more than I can possibly describe, but I've never been so scared as when I thought you were going to fall off that cliff."

"You risked yourself to save me."

"I never want to be that terrified again."

"Neither do I." He rubbed his thumb over the back of her hand. "What happens now?"

"I don't know, but since both of us need time to recover from our injuries, maybe we can find out who we are now that I know the truth."

Hope soared inside him. "I can't think of anything I would like more."

His eyes met hers. A thousand words passed between them in the single look, and Levi couldn't resist leaning forward. His lips met hers, and a sense of rightness fell over him.

The secrets between them were gone, and so were the doubts. Love swelled within him, bringing with it a new determination. Cassie was the woman he loved. Now he had to find a way to make sure he never had to let her go.

* * *

Cassie hung up the phone and let out a sigh of relief. Darius was going to make it. He had undergone a second surgery this morning, but Dr. Marois assured her he was now stable and on the road to recovery. That recovery would likely take at least six months, but his prognosis was good. Cassie couldn't describe the relief that flowed through her at the knowledge that all of the guards injured during the last shooting would recover fully.

She stood and tested her weight on her injured ankle. After three days of using crutches, she had graduated to walking on her own. She supposed it would take another few days for the limp to disappear completely.

She glanced at her watch. Almost lunchtime. Her stomach fluttered in anticipation. Since her father had canceled all royal engagements to give her family and their security force time to recover from the recent shooting, her days had been her own. Mostly. She rarely went more than a few hours without a conversation with someone regarding the upcoming drilling project, but at least she didn't have to worry about in-person meetings.

The past few days reminded her of when she and Levi had first started working together in Meridia. They did their work during the day and met for meals to spend time together. She had to admit, things were quickly returning to where they had been before her father told her the truth.

Already looking forward to seeing Levi, Cassie picked up the phone and dialed the kitchen. "Norman, has Mr. Marin already ordered lunch?"

"No, Your Highness."

"Could you please send something up to his room for both of us?"

"Of course. Do you have a preference?"

"Whatever you're making for the staff is fine. Thank you." Cassie ended the call and made her way to Levi's door. She knocked, not surprised when Ivan answered. "How's the patient?"

"Doing well. We finished his physical therapy a few minutes ago." Ivan opened the door wide to allow Cassie to pass through.

She walked into the empty living room and glanced out the french doors leading to the balcony, where Levi was sitting with a file open in front of him, his gaze on the horizon.

Cassie opened the balcony door and stepped outside, then closed it behind her to ensure privacy. "Mind if I join you?"

"Hey there." Levi started to stand.

"Don't get up." Cassie sat opposite him. "I spoke to the doctor a few minutes ago. Darius is going to make it."

Levi's shoulders visibly relaxed. "I'm so glad. Ivan mentioned Theo and one of the other guards returned to the palace this morning."

"Yes. We expect everyone will be back by the end of the week, except for Darius. It will take him another week or so before he can come home."

"They're all coming back here while they recover?" Levi asked.

"My father and I agreed that it would be best. This is their home," Cassie said. "Unfortunately, it's going to be a while before everyone is well enough to return to work."

"Which leaves the royal guard seriously shorthanded."

"Yes. I spoke to Annabelle this morning. Both of my sisters are anxious to come home . . ."

"But no one wants them here until their safety can be guaranteed," Levi finished for her.

"Yes." Memories of working with Levi rushed into her mind. She had trusted him with her family's safety once. Could she do it again, knowing he had deceived her for so many weeks? Wings of hope fluttered inside her. "The

doctor said you'll need a few more weeks of physical therapy before you're back
to full strength. How would you feel about helping me increase our security
force?"

"You want me to help hire new guards?"

"Yes."

"That's putting a lot of trust in me, especially after what happened."

"Are you talking about Julien breaching the grounds or you being CIA?"

"Both."

"From what the guards have pieced together, Julien and his friend came
through the east fence," Cassie said. "Had they waited another week, they never
would have made it onto the grounds."

"That's true," Levi conceded. "When will the enhanced fencing be done?"

"Saturday. The new scrambler for their communication system arrives
tomorrow."

"Really?"

"Yes, our security force saw the wisdom of your suggestion," Cassie said.

A knock sounded on the balcony door before it opened and Ivan carried
a tray outside.

"The kitchen staff sent this up for you." He set the tray on the table. "Are
you okay for a few minutes while I go get some lunch?"

"I'm fine," Levi said. "Take your time."

"Thanks. I'm going to check on our other patients, but I should be back
in a couple hours."

"Sounds good."

Ivan disappeared back inside and closed the door.

Cassie put a plate in front of Levi and took a second for herself. She motioned
to the notebook Levi held. "What are you working on?"

"Actually, I had an idea of how to augment your security forces without taking jobs away from those who were injured."

"What did you have in mind?"

"A combination of things actually." Levi waved at the food in front of them.
"Did you want to wait until after lunch to talk about this?"

"No. I'm curious."

"I don't know how your father would feel about it, but I have a friend who
works for the CIA. He has a K-9 partner. Together, they specialize in bomb
detection. They're available, and I think I could get the Agency to lend them
to your family for the next six months or so."

"Why would they do that?"

"You awarded a huge contract to an American company," Levi reminded her. "Even though Axion will hire a lot of locals, the US government has an interest in protecting its citizens."

"I'm not sure my father will go for that, and I'd prefer not to mislead him."

"The only way to know is to ask," Levi said. "And for the record, I have no interest in trying to sneak agents onto the palace grounds."

Cassie recognized the underlying meaning of his words. He wanted her trust as well as her father's. "What else did you have in mind?"

"Remember when we talked to your cousin Crispan?"

"Yes."

"He mentioned that he didn't trust Pantheon."

"That's right. You're the one who proved that mistrust was well founded."

Levi shrugged off her statement. "Regardless, your cousin does know which security companies are good."

"Wait. You're thinking about having the royal family hire a security firm?"

"Yes. I spoke to Crispan last night." He tapped on his notepad. "We found one that's headquartered out of Madrid that employs quite a few citizens of Sereno. Most of their other employees are Spanish or French."

Cassie considered the possibilities. In truth, if they hired enough guards to replace the injured, they would be overstaffed when they all returned. "How hard would it be to run the background checks on their people?"

"I already started." Levi handed her his notebook. "I listed their nationalities beside their names."

Cassie scanned the list. Four from Sereno, two from Spain, and another from France. Beneath those names, Levi had listed alternates from a number of European countries as well as two from Canada.

"This could work to augment our staff for the guards, but what do I do about Darius?" Though Cassie already knew who she wanted in the interim, she laid out the facts. "Paciano is doing his best to fill in, but he doesn't have the experience to head our security force for six months."

"If your father will allow it, I could work with Paciano while I'm here. With some training, he might be able to handle things until Darius returns."

Cassie took a tentative step onto the bridge of trust they had once shared between them. "Or you could take over until Darius comes back."

"I don't think your father would go for that."

"Like you said, we won't know unless we ask."

Levi took a bite of his sandwich, chewing slowly as though he needed a minute to ponder the possibilities. "Do you think your father would agree to meet with me?"

"I think so," Cassie said with hope welling up within her. "I can see if he will meet with both of us this afternoon."

"Maybe it would be best if I meet with him alone."

"Are you sure?"

He put his hand on hers. "I'm sure."

CHAPTER 47

LEVI WASN'T TERRIBLY SURPRISED THAT the king had put him off. He had rather expected it. What he hadn't expected was to be ignored for three days.

His wheelchair had been replaced by a cane, and Ivan now spent more time with the newly arrived patients than he did with him. Now Levi's days were filled with spending time with Cassie and working with Paciano to oversee the final details on the security enhancements. Whether King Alejandro agreed to let him stay on with the royal guard or not, Levi wasn't leaving until he was certain every precaution was in place.

As for what would happen with him and Cassie after he recovered, Levi wasn't certain. The sad truth was that the king wouldn't be here by this time next year. If Alejandro did object to Levi's presence, Levi could wait until after the king's death to continue his relationship with Cassie. He wanted better for Cassie though. He wanted her to have her father's approval for what he had in mind. It might be a long shot, but he owed it to Cassie to try.

He crossed the hall and was escorted into the king's apartment, only this time, the king's assistant showed him into the king's office rather than his living room. Alejandro sat behind an enormous desk, a thick file on one side and a coffee mug on the other.

King Alejandro nodded at the butler. "Thank you, Byron. That will be all for now."

"Yes, sire." Byron bowed slightly and left the room, closing the door behind him.

"Have a seat," Alejandro said.

"Thank you for making time to see me, Your Majesty." Levi sat across from Alejandro.

"I'm sure you are aware that your presence here occurred despite my objections."

"I suspected as much," Levi said. "I don't know if your daughter mentioned that I have been following through with the work I started on your security enhancements."

Alejandro straightened in his chair. "No, she didn't."

"Please don't be upset with Princess Cassandra," Levi said. "She allowed me access because she knows how concerned I am about her safety. Understandably, she wants her sisters to be allowed to come home and to know that they will be safe when they do so."

"Her sisters are as anxious to be here as Cassie is to have them home."

"I know I'm not an official part of your security staff, but I hope you'll let me finish what I've started," Levi said. "My time spent here was entirely focused on enhancing security. Whether you believe it or not, I never spied on you or your family, nor did I send information back to the CIA."

"I'm fully aware of that."

"You are?"

"My resources may not be as extensive as the CIA's, but it wasn't that hard to pull your phone records to see that you hadn't been calling Langley."

"I'm impressed. That's something I would have done."

The king leaned back in his chair. "We never did decide on your official title here, did we?"

"No, Your Majesty. We didn't. That conversation died when you learned of my heritage."

"From the amount of time you and my daughter are spending together, I'm guessing you are hoping I will overlook your loyalties."

"I hope to be allowed to serve your family."

"What did you have in mind?"

Levi drew a deep breath and gathered his courage. "I did give some thought to that. I believe there are a number of options for my future here."

"Oh, really?" The king's eyebrows lifted. "I'm listening."

"To start with, I have been working with Paciano on an interim security plan to hold you over until your guards are able to return to work."

"What does this interim plan entail?"

"Your nephew Crispan and I believe a private security firm out of Spain could enhance your staff for the next few months," Levi said. "I would also like to bring in a friend of mine from the CIA."

"Another spy in Sereno?"

"Alan isn't a spy. He and his K-9 partner work bomb detection," Levi explained. "He wouldn't need access to any sensitive information, but having him and his dog here can help strengthen security until your guard forces are back to full strength."

"I'll consider it," King Alejandro said. "Anything else?"

"Yes. I would also like your permission to take over for Darius until he recovers from his injuries," Levi said. "Considering his loyalty to your family, I assume you won't want him to be replaced. By allowing me to fill in for him, the job will remain his."

"Where would that leave you when Darius returns?"

Levi straightened his shoulders, and his gaze met the king's. Nothing ventured, nothing gained. "I would like to ask for your daughter's hand in marriage."

For a moment, the king said nothing. "My daughter, married to an American spy? Surely you can't be serious."

"I would be a former American spy if she says yes."

"You would leave your loyalties behind to marry my daughter?"

"I prefer to think of it as realigning my loyalties," Levi said. "Cassandra has been my priority since I met her."

"And you haven't spoken to her about this yet?"

"No, I haven't."

"Your deception hurt her deeply," Alejandro said. "I don't want her to ever feel that kind of pain again."

"Nor do I."

Alejandro fell silent, his gaze remaining on Levi. "Either you are very good at lying, or you're sincere about your feelings about Cassie."

"I am good at lying, but right now, I'm being completely honest with you."

Alejandro's lips curved slightly before he fought against the smile. "With time, I might learn to like you."

"I would like that very much."

"At the risk of poking my nose into your private affairs, I have to ask, Have you bought Cassie a ring yet?"

"No. I hope to go into town and shop for one after the security enhancements are complete."

"I believe I have another idea that might suit us both."

"What's that?"

Alejandro opened his desk drawer and retrieved a wooden box. He set it on the desk, opened it, and drew out a stunning diamond ring. Levi estimated the diamond in the center to be at least five times the size of the one his father had given to his mother. "This was the ring I gave my wife when I proposed. It belonged to my grandmother before her."

"It's stunning."

"I believe it would mean a great deal to my daughter to have it." Alejandro stared down at the ring before he held it up. "If I'm correct, it will mean even more to her if it is given to her by you."

"Your Majesty, I can't . . ."

"Of course you can." Alejandro held out the ring. "Consider it an early wedding present."

Levi swallowed hard. "Does that mean I have your blessing?"

"You do." Alejandro pushed to a stand.

Levi followed suit and shook Alejandro's outstretched hand. "Thank you."

"Promise to keep her safe and happy."

"I promise I will always do my very best."

CHAPTER 48

CASSIE SAT ACROSS FROM HER father and watched him move the food around on his plate. "Papa, you need to eat something. Mama always said breakfast is the most important meal of the day."

He took a sip of juice and set his glass down. "I'll eat something in a bit. For now, we need to discuss when we should have your coronation ceremony."

"My choice would be in twenty or thirty years from now."

"We both know that isn't going to happen." Alejandro reached out and patted her hand. "Dr. Lewis's treatments might prolong my life for a few months, but we need to face facts. By the first of the year, you will rule whether I am still here or not."

Cassie swallowed the tears that threatened suddenly. "I understand."

Alejandro pushed back from the table. "I'm going to rest for a few minutes. I can only imagine tonight will be draining when your sisters get home."

"They're anxious to see you," Cassie said.

"I'm anxious to see them, although I am not looking forward to letting them know the news about my health."

"I know. It won't be easy, but together, we'll be here for you and each other."

"Spoken like a true diplomat." Alejandro leaned down and kissed her forehead. "I'll see you later."

"Yes, Papa." Cassie pushed her own breakfast plate aside. As soon as her father disappeared into his room, she stacked the dishes on the tray and set them on the kitchen counter, where the staff would collect them later.

Her emotions churning, she left her father's apartment, surprised to find Levi in the hall outside her room. "Hey, what are you doing?"

"I'm going stir-crazy," Levi said. "I thought you might want to go for a ride with me. We can ride the perimeter like old times."

"You realize our 'old times' only go back two months."

"Almost three."

"It doesn't seem that long." Cassie looked up at him, barely able to remember life before she met Levi. "Then again, in some ways, it feels like forever."

"I know what you mean," Levi said. "Come on. The fresh air will do us both good."

Bad memories overshadowed the good. "I haven't been outside since . . ."

"Another good reason to go." Levi stretched out his hand. "Let's go to the gazebo. It's your favorite place."

"Are you sure it's safe?"

"I'm sure."

Cassie put her hand in his. "Okay. I'm trusting you."

"I like the sound of that."

* * *

Levi rode through the memories, determined to make today overshadow the events of last month. For the past few weeks, he had continued his recovery, assisted in the hiring of the new security firm, and even managed to convince Alejandro to allow Alan to work in Sereno for the next few months.

Work had taken priority, but now, finally, it was time to put his personal life in order.

He had no doubt today would be memorable. Whether it would turn into the best day of his life or the worst, he wasn't sure. He prayed it would be the best.

They reached the gazebo, and Levi swung down out of the saddle, careful to land on his good leg. He had gotten rid of the cane, but he suspected it would be a while before his limp disappeared.

Cassie led the way to the gazebo, her limp already gone. She stopped and looked behind her, scanning the trees.

"You okay?" Levi asked, even though his palms sweated and nerves battled in his stomach.

"Yes. It's just hard to believe that a few weeks ago we were only a couple hundred meters from here when someone tried to kill us."

"Julien is gone, and from what I've learned about Theo, he already officially abdicated his claim to the throne." Levi took her hand and led her up the steps. "In essence, he has neutralized the threat against you."

"What do you mean?"

"The Escobar family would believe Theo is next in line for the throne. Since only your family knows he gave up his claim, the Escobars would assume only Theo would benefit from the loss of your family."

"I suppose that's true." She ran her fingers through her hair.

Levi shifted so he was facing her. Tears shimmered in her eyes. "Hey, if this is too hard being here, we can go back."

She shook her head. "No. It's not that."

"Then what is it?" Levi asked. "Your sisters will be home tonight. The enhanced security is finally in place. Your life is finally yours again."

"My life is mine, but everything is about to change."

"You're talking about your father."

"I can't stop thinking how much of my life he's going to miss. He won't see Annabelle graduate from college or Victoria get her advanced degree. He'll never get to walk any of his daughters down the aisle or meet his grandchildren. He won't see what our country can become now that we have new natural resources to benefit our citizens." A tear spilled onto her cheek. "I've had months to get used to it, but my sisters still don't know our father has less than a year to live."

"All anyone can do is help him live his last months the best he can," Levi said. "Help everyone have happy memories to look back on."

"I'm not sure I know how."

Levi's pulse picked up speed. "I do have one idea."

"What?"

Levi swallowed. "What if your father could see you get married?"

"I don't understand . . ."

"Cassie, I love you more than anything. I know it might seem crazy since we've only known each other for a short time, but I want to spend the rest of my life with you."

"Are you saying . . . ?" Cassie's voice trailed off when Levi lowered to one knee.

"I'm asking if you will spend your future with me." Levi drew the ring from his pocket. "Cassandra Rossi, will you marry me?"

Cassie's jaw dropped, and her eyes widened. Levi watched her work through her shock, his chest aching with each heartbeat. When he was certain he was going to die of anticipation, she nodded. "Yes. Yes, I will marry you."

Joy swelled within him as he slipped the ring onto her finger. She looked down at her hand, a new look of surprise dawning on her face. "This is my mother's ring."

"Yes." Levi pushed to a stand, Cassie's hand still in his. "Your father wanted it to be yours."

"You talked to my father?"

"I did." Levi slipped his arms around her waist. "I think the idea of being able to walk you down the aisle overshadowed his concerns about who I work for."

"How do you feel about resigning from the CIA?"

"It depends. How do you feel about short engagements?"

"Is three months short enough?" Cassie asked. "I think October would be a lovely month to get married."

"I'll send in my resignation today," Levi said without missing a beat.

"Are you sure? I don't want you to regret your choice."

"You are my choice." Levi lowered his lips to hers and let himself fall into their future. "I am the luckiest man alive that I'm your choice too."

"You are my choice." Her hand lifted to his cheek. "For always."

Joy overwhelmed him, and he had to swallow before he could respond. He leaned down and kissed his bride-to-be before he gathered her into his arms. "I promise to love you always. Always and forever."

"Always and forever," Cassie repeated. "That sounds like happily ever after to me."

"Yes, it does."

About the Author

TRACI HUNTER ABRAMSON WAS BORN in Arizona, where she lived until moving to Venezuela for a study-abroad program. After graduating from Brigham Young University, she worked for the Central Intelligence Agency for several years, eventually resigning in order to raise her family. She credits the CIA with giving her a wealth of ideas as well as the skills needed to survive her children's teenage years. She loves to travel and enjoys coaching her local high school swim team. She has written more than twenty-five best-selling novels and is a five-time Whitney Award winner, including 2017 Best Novel of the Year.

bookbub.com/authors/traci-hunter-abramson
@traciabramson
facebook.com/tracihunterabramson
instagram.com/traciabramson
traciabramson.com